DATE DUE			
JUL 2 8 1992			
NOV 1 9 1992			
DEC 3 1992			
DEC 1 4 1992			
JAN 1 9 1993			
OCT 0 6 1998			

Also published by Ballantine Books:

REGGIE by Reggie Jackson with Mike Lupica

DEAD AIR

Mike Lupica

BALLANTINE BOOKS • NEW YORK

TO MY MOTHER AND FATHER,
PARENTS BEYOND CATEGORY,
LOVE AND WISDOM NO MATTER
WHICH WAY YOU TURN.

CHAPTER

1

FINLEY'S guide to gracious living has always gone something like this: Slip on as few banana peels as possible. Keep all other slapstick to a minimum. Unless all other options have been exhausted, try like hell not to break your ass.

Most important, no heavy lifting ever.

I'm Finley, by the way. P. Finley, for Peter. I'd been having the Tournament of Banana Peels Parade lately, complete with floats and marching bands. My next piece of slapstick had a chance to be an alimony check. My ass felt like it was in traction.

And as for heavy lifting, I was beginning to think of myself as the Incredible Hulk of late-night New York. When it came time to leave O'Rourkes, the saloon that was home away from home, they'd just call Nick's Exxon Station and order a tow truck to go.

Which is why I had told Delores, the black Gracie Allen who is my secretary, that any interruption of any

1

kind on this particular Sunday would be viewed as a violation of the terms of the Geneva Convention.

I said, "Honey bunny, think of it this way. I am the Lindbergh baby today. You are the nanny. The Lord has given you a second chance."

I did not need any spanking-new problems. The next annoyance of any kind, great or small, was going to make me an entry in Mr. Guinness's book. It was also going to make me nastier than a slumlord's breath. I did not want the phone to ring, I did not want to hear from the answering service, I wanted no one with a sad story knocking on my door. I never again wanted to execute a one-and-a-half backflip—degree of difficulty three—into a glass of Jack Daniel's. Captain Humidity had Manhattan by the throat. The Red Sox were in fourth place. And those were just the appetizers. I wanted to be left alone.

As I sat across from the Ted Williams poster in my quaint office at Channel A—I call it quaint, incidentally; my right hand by way of Vassar, Natalie Ferrare, refers to the office as being decorated in Art Yeccho—I decided to make one of my periodic lists. I am a list maker of some repute. With the barest encouragement, I will tell about my ten favorite movies of all time, my five favorite World Series games, my three worst dates. I am constantly revising my list of the Ten Most Despicable People in History. The president of Shearson American Express was one that week. Hitler was two.

The list was headed "Finley's Laments." I wrote it out longhand on my trusty yellow legal pad. It went like this:

1. Wife still gone.
2. Wife now dating stockbroker (note: stockbroker to be tortured, then killed).
3. Mortgage payment on charming Bridgehampton cottage past due.

4. Jimmy O'Rourke, saloon keeper and alleged friend, enjoying his Bridgehampton summer in my charming cottage because mortgage payment used to pay bar tab.

5. Big Tony Altamero show unfinished.

6. Altamero show anxiously awaited by boss and vicious dwarf, Charles Davidson, Esq.

7. Red Sox in midst of six-game losing streak thanks to relief pitching scum, who should die along with wife's stockbroker.

8. Hangover now the size of *Queen Elizabeth II*.

My wife had been at the top of the charts for months. The fabulous and headstrong Jeannie Bogardus Finley had been gone since Valentine's Day. Some wives send flowers; she had left a cute little card with her new address on the kitchen table, next to the toaster-oven. It was one of those Hallmark things with two small children on the front. The message was short but full of Jeannie:

> Hi fella. This is from J. B. Finley. You remember me, wife and chief sparring partner. Just to follow up on last night's pleasant replay of Guadalcanal, we are no longer living together. The address of my new apartment is at the bottom. Don't use it anytime soon, okay? Good luck with growing up. I know you can do it. Go, Red Sox! Love, Jeannie.

I had spent an entire lifetime surrounded by comedians.

Normally I would have been at Yankee Stadium on such a Sunday, braving the heat, watching my team play the hated Yankees and try to end their losing streak before the divisional race got out of hand in September. But another ambitious patch-up dinner with Jeannie had turned into a train wreck the night before, so I had ended

up on Second Avenue at O'Rourkes, singing the score of
High Society with James O'Rourke at four A.M., and my
Sunday had begun with me waking up with someone
screaming in my bedroom. The voice turned out to be my
own. So I was punishing myself with an afternoon in the
office, mainlining black coffee and cream soda, hoping to
make the Altamero retrospective into something that
would make the boys at "60 Minutes" break down and
cry.

That was the plan, anyway.

The offices of Channel A, my station, are on Fifty-
seventh Street between Tenth and Eleventh, on the sixth
floor of a building that urban renewal forgot. You go
through a Crazy Eddie's television/stereo equipment
store on the ground level, make a right at the back, then
take a freight elevator as old as Bob Hope to six. Once
there, you find a tiny, cluttered newsroom, the modest
set for our modest nightly news show, a row of offices, a
control booth, and a tape room, all thrown into a shot
glass. It is nothing that would make Brokaw or Rather
rethink their careers at the networks. Imagine a bomb
going off on the old Mary Tyler Moore set and you've
got Channel A.

But the place happens to do quality work, specializing
in old movies, sports events, public service shows, cracker-
jack local reporting, and me, Peter Finley, electronic
gumshoe. At my best, I am a detective who packs a minicam instead of a gun. People talk to me and I listen, and
I get mad a lot. I used to do all of this with my column
at *The New York Herald.* Now I use pictures supplied by
Marty Pearl, a bearded bear of a man who, in addition to
being my best friend and my muscle, is the best television
cameraman alive. I do occasional spots on the evening
news when something hot is breaking, and once a month
I do an hour-long documentary about stories that have a

little more meat to them. The show is called "The Finley Report." This is the number that has been acquiring local Emmys the last few years the way housewives stockpile coupons. If someone big in New York City is doing something bad to someone little, I have this habit of finding out about it and getting it on tape.

Through the years, I have also managed to solve my share of problems in the crime family, which is a joy to the station and a source of endless pride to my father, Andrew Jackson Finley, known as Jack in all his years working the streets of Boston as the most colorful detective the BPD ever saw.

"I taught the kid everything he knows," Jack Finley is fond of telling interviewers. "Not everything *I* know, mind you. I had a real job. But it's enough to get the kid by in show business."

My father refers to everything television-related as show business. He thinks just about everyone in television is a no-talent sissy. Except his son, of course.

After my father retired from the force in Boston and my mother died, he moved to New York as an occasional consultant to the homicide branch of the NYPD. He lived in a house in Forest Hills not far from the West Side Tennis Club, where he terrorized the local matrons with an amazingly smooth line of Irish con and a surprisingly solid clay court game for a man sixty-three years old. We were supposed to have gone to the Red Sox–Yankees game, but I had told him about my date in the tape room, so my ticket behind the Sox dugout was being used by a rich widow whose first name was Muffin.

"I met her during a mixed doubles tournament at the club," he explained over the phone. "She thinks because I carried a gun once I'm a character, sonny."

He had told me about her before. "Pap," I said, "is she the one who also has the place in the south of France?"

"God is good, Peter," he said gravely. "Tomorrow night she's taking me to see *La Bohème.*"

"Fat lady sing in that one?"

"Dies too," he said. And hung up.

So he was at the ballpark with Muffin and I was in the office on Sunday, wondering why the air conditioner made me feel like Kenya, trying to figure a way to fire some life into Big Tony Altamero without having to interview the old fake again. The newsroom was fairly deserted, since the station was doing a weekend-long Tracy and Hepburn festival, and only occasional news updates were required by the skeleton staff. I had told Delores that if there were any calls to say Mr. Finley had died. In lieu of a funeral, his remains were being scattered over O'Rourkes. That was the message for everyone except Jeannie. I told Delores to skip the wit if Jeannie called and buzz me with electrifying speed.

I wanted the Altamero piece to work, since it was Big Tony who had been the reason I made the jump out of newspapers, onto the best-seller list for about ninety seconds, and finally into television journalism. You probably remember Big Tony's disappearance five years ago. He was the Jersey union boss who got himself into deep water with an array of wise guys from the mob and proceeded to do a Jimmy Hoffa impersonation, dropping completely out of sight for six long months. Most of the English-speaking world assumed he was sleeping with Jimmy and was thus extremely dead. Everyone except Finley of the *Herald.* I thought he was alive and convinced the paper to let me prove it. I stayed with the story from the moment Big Tony went out for a pack of cigarettes and didn't come back. I worked a series of reliable informants I had met in my travels, became extremely close to an old girlfriend of Tony's, crisscrossed America more than Charles Kuralt, and finally found Tony living above a pizza palace in

Santa Clara. By then he was tired of running and wanted to make a deal with the feds. I acted as go-between, and the day he went public I began an exclusive series that ran for two weeks and made me a celebrity.

And Big Tony Altamero liked me. When the publishing houses ran their lottery for his life and times, he decided that I had to be his Boswell. The book was done in a hurry and was nothing special, but the money was, and so was the exposure. Charley Davidson, who runs the show at Channel A and is an old newspaperman himself, saw me on some interviewer's couch, offered me my own show and my own team—which turned out to be Marty and Natalie —and I left newspapers without looking back.

Finley, troubleshooting reporter. Full of laments on an August Sunday. The marriage wasn't working, the book money was long gone, Big Tony wanted to talk more about growing tomatoes than the mob, the Red Sox were still losing 6–3 in the sixth, and I was more finicky than Morris the cat.

Delores chose that perfect moment to buzz me. I had swiveled my chair away from the television set and was staring down at Fifty-seventh Street, where a cop was pulling over a kid on a skateboard who had run a red light. Skateboarding to endanger.

"There's a man out here to see you," Delores said cheerily.

I swiveled back around and pondered my dirty Tretorns, balanced precariously on top of my desk.

"If the man is not here to tell me I have won the Lotto instant jackpot, then give him my dead message."

"Peter," she said, "the man says he knows something about the Peggy Lynn Brady disappearance."

I reached over to the remote control switch on top of my desk and turned up the volume on the game. Second and third. Rice at the plate, bat straight up and down and steady as a scalpel, eyes like slits as he glared out at Guidry.

"Delores, honey. Every maniac who can call a newspaper or television station knows something about Peggy Lynn Brady. What's his name?"

"Billy Lynn, Peter. He says he was married to her once."

I turned the television set off—Rice was on his own—and I snapped to attention.

"Married to her?"

"I believe there's an echo on this line. Married to her, sweetness."

"You believe him?"

"Peter, if this guy is a liar, my name is Ella Fitzgerald."

I could feel my heart starting. I told Delores to send him right in. Of all the things that all the world knew about Peggy Lynn Brady, missing television star, no one had ever heard of a husband named Billy Lynn.

I crumpled the list of Finley's Laments into a tight little ball and hooked them into the corner wastebasket like Jabbar, smiling for the first time all day.

Little did I know.

HE looked a lot like the young Henry Fonda, the one from *The Grapes of Wrath,* his manner so earnest I could hear alarms sounding faintly in the distance. A long face that was all angles and planes and had spent more than a little time outdoors. Short, careful black hair with just a hint of cowlick. Eyes that looked sleepy at first, but only at first. A thin-lipped mouth locked into half a smile. A flagpole of a man, wearing a heavy blue suit all wrong for the heat, pressed white shirt with one collar snaking over one lapel, red tie of simple print that was slightly too wide for fashion. Sunday-come-to-meeting clothes. Except he'd come to Channel A.

I, of course, was in the tennis shorts that looked like Bill Tilden hand-me-downs, and favorite *M*A*S*H* T-shirt. Billy Lynn made me feel like he'd find my picture next to the word *slob* in the dictionary. I tried to pull my own slouching six-one up a little straighter as I shook his hand.

I half-expected him to start by telling me he was packing mama and the kids into the pickup and heading to California. Instead he began, "I hope I haven't come at a bad time, Mr. Finley."

The accent was soft, full of honey, produced somewhere between Virginia and Florida. I guessed Alabama.

"It's Peter," I said. "Don't worry about this being a bad time. If you are who you say you are, I'm probably going to want to take you to the prom."

He let that one slide, and surveyed my office the way a man surveys a ghetto for the first time. The Williams poster. The piles of cassettes underneath the Sony in the corner. What looked to be a hundred years worth of the Sunday *Times* to the right of my desk. An open locker filled with my baseball glove, a bat, a running suit, my Jack Kramer autographed tennis racket. A framed photograph of Jeannie, next to the Fifty-seventh Street window. Empty pizza box on the desk. At least I thought the pizza box was empty.

"I didn't know if you'd be in on Sunday, but I figured I'd take a chance, since I didn't know who else to come to in New York," he said. "I figured if I went to the police first, I'd probably be readin' about myself in the Monday papers, and I didn't want that to happen. It's not my way, Mr. Finley."

He'd said PO-lice.

"Call me Peter," I said gently.

"Peter. Sorry. Where I come from, we tend to be a little formal with strangers."

I threw the latest Sunday *Times* off the chair on the visiting team's side of my desk and motioned for him to sit as I kicked the door shut behind him. I noticed that the seat of his pants was shiny, like the shoulders of the jacket. I sat on the home side of the desk and lit a Marlboro.

"You better tell me what all this is about, Billy. Delores said you had been married to Peggy Lynn Brady. Is that true?"

"Yes sir, it is. A long time ago and not for very long, 'cause it didn't take either one of us much time to figure out Peggy was headed for places I couldn't go. Not many people back in Guertin knew about it. We kept it a secret when she entered her first beauty contest, and by the time she won that, she was ready to come up north, so we ended it quiet. When she started to get big on television, she just sort of told a different story about her growin' up years. She always did have a flair for that. Peggy Lynn could always dream her life better than it was, at least when she was in Guertin."

"Where is Guertin, Billy?" He was going to have to tell this at his own pace, that was plain enough. He had probably worked it out beforehand.

"It's in Alabama. I run a general store and own a gas station. I used to farm some until that dried up."

"Why are you here now? Do you know something about where she is? Did she contact you?"

"Oh, no, nothin' like that, sir. I'm here because she's dead."

Dead. I let that one sit between us on the desk for just a second. Peggy Lynn Brady. Dead. He said.

Her disappearance had been the hottest story of its kind since Aimee Semple McPherson had taken her little vacation sixty years ago. Peggy Lynn had been a big name, maybe the biggest female name, in television talk lately. Her story was a perfect fan magazine legend. From Miss Alabama to New York model. From model to a job as a sportscaster on a local New York station. From sports to anchor and from there to a network shot with the Global Broadcasting Company, the struggling new fourth network with all the Arab money behind it. Her current show, "Midnite," was the only top-rated show GBC had. She was beating Carson, beating "Nightline," beating CBS reruns and movies.

And eight days earlier, after taping her last show for the week, she had walked out of the GBC studios onto Forty-second Street and vanished. No hint of foul play. No ransom note. No word. No nothing. The story had not been off the front pages or away from the nightly newscasts for one day. The cops were wringing hands and offering cop talk disclaimers. There were whispers about it being a grand publicity stunt, since Peggy Lynn was in the process of negotiating a new contract with GBC at the same time GBC was supposed to be in the process of being sold to the Reverend Eugene Endicott's World Christian Network. There were blind rumors about a secret rendezvous with some secret lover. Whispers. Rumors. Theories galore. But nothing to go on really. Aimee Semple Lynn McBrady.

Now I had a husband with a blue suit and sad, hound dog eyes looking at me like I was the Pope and telling me she was dead. I got up and walked over to the air conditioner, pleading with the dials one last time. I opened the door to my tiny refrigerator under the picture of Jeannie and grabbed myself another Dr. Brown's cream, which is mother's milk on hangover days. I held up the bottle to Billy Lynn and he shook his head no. I drank some Dr. Brown's and studied him. He was sitting tall in his chair

with hands on knees waiting for me to say something
brilliant. I lit another Marlboro instead.

August had not been a month for quitting smoking.

"Dead" is what I finally said.

"As sure as I'm sittin' here, Mr. Finley."

I could see that the "Peter" business was out of the
question without putting a gun to his head. He just wasn't
the type.

"How do you happen to know that, Billy? Everyone
from Sam Spade to Luke Skywalker has been working on
this thing since Peggy Lynn went away, and nobody has
come up with clue one. The *hint* of clue one. Now you
show up from Alabama and tell me she's gone toes up. If
you have a little more to go on, I'm all ears."

He leaned forward and put the big hands on my desk.
The eyes didn't look sleepy at all now. I had the feeling
that for Billy Lynn, this was the equivalent of a tantrum.

"There are things a man knows, Mr. Finley. In all the
years since she left, there hasn't been a week that's gone
by without me talkin' to her or gettin' a letter from her.
I saw her change from the girl I knew without seein' her
much at all. I saw what this life could do to her. She was
driven, Mr. Finley. She'd climb higher and higher and not
know what the next step was gonna be, and not care. She'd
laugh and tell me she was gettin' better at playin' their
game. Whatever that game was, she played it so well it got
her killed, sir. Lately, on the telephone and in her letters,
she said there was some trouble she was in, but that she
could handle it. I asked her what she meant the very last
time she called and she told me not to worry. Whoever did
this was someone she knew. And that's a fact."

While he was talking, I had casually jotted down
"something written in letters?" with my cigarette hand.

"Billy, why didn't you go to the police with any of
this?"

"Mr. Finley, would you go to the police with what I just told you?"

I smiled. The cops would take a quick statement from the earnest Alabama man, file the statement in their crack-pot file, maybe make a couple of phone calls to Alabama to check on the marriage license. They'd have him back on the streets in thirty minutes. Then one of the cops who liked seeing his name in the papers would call the *Post,* and Billy Lynn would be a brand-new poster boy for a story that had begun to flag without fresh information: PHANTOM HUSBAND SAYS PEGGY LYNN DEAD!

Or something comparatively tasteful.

"No, I wouldn't go to the cops, Billy," I said. "But why come to me? I dated Peggy Lynn a couple of times when she first came to the city, but it's been a hell of a long time since we traveled in the same circles. I've just been follow-ing her on television same as everybody else."

"She wrote me about you a long time ago. I remember the letter same as I do all the other ones, which I suppose comes from rereadin' 'em so many times. She said she'd met an important newspaper writer who helped people. She said that was what she planned to do, once she had it figured out on television. This was all back in a time when I still thought she was on the right road. I'm a religious man, Mr. Finley, and I believed that our Savior, the Lord Jesus Christ, was goin' to take care of Peggy Lynn, maybe even bring her back to me. Are you religious, sir?"

I said, "The Lord and I have a nodding acquaintance. When I misbehave, he doesn't take me to ballgames."

I felt like a shit immediately. He looked like I'd slapped him.

"I don't think none of this is funny."

"I'm sorry, Billy. Go on."

He continued, but a little more cautiously, a little less

sure I was the terrific guy I was supposed to be. "Anyway, the next time I heard about you was when you found that gangster a few years back. I try to read as many papers as I can, so's to keep up with what Peggy Lynn is . . . was doin'. I even saw you interviewed on television a few times. I figured if you could find that man, him a real gangster and all that, you could find just about anyone, or anything. So I bought myself a plane ticket when it was clear the police was all wrong about this—she's dead, not disappeared—and I came here to you. I figured you was the guy to find her killer."

He sat there in the stuffy office looking at me with a confidence I wished I deserved. The look made my head hurt. All I wanted to do was to finish the Altamero story and drive out to the beach and watch more baseball and drink at Bobby Van's bar in Bridgehampton and ponder the ebb and flow of the currently sorry life of P. Finley. I needed to start running again, work the heavy bag every day, and pull myself out of what Mr. Cole Porter called "the old ennui." But I was being double-teamed by two nasty forces. I liked this simple man. That was one. Two was even worse: I was actually starting to get curious about what had happened to Peggy Lynn Brady, of Guertin, Alabama, and the world. Ego is ego and Billy was right. I *was* good at finding out things. I could always go to Bridgehampton in September, when the riffraff was gone.

"So you want me to find out what I can, if I can, is that right? Without cops." I had finished the cream soda, so I lit another Marlboro.

"You know her world, Mr. Finley. You know all the people in it. I'm thinkin' you might see things others missed. I'm askin' you to find out who killed her, and how. And why. I'm prepared to pay you for your time."

"I'm a reporter, Billy, not a private eye. What you're talking about, if it happens to be true, is a good story. Good stories make my job easier. I'm going to talk to my people about doing this one. I can't promise you anything, and I don't want you to get your hopes up, but maybe I can work this better than the police, with a little luck. I don't know. You keep your money. I'll see what I can do."

"That's all I can ask." We both stood up. I walked over and opened the door for him. We shook hands again. Two old pals. He looked so damn grateful I wanted to change my mind right there.

"Where are you staying?"

"The Holiday Inn. Just up the block."

"Those letters from Peggy Lynn you talked about. Did you bring any of them with you?"

"Yes sir, I did. At least the most recent ones. I've got them back at the room. If you'd like—"

I stopped him with a friendly forearm shiver.

"I don't have to look at them today. I'll call you in the morning at the hotel. If you're out, I'll leave a message."

"I'll be there, Mr. Finley."

I stood in the doorway and watched him walk through the newsroom, looking this way and that at the teletypes and the computer terminals and the various sets, a country boy on a tour of another planet, searching for a girl he'd lost a long time ago, a long way from home.

When I turned the Sony back on, the Red Sox–Yankees game had been replaced by an Abbott and Costello movie. I called SportsPhone to get the score. According to some fast talker named King Wally, the Yankees had won 6–5. Guidry struck out Rice with the bases loaded in the ninth.

While I pondered the possible symbolism in all that, I

dialed Marty Pearl's number. I wanted Marty and Natalie in the office early Monday.

When he picked up after about fifteen rings, I told him we were going a-hunting for Peggy Lynn Brady. Marty greeted this news with a typical burst of enthusiasm.

"Deal," he said, and hung up.

CHAPTER

2

AFTER Marty I tried Natalie but she wasn't home, so I left a message on her answering machine to be in the office by nine the next morning. Just about every upwardly mobile person in New York City has one of those phone machines. It is some sort of rule they passed a while back. I have an answering service, a habit from my free-lancing days. I am opposed on religious grounds to conversing with a recording.

After Billy Lynn started my heart for me, I spent two serious hours in the tape room with Dwan Bagley, my favorite editor. Dwan is just a shade under six foot six, has skin the color of Häagen-Dazs chocolate ice cream, bears more than a passing resemblance to the young Harry Belafonte, and is constantly taking hip to dazzling new frontiers. He is a fascinating mix of anger and humor, militance and charm, and could not have been produced anywhere except 125th and Amsterdam. He likes to come on like the sixties aren't over and Malcolm isn't dead, and he occasionally likes to spread the Harlemese so thick you need a machete to cut through it, but I happened to know that the radar gun had clocked his IQ at an icy cool 145 once. He is a surgeon with both tape and film, a talent that has earned him the nom de plume Doctor D.

You give Dwan ten minutes of show and tell him to make it eight, and he goes into a room, shuts the door, and in a little while he comes back with eight. You ask him to move things around and he does it like a three-card monte player. I found him when he was seventeen, terrorizing the audio-visual department at the New School downtown. I liked his smart mouth and a merriment behind the eyes that Harlem hadn't killed, so I put him to work as a summer intern at the station, figuring a job was better than Stoop Sitting 101. In the four years since, he had dropped most of the vulgarity from his routine and become my friend. The next stop for Dwan was going to be directing; after that all of the Shiite Muslims weren't going to be able to hold him back.

"Doctor D," he had told me more than once, "is going to be Spielberg in off-white."

It took some sweat and more time than we expected, but we finally transformed Big Tony into a reasonably interesting subject, thanks to Dwan's usual wizardry and a few helpful edit suggestions from me. The last piece of business was laying down new voice-overs for the open and close.

But Dwan was less than thrilled with the finished product. I had to fight off a grin as I watched the huge, gifted man-child pace and growl in the tiny room. He was wearing his normal summer work clothes: two-toned Dolphin running shorts, fishnet T-shirt, New Balance running shoes the color of coral. The earring was one I hadn't seen before. I was hoping it wouldn't be a lengthy tantrum. If

I didn't get a cheeseburger soon, I was going to get the bends.

"You should have left this dude with the pepperoni pizzas" was the thrust of Dwan's critique. "Big Tony my *ass*. He probably used to burn people if they used the wrong fork, and now he acts like he's lead singer for the Vienna Boys Choir."

I was packing up my leather satchel, the one Jeannie had brought me from Phoenix a few years ago. I noticed one of the brass clasps was missing. Perfect.

"Doctor D," I said, "if I'd left him with the pizzas, I would still be bleeding out eight-hundred-word newspaper columns three times a week instead of breaking bold new ground as I explore the limitless potential of cable television."

A perceptive critic had written that last part, in the *Times*.

I got the satchel closed, gave Dwan a little salute, and walked out of the office.

"Hey, Finley," he called as I headed down the hall toward the elevator. "What's ten inches long and white?"

I didn't turn around, just kept walking. I didn't know the punch line, but assumed it would portray the sexual prowess of Caucasians in a less-than-flattering light. Most of Dwan's jokes did that.

"Okay, Slick. I bite. What's ten inches long and white?"

"Nothing" was the punch line. Followed by cackling. Before the elevator doors closed, I gave him the finger.

The mugginess had taken its big hand off the city's throat at twilight. I decided to walk across town to my apartment at Sixty-fifth and York. That is the other side of Manhattan to the extreme. But Fifty-seventh Street, the whole show west to east, is my favorite walking stretch in Midtown. It is filled with all of Manhattan's special variety, from the pastrami at Wolf's deli to make-your-own

T-shirt shops to Henri Bendel's frosty elegance, from Bur-
berry to the Irish Pavillion to the Magic Pan, where you
can find good crepes, if you think there are such things as
good crepes. You get all of this on Fifty-seventh. Plus a
Dunhill tailor and Tiffany's. There are book stores and
leather stores. There is the First Women's Bank. There is
the Festival Theatre, old and cozy, where you can watch
first-run movies in the afternoon. The Russian Tea Room:
home of the movie deal and the twenty-five-dollar omelet
and all the chicest of the chic who want to be seen being
seen. And there is Carnegie Hall, still an imposing broad
after all these years, despite some of the fakes they let in
now. Someone named Rick Springfield was performing
that week at Carnegie Hall. Neil Sedaka had been in the
week before.

The thought of Neil Sedaka on the stage at Carnegie
Hall made me want to beat up a nun.

I was thinking about the first time I saw Sinatra there,
how he came strolling onstage with all his flinty style in
the sleek tux, just picked the microphone off the stool with
no introduction, and began to sing "All the Way," when
I found myself standing in front of O'Neals at Fifty-
seventh and Sixth. And O'Neals wasn't about Sinatra.
O'Neals was Peggy Lynn Brady. It had been at O'Neals
that I first met her, ten years ago.

God, I thought, could it be ten years? It was, it was. I
was young then, and so was she, and the city was younger.

It seemed that way at the time, anyway.

EVERYTHING about the night was still vivid. A good
print.

It was a book party for Norman Mailer's most recent
collection of essays, most of which dealt with Norman's
favorite subject: Norman. A lot of the free world had

been invited and a lot of the free world had shown up—
the party was free—hoping to see Norman get drunk
and pop somebody. I was there to do a column about all
that, having recently scratched my way off the police
beat.

Peggy Lynn had just started doing sports for Channel
2, the CBS-owned-and-operated station. She didn't know
a curve ball from a jock strap, but you could see even then
how much the camera loved her. She could be interviewing Reggie or Namath or Ali, and you could not take your
eyes off her. It was as if her guests were standing there next
to the sun. Peggy Lynn could have been reading the phone
book and it would not have mattered a bit. Whatever star
is, she was star from the beginning.

She had been moving around O'Neals doing quick bits
with some of Norman's boxing friends, and when she was
finished and her crew had left, she snuck up behind me at
the bar. I am always at the bar during any sort of cocktail
party. I do not mingle unless provoked. If you attempt to
mingle there is a far greater chance that you will be run
over by a photographer or a producer making a broken-
field run at a starlet. Or vice versa.

At the bar, you can also set your drink down while you
light your cigarette in a dignified manner.

"Excuse me," I heard a musical, slightly Southern voice
say. "You're Peter Finley, aren't you?"

I casually turned around. And casually wondered
where I'd left the old oxygen mask. Up close the whole
package was startling. The blonde hair had been poured
like batter over the perfect face; the cheekbones were
merely high enough for one of those George Willigs to
climb. The green eyes were pale emeralds, set against the
whitest of healthy white backdrops. The smile brought the
word *sunrise* to mind. Peggy Lynn Brady could have been
wearing a uniform from the Hitler Youth and I would not

have noticed. She had to be in the neighborhood of six feet if she wasn't in heels. I didn't particularly care if she was in heels.

"I've seen your face on wanted posters," I said finally. "Crossing state lines for the purpose of home wrecking. Smiling to endanger. Four counts of heart breaking. Consider this a citizen's arrest. I'd better frisk you."

She laughed. A good, throaty laugh, real, not something from the Actor's Studio. My thoughts at that moment were running to blood tests, licenses, and a justice of the peace who resembled Barry Fitzgerald.

"You talk as funny as you write, Peter Finley," she said, still smiling brilliantly. "Buy me a drink and I'll let you recite three columns of your choice. But only if you start with the one about the blind kid who runs the newsstand over by the Garden. I loved that one."

"Me too. What're you drinking?"

"Jack Daniel's. Neat."

I waved at the bartender for two more. I had never met a woman who drank Jack Daniel's neat and did not sleep in doorways.

We finished our drinks there, then I invited her to dinner. She accepted. We left the Mailer party like hostages being released. Dinner was at a little Italian place on Forty-ninth between First and Second called Antolotti's. The wine was good there, the pasta homemade, the waiters weren't aspiring actors, and you didn't have to worry about a Carmine getting gunned down while you signed the American Express receipt.

I am rarely enchanted by someone outside a Red Sox uniform. Enchanting is the only way to describe Peggy Lynn that first night. She told funny stories about the modeling business, about growing up in jerkwater towns like Guertin, about beauty contests, about finding an apartment in Manhattan, about her very first audition as a TV weather girl. I did not get to recite three columns. I was an eager audience of one, laughing in all the right places, ordering more wine, deftly lighting cigarettes like some South American gigolo.

She was totally self-absorbed in a totally charming way. She was performing for me, posing, mugging for an imaginary camera, and we both knew it, but it was all right. Her face was so full of expression and life it gave her whole body the illusion of constant movement. She was a toucher in an innocent way, reaching for my hand or my arm to give emphasis and punctuation to her stories, leaning close and whispering like a young Bacall, husky and intimate when a punch line was a bit raunchy.

And way behind the smile, I could see she was ambitious as hell. That slipped out in drips and drops, and the smile couldn't hide it all. Somewhere along the line, she had learned how to handle herself in the clinches. She was going to have it all. She had no doubts about that.

Neither did I. I pick up on things very quickly. Sometimes.

"I thought television was going to be hard when I first started, Peter," she said at one point. "But television is easy, once you can fight your way in front of the camera. It's getting there that's the trick, and staying there. You just have to know who to flatter and whose jokes to laugh at and who to listen to. It's not all that political. It's just a little talent and a lot of common sense. Those moguls think they're the only ones who know the rules to the game. Hell, anyone can pick those up. All those men who make the big decisions look at you and think they must be seeing dumb if they see pretty. I want them to always see that. Because one day they're all going to wake up and I'm going to own them, and they're going to wonder when it was this stupid blonde got so smart."

She stopped, as though sensing she'd said too much.

She'd had a lot of wine but somehow I didn't think it was the wine talking.

"Peggy, I'm no big fan of television," I said. I wasn't then. "But isn't this attitude of yours a little cold-blooded, this early in the game? I'm not saying you should be Shirley Temple. But you're starting to sound like Lizzy Borden."

"I'm not cold-blooded at all," she said. "And I'm not Lizzy Borden, hacking my way through the business. I'm just being a realist in a world where there ain't too much that's real. That's all. I plan on being the one doing the using instead of the one being used."

Much later that night, when we were lying in my big bed and watching one last tugboat make its way up the East River as we sipped Hennessy, she leaned over and kissed me sweetly on the cheek.

"There's still a lot I don't know about the big city, Peter Finley," she said softly. "I want you to teach me."

After the blessed events of the previous hour or so, I assumed she didn't mean in bed.

She didn't. Our affair, if it can be called that, lasted about three months. We went to movie premieres. We spent smoky nights in little jazz clubs in the Village. We ate and drank at all my favorite writer hangouts, O'Rourkes and Clarke's and Elaine's and the Lion's Head. I took her to ball games, and prize fights at the Felt Forum. She would come out and watch me put a column together on the street, whether it was with a cop or a bookie or a kid who'd held up a liquor store for sport. And Peggy Lynn was full of questions, full of observations. She had a clear eye. I could see her becoming more of a reporter, a better asker of questions, in her own work.

Finley, in the early going, was still enchanted. It took me too much time to look past the mattress and realize I was nothing more than a post-grad course in journalism for her; she was just filling in some gaps in her education. She may have been mildly amused by my wit and entertained by my affection, both in and out of bed, but mainly what she was doing was going to school with someone she thought knew the ropes: I was reference material. It dawned on me finally that if she hadn't accidentally met me at the Mailer party, she would have accidentally met me at one of my saloons. Or at the office. Or at the ballpark. It was fairly flattering. But she wasn't lying about being a user.

Hazardous to Finley's ego. End of affair. We lost touch after that. I told myself it was my idea. I lie to myself a lot. And I knew there would be other courses for her, other Finleys who would fall the way I did, like an Italian government. She was good at it. I watched her move through the television heavens like a comet, noting her progress with a bitter sort of amusement.

As they say in all the Noel Coward plays, bitter amusement generally follows after I have been dumped on.

AS I slowly made my way east, I thought briefly about calling Jeannie and asking her to meet me in the Oak Bar at the Plaza for a drink that might patch up the patch-up dinner. A lot of weekends in better times had ended there on Sunday, after the *Times* and brunch and the park and maybe a movie. The movie was always a comedy; we went to comedies on Sunday. Then the Oak Bar, where we would drink civilized martinis and speak in hushed, Oak Bar voices and make conspiratorial jokes about the other customers, especially the old ones. Then after we were done with too many civilized martinis and limp from holding in laughter we would walk hand in hand back to the apartment on York. There we would shut doors and pull down shades and write a final chap-

ter to the weekend with a different sort of style, a better
conspiracy.

But I did not call, because I was afraid she would still
be spitting angry about the previous night's version of an
Israeli-PLO band concert. Or I was afraid that she might
not be home, might be sitting in the Oak Bar at that very
moment with the stockbroker she was seeing. Or I was
afraid that a drink at a special haunt would wound with
special memories. Conclusion: afraid. So I decided to stop
at Clarke's for a therapeutic bacon cheeseburger and a
rundown of the rest of the baseball scores from Tommy,
the headwaiter in the back room. I also wanted to talk
with Lt. Mick Dunphy from homicide.

A military sharp right turn on Third Avenue immediately followed that decision.

I wasn't sure if homicide had been invited to the Peggy
Lynn Brady party yet, but I was fairly certain Dunphy
would be at Clarke's, maybe with my father. The Giants
had opened their exhibition season that afternoon over in
the Meadowlands. For Mick Dunphy, once the football
season started, Sundays belonged to the Giants, if he
wasn't cracking a case about a dead cover girl or an Arab
banker or an ex-Nazi somebody had discovered in SoHo.
Mick would watch the game from Wellington Mara's box
at Giants Stadium, which was perfectly lovely if you considered that Mara owned the team. When the game was
over, Mick would move it along to Clarke's for the post-
mortems, same as in the old days. His priorities ran to
dead people, football, tradition. Stewardesses were also in
there somewhere.

Dunphy, who played for the Giants briefly before his
knee went one way and the rest of him went another one
Sunday in Cleveland, was New York's celebrity cop, and
its best. It had been that way a long time. He started out
on the emergency squad back in the fifties, one of the

crazies who climbs up on the bridge and grabs the certified crazy before he makes like Esther Williams. Now he was a legend uptown and down, and the object of a lot of envy. Mick Dunphy answered to no one, mostly because no detective anyone could remember had ever been in on the finish of so many big ones. I had always been very impressed by Dunphy for other reasons. He once got to sit on Johnny Carson's couch. He made an annual trip to Tobias's of Savile Row to buy his suits.

He was also one of the two or three greatest Scotch drinkers I had ever seen.

When I walked into the back room, he was sitting alone at his usual table, inside left, front corner. He also looked like he was settled in: Dunhill lighter and Luckies to his right on the table, a bowl of chili the size of a catcher's mitt in front of him, coffee and tall Scotch to his left. He was studying a football stat sheet.

"Winners or losers?" I said.

Dunphy gave me a disinterested look over the top of his reading glasses.

"Losers," he said. "Our rookie quarterback throws an interception after the two-minute warning, Montana throws one ten miles to one of his greyhounds, and we lose, twenty-three to twenty. I would also like to mention at this time that our new rhythm and blues halfback, the kid from Notre Dame, plays like an interior decorator."

"Thanks ever so much for the game story, Reverend King. Mind if I sit down?"

Dunphy took a hand off the stat sheet and waved it at one of the empty chairs.

"Is this a chance meeting on a Sunday in New York, or might you be nosing?"

"A little nosing, a little cheeseburger withdrawal."

"Nosing about whom? Or would this humble civil servant be prying?" In a squad room, or out on a case,

Dunphy often felt compelled to talk like someone out of *Raging Bull*. Fuck this. Gimme that. Scumbags all around. Side of the mouth stuff, usually. But when he let his guard down, he sounded more like Alistair Cooke. He confided to me late one night that his favorite author was Evelyn Waugh.

"I'm suddenly very curious about Peggy Lynn Brady."

Dunphy's dark, hooded eyes looked like the middle of the night. "My heart leaps," he said.

"You in on it yet, Mick?"

"Officially or unofficially?"

"Officially?"

"No sir."

"Unofficially?"

"Let's just say I've made a couple of phone calls and received a couple, just to be sporting." He spooned some chili into his mouth, frowned, and added more Tabasco sauce.

"You have any theories, official or otherwise?" I said.

Dunphy smiled. I couldn't tell if it was me or the chili. He had a smile that always looked like trouble to me, and a lot of wavy gray-white hair, the kind of wavy hair you don't see anymore, and a nose that hadn't been straight since Studebakers were all the rage, and a jaw as square as three meals a day. Character actor. In the movies he would have played somebody's best friend. He put down his spoon, took off his reading glasses, folded them up, placed them neatly in the breast pocket of a cream-colored suit that looked softer than Linus's blanket. Then he shook a Lucky out of the red-and-white pack, tapped it once on the back of his hand, lit it with his Dunhill lighter.

There are very few people left who can carry off tapping an unfiltered cigarette on the back of a hand with any panache. Dunphy could.

"I have theories about everything," he said.

I waved at Tommy and pointed toward Mick's coffee cup.

"You think she's dead?"

"Deader than disco," Dunphy said.

"There are those cynics who think she just might have taken off for a while," I said.

Dunphy harrumphed, smoke bursting from both nostrils. I had this feeling that the Alistair Cooke segment of the show might be ending. It was. Now he was business.

"Try to think like your old man for a second, okay? This is no publicity stunt, dickhead. You take off the way she took off, somebody knows where you are, even if you want to hide. Boyfriend, boss, secretary, flack. *Somebody*. People like Peggy Lynn Brady don't go to the fucking toilet alone. Nah, this one is too clean. It doesn't happen like this unless somebody wants it to happen like this. It's no kidnapping either; there'd be a note or something by now. Kidnappers are not known for patience. She's dead, Peter. I'm going to work on this one tomorrow. It's going to be more fun than a fucking cookout."

I had to grin. Tommy brought me a fresh coffee as Mick's battery was running down. Tommy also set down a piece of paper with the American League scores from the West Coast games scribbled on it. The Angels had beaten the Orioles. The Mariners had beaten the Tigers in the tenth. At least the Sox hadn't lost any more ground. I waved Tommy back after I looked at the scores and celebrated by ordering a beer.

I said to Mick Dunphy, "You said you made a couple of phone calls already. Find out anything wonderful?"

I got the killer smile again. "As a matter of fact, I did. Maybe you already know this, but Miss Peggy was a very unpopular lady around the office. If she had any friends over there, other than a producer fellow named Sam Cummings and a woman named Kris Stanford, they're all on vacation in the Poconos or someplace. You talk to some of the camera people and technicians and the word 'bitch' keeps cropping up. Her co-star, Mr. Brant, I hear he wants to wring her little neck. There was talk of throwing a party as soon as she took a walk. She's the biggest star they got over there and even the head of the network, Harrold, who needs stars right now, *he* isn't pining away for her either."

I lit a Marlboro with his Dunhill lighter, which felt fine.

"You found all this out with a couple of casual phone calls?"

"I'm a trained detective," he said. He took the Dunhill back when he saw me fondling it. "I even manage to get by without makeup."

"Quote ha-ha unquote," I said. "Could someone over there have wanted to kill her? You think Huntley ever wanted to off Brinkley?"

"I'll decide that when I talk to some of those TV maniacs over there in person."

"So you're in for sure?"

Tommy brought the icy beer and I drank half of it down in a gulp. Cold beer on a summer day still made me want to hit Pavarotti notes.

"Yeah, I'm in all right," Dunphy said. He put a twenty-dollar bill underneath his coffee cup, collected cigarettes and lighter and stat sheet, stood up, smoothed out the front of his slacks, adjusted his tie.

"I take it we might be bumping into each other here and there?" he asked.

"Stay on your toes, Mick," I said. "You know me. I've got more moves than a halfback."

I thought I might have detected a smile in the semidarkness, but I couldn't be sure. Dunphy walked toward the front room in that light, confident jock's step he never had lost. Tough guy in a cream-colored suit. I took a felt-tip out of my satchel, picked up the ordering pad they leave

on the tables at Clarke's and wrote "bacon cheeseburger,
rare, home fries."

WHEN I got back to the apartment I decided I needed a
little exercise to work off cheeseburger one, and its sequel.

One of the first things I'd done when I took the apartment was turn the guest room into a miniature gym. It was
after I got the book money, before I married Jeannie.
There was a speed bag, heavy bag, portable rowing machine, board for doing proper sit-ups, with the legs ele-
vated. I tried to do an hour in there every other day or so.
I had hated to jog even before my knee operation, though
Jeannie used to drag me along with her to the park when
she was having a burst of fitness fervor.

I had gotten the operation instead of a varsity football
letter my junior year at South Boston High, while I was
returning a punt the first game of the season. A future
felon from Charlestown chose to ignore my passionate fair
catch signal and broke open my medial collateral ligament
like a fortune cookie.

The message inside the knee could have read, "I can't
dance, don't ask me."

So now I had Finley's Gym. All of this would have been
a lot more meaningful without hobbies like cigarettes and
bourbon and beer.

I started slowly at first on the speed bag, using a precise motion with both hands, not unlike someone knocking on a door. This is terrific for hand-eye coordination,
and you can work up a surprisingly good sweat once you
get rolling. I am good at this one. Pretty soon the bag
was a blur and the room sounded like gunfire, and my
hands were a couple of pistons. I've still got it, I
thought, smiling like a champ. It had been seventeen
years since I won the middleweights in the Boston

Golden Gloves. But the hands were still fast and true. I finally stopped the bag and gave it one last solid right, trying to knock it off its hook.

I pretended the bag was the face of Jeannie's stockbroker. Phillip his name was. Yale. Killer handshake. My father and I had run into them coming out of Elaine's a few weeks before. After they got into a cab, my father shook his head wonderingly.

"Sonny, I don't believe I've ever seen a talking hairdo before" is the way he described my wife's boyfriend.

After the speed bag, I made a quick tour of the room. Sit-ups, seventy-five of them; I usually did more, but I usually worked out in the morning. Ten hard minutes on the rowing machine. Ten hard minutes on the heavy bag, hooking hard and low with both hands, circling, hooking more. Nothing fancy. When I finished I put some Willie Nelson on the stereo. Good old Willie. Face like a cactus, voice like an angel. I passed through the kitchen and picked up a cold Coors, then went into the bathroom and filled up the sunken tub—one of Jeannie's relics—with hot-hot water, and settled in, listening to Willie sing about redheaded strangers and cowboy heroes and uncloudy days.

Willie was easing his way through "Railroad Lady" when the phone rang. I reached out with a soapy arm and picked up the receiver. It was Jeannie Bogardus Finley.

"I've got to come over and pick up some sweaters before Thursday. I've got to go to London for a few days, and I thought I had more sweaters here but I don't. So maybe I could come over some night and pick them up, if you're going to be home."

Jeannie never said hello on the telephone. She just started in and expected you to be caught up when she stopped for a breath.

"I'm sorry," I said. My heart felt like a triphammer.

The sound of her voice could do that to me, especially when I wasn't counting on hearing from her before the next administration.

She said, "You're sorry about the sweaters? Or you're sorry I'm going to London?" Jeannie was editor in chief of *Era,* the newest and best of the women's magazines, *GQ* for their side. She also wrote for *Era* occasionally when the spirit moved her to travel.

"About last night. I'm sorry I got drunk. I'm sorry I lost my temper. I'm sorry I made such an issue of the check. I'm sorry I called your stockbroker friend a hairdresser. That should clear the bases."

I thought about lighting up a cigarette, but she would hear me inhale. She wasn't happy about me being a smoker. I didn't want to apologize for smoking too. It was exhausting being so sorry.

"I accept your apology." The voice was flat. The words tasted like melba toast. "What about the sweaters?"

"Anytime you want. But listen, J.B., I really would like to talk when we're both a little more calm."

"I was calm last night, at least for a while. You were Richard Speck."

I let that one slide, mostly because she was right.

"So what do you think? How about lunch sometime before you go? I'm great at lunch. We'll go to Twenty-one. I'll wear a tie."

"Peter . . . maybe. I don't know. We'll talk about it. I'm a little late right now."

My stomach dropped toward the Gulf Coast.

"Date?"

"Does it matter? God."

"Call me a silly romantic. I like to keep up with my wife's social whirl. By the way, wife, is London business or pleasure?"

"I've really got to go, Peter. Good luck with the Al-tamero piece."

She hung up. We were clearly making real progress. I finished my beer, lit a petulant cigarette, climbed out of the tub, slipped on the venerable blue robe, had a passing thought about popping *The Philadelphia Story* into the VCR. I decided against that. I was in no mood for Grant and Hepburn to work it out in the end after saying witty and charming things to each other for two hours. Plus, I had the movie memorized.

I sat down on the couch, butted out the cigarette, and closed my eyes. Next to New York, London is my favorite city in the world. I remembered when Jeannie and I stopped there at the end of our honeymoon, and had stayed in the flat at Dolphin Square, and how I made her walk with me all the way to Trafalgar Square the first day we got there so I could see the statue of Lord Nelson.

When I woke up it was a few minutes before twelve. I put the television set on and flipped the dial to Channel G. For God. It was where you found the Reverend Eugene Endicott's World Christian Network on Manhattan Cable. At midnight, they reran Endicott's own show. It was called "The Living God Live!" Even when it was on tape.

"The Living God Live!" was first shown at seven, before the kiddies went to bed. Then again at midnight, as the network closed its broadcast day. Then one more showing at seven in the morning, when the WCN started up all over again. It was a combination of telethon, Billy Graham revival, and the Circus Maximus showroom in Las Vegas. There was faith healing and country Baptist church and then there was the Rev himself, the most riveting and mesmerizing speaker I had ever heard. Endicott could turn one word, *Jesus,* into the damned Gettysburg Address.

In the televised age of the huckstering, Bible-thumping, used-car salesman, entrepreneurial showman evangelist, Endicott was top of the line. I thought his act was silly, campiest of camp, and shameless. Lots of flash and illusion. He even had music videos set to gospel music; they were funnier than the Three Stooges. Some people thought he was a political beast-in-waiting, like oily Falwell, though Endicott had stayed away from politics, so far.

To me he was as real as professional wrestling, just a guy selling fast-food Jesus. But he had my favorite show on television, next to Letterman's and my own.

"The Living God Live!" always opened with a huge production number starring the World Christian Network Chorus, Endicott's version of Welk's champagne ladies. It was always really good, Broadway quality. Then Endicott's Ed McMahon, a good-looking aspiring evangelist person in a tuxedo, would introduce Endicott to the studio audience and all of us watching at home. He was doing it as my set finally cleared up. The WCN singers were behind the announcer on some steps. They all wore white robes and frozen smiles. I assumed the director was a born-again Busby Berkeley. Slowly, the women began to peel away down the steps, moving off to the sides.

Then there was the Rev, sitting on a throne. He wore a different-colored robe every day. This one was royal blue. The people in the studio audience gasped. Always did. I laughed in the living room and said out loud, "Liberace." Endicott—with perfect white hair and a face that was almost girlishly detailed—stood up and stretched out his arm and, in a Judgment Day voice, offered the same opening invocation he did every time out on "The Living God Live!"

"We have *arrived* at the hour of the day reserved for inviting the *Living God* into the houses that are your *souls!* And now I must ask you, brothers and sisters and little children, the blessed and the sinners: Is your house *clean enough* today?"

In the living room, I said, "Say amen."

Endicott slowly walked down the steps from the throne and the members of the chorus converged on him from left and right, and in his own lovely baritone, Endicott began to lead them in a song that used the word *Savior* a whole lot.

The show often featured a guest star from show business. Tonight's was a country and Western singer with a speech impediment. The show was by the numbers after that: An 800 number flashed on the screen, and we saw a bank of young Christian soldiers working pledge phones. Endicott healed an arthritic. There was someone for him to heal every day. He never ran out of gimps.

He had the regular segment where he read items from the day's newspapers, offering his own comments and editorial opinions. The gospel video came in the last half hour, then a ten-minute sermon that was guaranteed to bring the house down. I passed on it and called the answering service and told Gina, the night operator, to handle everything until morning unless a man named Billy Lynn called.

I had been even more mesmerized and amused than usual by Endicott, probably because I idly wondered if there could be some connection between Peggy Lynn's disappearance and the good Rev's rise to mainstream media control. Sometimes even I got sucked into believing the Rev could move mountains, part seas.

"The Living God Live!" originated in Dover, Delaware, home base for Endicott's network and his church. When the Rev was on tour, the WCN used reruns, but kept the pledge part of the program live from the Dover studio. Endicott had done it all in five short years. He had started out with a Sunday morning FM gospel hour in Morgantown, West Virginia, then got a calling from a Higher Power about the higher power of television. His first show was on UHF in Wilmington. Then the whole business took off. Now Endicott was tied into every important cable system in the United States and his WCN Living Church—corporate name—was worth billions. Endicott University in Dover had received full accreditation the previous September.

I figured their football team would be beating the goo out of Penn State before the end of the decade.

And now Eugene Endicott was getting ready to go mainstream if he could merge with, buy really, Global. He was ready to challenge the big boys, according to a recent cover story in *Newsweek* entitled "God Goes Prime Time." He wanted an even bigger audience than cable afforded him, and Global, which had fallen on hard times, was the network available.

I thought, Maybe he can even bring Peggy Lynn back from the dead. Live!

When the show ended I switched off the set and climbed into a bed that seemed big and cold as Greenland without Jeannie Bogardus. I dreamed about Jim Rice. Eugene Endicott was pitching to him but Jimbo couldn't get a hit because the bat kept slipping out of his hands.

CHAPTER

3

THEY started dying on me Monday.

I didn't know anything about that in the morning. All I knew then was I had set the wake-to-music alarm on the Panasonic for 7:30 and the buzzer on the digital next to it for 8:00. Back-ups are crucial in life. Before the alarm I could get thirty minutes of "Imus in the Morning," then bound out of bed like the star of a Rice Krispies commercial.

Only this morning, Don Imus, the outrageous WNBC disc jockey, never made it to my room. Andrew Jackson Finley beat him by a half hour. The exact time was burned into my memory. I saw the time before I tried to throw my digital at my father.

At 7:03 A.M. the guys building the new condominium across the street hadn't even started to play Beethoven's Fifth on the jackhammer. My eyes felt like Orson Welles was sitting on them.

"Get up and have breakfast with your old man, sonny,"

my father was saying. I was trying gamely to crawl back into the fetal position under the covers. "And forget about throwing that clock. You know you never have your best stuff at this time of the day."

I groaned like an X-rated video.

"There is no this time of day. This time of day can only occur after I've read 'Doonesbury.' "

"Sonny, I'm here on a matter of grave concern to both of us. Our baseball team is playing like the Joffrey Ballet."

That called for surrender. I laughed, threw the sheets aside, propped myself up on an elbow. I blinked a couple of times until my light meter was adjusted. My father had a Food Emporium bag full of groceries under his arm. He looked, always and forever, illegally chipper and natty as hell. He has a morning face. His cheeks are the home office for ruddy. His white hair, curly and soft and short, always looks like baby powder. His outfit looked like three scoops of sherbet: pink Lacoste, seersucker sports jacket, lime-green slacks.

He was grinning the rakish grin he likes to throw at everyone. Deadbeats, matrons, uppity bartenders. And me. He smelled like a barbershop, even at twenty paces.

He had been waking me up a lot lately, never worrying that my bed might be occupado. My father just assumed that since Jeannie left I had made a devout vow of celibacy only the Supreme Court could overturn.

"I took the liberty of bringing some supplies with me," he said. "Good that I did. Your refrigerator looks like the gulag, as usual. Is that a head of lettuce in there, or the brain that wouldn't die?"

I coughed a Marlboro cough that began in my shins.

"C'mon," he said. "Up with you. I'll cook us some eggs and then we'll look through the dictionary to find a word that describes what Muffin did to your father's poor old bones last night."

"Do I get a vote?"

"We're having omelets," he said, and walked jauntily off toward the kitchen, whistling "Galway Bay," enthusiastically and off-key.

I headed for the bathroom, trying to decide whether to shave first or shower. I put on the light and looked in the mirror. I groaned again. My eyes looked as if little tiny men in dirty sneakers had been running laps around them all night.

Same face as yesterday. Not twenty-five anymore.

I decided to shower.

"I take it you didn't tell Mick Dunphy about this Billy Lynn fellow," my father said a little later.

"Do I get disowned?"

"You were deceitful, Peter," he said. "You were brought up to think of the policeman as your friend."

We were sitting in the living room doing second cups of coffee while Bryant Gumbel interviewed some Joint Chief of Dandruff on the "Today" show. The jackhammers had begun their concerto. The maid had called to say she'd be by in an hour or so. I had checked in with the answering service. No Billy. No Jeannie. Breakfast had been Jack Finley omelets: three eggs, chili sauce, cheddar cheese, scallions, picante sauce. It was a wonderful and terrifying concoction; around noon my stomach would feel like the inside of a jet engine.

While we ate, I laid out the events of the last twenty-four hours, starting with Billy's visit, concluding with Dunphy's observations about GBC and Peggy Lynn, and my own sour memories of the lady. My father said little, absorbing it into a cop mind that had always worked like a fancy computer. The good ones are supposed to know how to listen.

"Billy's my own pet for now," I said. "At least until I can get some sort of handle on everything. I feel like someone who parachuted into an Agatha Christie on page one-sixty-eight."

"Um," my father said.

He was in the process of getting his first Partagas of the day lit. It was a familiar ritual that always seemed to belong in a church service. Consecration. Communion. Cigar.

1. Delicately remove cellophane wrapper.
2. Pass cigar lovingly under nose, like Julio Gallo sniffing a new burgundy.
3. Snip off one end with cutter your son bought you last Christmas at Nat Sherman's.
4. Roll mouth end around between lips. The R-rated part of our program.
5. Light match, apply flame carefully, take first puffs.
6. Take first serious drag, then lean back like someone who just picked the winner in the Irish Sweeps Derby.

The process would be repeated five more times before he had his bedtime Hennessy. My father liked his cigars.

"You trust this Billy Lynn, I take it?" he said finally.

"He makes Billy Graham look like a lying snake. How can you smoke those things this early in the morning, by the way?"

He dipped the tip of his cigar into his coffee as though it were a Dunkin' Donut, and smiled a smile you could bounce on your knee.

"Don't deny an elderly gentleman one of the few pleasures he has left. You'll be old one day too. From the looks of you, Peter, that one day might be Wednesday."

"Old, my ass. I thought you gave Muffin a case of burning loins, as we say in the Gothic novel."

"Do you eat with that mouth?" my father asked placidly, blowing a perfect smoke ring toward the ceiling. "I only titillated you with smut to get you out of bed. You know I never kiss and tell."

"Not this morning anyway." I lit up my leadoff Marlboro and asked him the question I didn't want to ask. "Seriously, do you think she's dead, Pap?"

Out the window, I watched the Roosevelt Island tram snaking across the high wire toward Manhattan and waited for his answer.

"Oh, Mick and the poor husband are right. She has gone to her reward somehow. Kidnappings do not go anything like this, not anything like this at all. Do you have any idea how you're going to start?"

"Sort of. From what Mick said there seem to be several thousand suspects running around the Global Broadcasting Company, starting right at the top. I'm going to have Marty and Natalie wander over there and interview some of the notable quotables at random. People talk to Natalie the way they don't talk to everybody else, and she's got an ear. Marty's camera has this way of spotting lies. After I see what they've got, I'll follow up with the interesting ones, and the game'll be on. I need to make a first down in a hurry."

He poured more coffee for both of us. I tasted mine. I thought there might be a touch of brandy in there, but I was too well-bred to ask about it.

Plus it tasted fine.

"You're coming in cold on this one, and late," he said. "I don't mean to be sounding like a cop all the time, but the department is way ahead of you, despite what Dunphy said. Don't think for a second he told you all of it. He held back things, same as you did. There seem to be a lot of sides to this one, sonny. Even in the age of Hinckley and Mark David Chapman, it isn't such an easy thing to murder the cover of *People* magazine and get away with it. Do you really think you can find out things the police haven't?"

"I usually do. It's why I get such good tables."

"True enough. You have excellent bloodlines."

"A thoroughbred, old-timer. Daddy was Secretariat."

"Anything the daddy can do to help?"

I said, "Couple of things, if you can. Hang around the station the next couple of days. It's the biggest case around, so it would be perfectly natural for you to be asking questions. They might be holding something juicy back. Also, call down to the cops in Guertin, Alabama. If there *are* cops in Guertin, Alabama. Check on Billy Lynn. You might even want to go down there for a day or two, check out his story. Channel A will pay expenses."

"Goody. And what is my resourceful son going to be doing whilst his daddy makes like an aging Hardy Boy?"

I knew what I was going to do first. I was going to pay a call on Kris Stanford. She was Peggy Lynn's personal secretary and best friend, or so she said. Professional best friend. Did all the things an agent did, according to the newspapers. I had met her here and there along the dusty old trail, at the odd awards banquet and press conference; she did a lot of Peggy Lynn's legwork, the way Natalie did for me. According to the newspaper stories, she even had an apartment of her own in Peggy Lynn's brownstone on East Seventy-fourth. And she had been interviewed a lot, both in the papers and on television, right after the disappearance. Then she had suddenly, and inexplicably, gone into seclusion. I planned on unsecluding her, if I could. With someone like Peggy Lynn Brady, who had so many planets revolving around her, I figured it was best to get as far inside the circle as I could, then work my way out.

I told my father all that. He nodded a lot.

"That makes sense. Sometimes when you think like a cop you make me want to dance like Fred Astaire. Are you going to visit Miss Stanford dressed like that?"

I frowned and looked down at my work uniform. Tretorns. Blue jeans, pressed and clean. Blue buttoned-down shirt. Knit tie, maroon. My summer blazer was draped over the end of the sofa. I had shaved.

"I always dress like this for work," I said defensively.

"I know," my father said sadly. "I know." We both laughed.

He put the coffee pot and cups on a tray and carried them into the kitchen, fastidious as always, cigar sticking out of his mouth. Jack Finley had cut his teeth as a policeman walking a beat in one of the roughest black-white sections of Boston, near Columbia Point, where they used to kill you if you didn't pronounce your a's hard enough. Over the years, as he moved his way up through the ranks to detective, they had put a few more bullet holes in him than I cared to remember. Once—when I was fifteen— they nearly killed him during a mob shoot-out at a saloon near Logan Airport. He never took dumb chances, but he took enough, and waiting for the phone call in the night had finally killed my mother. But when he was around me he had always laughed a lot, and despite what the job was, he had never shown me anything except elegance and cheer; he had taught me all about being a man just by walking around in my vicinity. The Lord made my father a cop, but I think He always had Cary Grant in the back of his mind.

"Always remember one thing," he told me during a bad time in college, when my diploma seemed to be parked on top of Mount Everest. "Life is not a melodrama. It's a situation comedy."

He was whistling what sounded vaguely like "Danny

Boy," his great face wreathed in cigar smoke, as he made short work of the breakfast utensils in front of my sink. And I was thinking again as I watched him there that if anything ever happened to him it would be like someone cutting a hole in my universe.

When he got the dishwasher going, he came back into the living room, checked the seersucker jacket for wrinkles like an actress tracking gray hairs, then put it back on.

"Have you talked to Jeannie?" he asked casually.

"Last night."

"How did it go?"

"Pap," I said, "my marriage is currently in sorrier shape than the Red Sox."

A cloud started to pass across the sunny Irish face. He stopped it short, came over to me, worked a smile around the cigar, patted me on the cheek.

"You got your keys?"

I nodded. There were times when he could still make me feel like a kid. This was one of them. It felt good.

"Well then. Let's go solve a crime," he said. He opened the door with a flourish and glided out with a smooth little two-step that did indeed have some Astaire in it.

MARTY and Natalie were waiting for me in my office when I got there at nine. I had stopped by the Holiday Inn to see Billy, but he was out, so I left him a message that I would call before noon, and to wait for me. I wanted to look at some of those letters. I didn't think there would be any Elizabeth Barrett Browning in there, but I was hoping there would be something that could help.

Marty was sitting in my chair and seemed, as usual, to be in a semicomatose state. His full red beard was resting on his chest like a soft pillow, and his eyes were half-closed behind his reading glasses. Red hair escaped in all directions from under his Brooklyn Dodgers cap. He was doing the *Times* crossword. It wasn't an official day for Marty Pearl unless he'd finished the *Times* crossword. I noticed he was wearing the same basic outfit he always wore, winter or summer, good weather or bad. Khaki bush jacket. Painter's pants roomy enough to park a Volkswagen Rabbit in. Bowling shirt. Marty is six foot six. My mother would have described his figure as "lush," which is what she said when she didn't want to say "fat."

"What's a word for *soft,* beginning with the letter *f*?" he asked as I shut the door.

"Finley," I said. "And it's nice of you to be worrying about my manhood."

"Seven letters."

"Flaccid."

"Bingo," he said sleepily. "And good morning."

"Good morning to you, scout," I said. "And to you, Ms. Ferrare. You still single?"

"Morning, Finley," she said. "I've already made a list of people Marty and I should see over at Global today. It's on top of that disgusting pizza box if you care to look at it."

She was curled up on the small leather couch next to my locker, feet tucked underneath her, wearing one of those one-piece jumpsuits the color of army fatigues, nervously smoking a cigarette. Her black hair was in a ponytail, pushed back in front by a bandana the color of the jumpsuit. Even on a Monday morning, she looked like she had come directly to the office from the cover of *Seventeen* magazine. Her usual supply of nervous energy had the office humming.

I noticed that the zipper on the front of the jump suit had traveled far enough south to command my attention, and Marty's.

"Listen, before I do that, would you mind if I sit a little

closer to you, Natalie? At least until Delores gets here with the coffee."

Marty snorted from across the room. It is as close to laughter as he gets. Natalie just blew a jet stream of smoke in my direction.

"Is that going to be the quality of the repartee this morning?" she said disgustedly. "Must have been another big weekend in bachelorville for you, Finley. You used to look at me like I was your nephew."

"You've just got to hang in there, Natalie," I said. "If you don't marry onto the big board soon, you may yet have your way with me."

She reached beside her for the notebook that was never far away and began to scribble in it.

"Dear diary," she said in the fluttery, schoolgirl voice she trotted out for such occasions. "Perhaps my ship has finally come in. . . ."

Natalie had always been able to ad lib, from the first day. I made one of my frequent mental notes to fall in love with her if Jeannie Bogardus Finley continued to act like Heinrich Himmler.

I was starting to make mental notes like that as often as I brushed my teeth.

When Delores was a little slow arriving with the coffee for Team Finley, Natalie sighed the way girls from Vassar are supposed to sigh and jumped up from the couch.

"Belly up to the bar, boys," she said, thrusting out a delicious hip as she vamped through the doorway. "I'll go check on the horses."

I looked over at Marty, who nearly smiled as he flipped me a thumbs-up sign.

"You surprised she's already got a list made up?" he asked.

"Not in the slightest."

"She got back early last night. Was in here at seven.

Ransacked the clip files. Checked out a couple of cassettes. Called a couple of flacks she knows, one from GBC. Used to date one of those prime-time baby moguls over at GBC. Woke him up and grilled him, too. When I got to the office, she was drumming her fingers on your desk with one of those 'where the hell is everyone?' looks. Ever notice how Natalie sort of treats life like a final exam?"

"I knew it the day I interviewed her. After she rattled off her credentials, critiqued my last three pieces, and then told me I ought to hire her while I could still afford her, I didn't know whether to give her the job or vote for her."

She came back in with the coffee. I looked at her the way I imagine Wally Pipp looked at Lou Gehrig when Gehrig was still second string.

"Okay," Natalie said, curling back up on the couch, looking over her notes. "Here's what we got: Peggy Lynn fucked around."

I choked a little on the coffee.

"Something wrong?"

"Hot," I whispered, pointing at my cup.

"Well, she did. As good as she was or is, she didn't move up as quickly as she did because of her winning smile and sunny disposition. She picked her, uh, friends very carefully. I didn't talk to as many people as I would have liked to this morning, but they all gave me that message. The consensus is that Peg o' my heart was real good at what we used to call Upward Boudoir at school."

"Catty," I said. "Very catty."

"What is this, a scoop of some sort? I *know* you dated her, remember? Anyway, if I may continue, here's who we should get to, in no particular order:

"Kris Stanford. Secretary, gofer, almost agent, friend, housemate. They're not as close as Kris would have everybody believe, in the sense of being equals, but she does run a lot of interference, handles a lot of details. Word I get is that she may have seen *All About Eve* a few too many times. My friend at GBC says compared to her I've got no ambition at all."

Marty said, "Got a scoop now."

She stuck her tongue out at him, cleared her throat theatrically, and went on.

"Thomas Harrold. Runs GBC with the proverbial iron hand, but is running a little scared right now because of the Endicott takeover. Might be some bad blood between Harrold and Peggy Lynn, because of the contract negotiation. Or they might have something going on, on the side. Peggy Lynn is supposed to be having a hush-hush romance with somebody. No one knows who. Could be Harrold.

"Johnny Brant. Peggy Lynn's co-star on 'Midnite.' Mortal enemies the two of them, now more than ever. At least the now before she went poof. We're talking hate here. If Brant were on shore and he saw Peggy Lynn drowning, he'd go get a hot dog."

"Worked with that sucker once," Marty said. "They just turn on the red light and wait for his brain to back up."

Briskly, Natalie gave us the rest of her list, dark eyes aglitter and alive, offering punchy asides as she went.

Sam Cummings. Peggy Lynn's producer on "Midnite." According to Natalie, Cummings was really her best friend at the network. He could do more for her than Kris Stanford. Had come over with her from Channel 2.

Seth Parker. The flamboyant ex-husband. Broadway director and choreographer. Boy Wonder of the Great White Way. They had been married for two years. The divorce case looked like a dilly starting out, then ended suddenly and quietly in Peggy Lynn's favor. Natalie smiled an evil little smile when she told us Seth liked boys now.

Reverend Eugene Endicott. The man quarterbacking the GBC takeover, mostly because he *was* the World Christian Network. He apparently had gotten involved in the Peggy Lynn negotiations but had left for a European tour a couple of days after she disappeared. Due back any day.

That was it. A simple morning's work. When Natalie finished, she flung her notebook into a duffel bag that surely had Gucci or Vuitton written on it somewhere, and sat back smugly, arms folded.

"You make me feel inadequate and irrelevant," I said.

"You ought to," she said. "Incidentally, before Marty and I get to GBC, I'd like to try and find Kris Stanford, if that's all right with you."

"I'm going to see her myself, without you guys. You just go over to GBC, dazzle them with your razzle, and get some of those folks from your dossier on camera. If you've got time after that, find out what Seth Parker is doing, and if I can get to him. He sounds like a thing of beauty and a joy forever."

"Going to see the secretary alone?" Marty asked. He had lifted the top of the pizza box an inch or so and was peering suspiciously in.

"I think I'm going to bring a friend," I said, and gave them the details of the Billy Lynn meeting, in *Reader's Digest* form.

"A husband!" Natalie shrieked. "Why did you wait so long to tell us?"

"I was going to, but then you walked all over me, as usual."

"You get him over here right now," she said sharply. "God. A husband. From Alabama. No shit."

"I'll introduce you to him later if you're a good girl. I'm going to bring him with me to see Kris Stanford. If the conversation starts to drag a little, I'll tell her who he is, and maybe we'll have ourselves a sock hop."

I took one last sip of my coffee, which now tasted like carbon paper.

"Let's all try to get back here by three," I said. "Any questions?"

"One," Marty said over his shoulder as he and Natalie headed for the door. "How long has that pizza been lying in state?"

I watched the big man leave, marveling once again that I was lucky enough to have Marty as sidekick, and friend. It was difficult for me to remember a time when Marty wasn't around for me. He had never revealed a lot about himself, the way friends do. I knew he had grown up in Brooklyn. I knew he had been to Vietnam and that he was divorced and that he had a son somewhere. I knew he was the best I had ever seen with a minicam. But even at his most drunken moments, Marty had never been what you would call chatty.

The first week I was at Channel A, we had been sent up to The Bronx to cover a gang war among some Puerto Rican kids that had paralyzed a neighborhood. In the middle of it, a murderous kid named Jesus pulled a knife on me. Marty never put the camera down, just broke the kid's nose with one punch. Jesus went down as though a building had fallen on him.

"Don't think he understood the question," Marty had said. The interview went swimmingly after that.

I chuckled at the memory of Jesus sitting there with his mouth open, sat down behind my desk, and buzzed Delores.

"Call the Fifty-seventh Street Holiday Inn and get me a man named Billy Lynn," I told her. "He's registered."

"Charley's looking for you, honey," Delores said. "And

I don't think he wants to take your bones over to La Grenouille for lunch."

"Stall him."

"How?"

"Lie."

"I thought it might be something like that," she said.

I wheeled around the chair and looked outside. It was one of those brilliant New York mornings they slipped into August every so often. The humidity was gone and the temperature had dropped into the high sixties. It was more like early autumn than anything else. I sat there grinning. I was alert. Alive. Eager even, for the first time in a while, maybe since Jeannie had left me. The hunt was on. I didn't have any answers yet but I was full of questions.

Finley on the case?

Out loud I said, "Why the fuck not?"

The phone rang. I picked it up. It was Billy Lynn, as earnest as ever. I thought his tail might be wagging.

"Sorry I wasn't there when you stopped by, Mr. Finley. I was around the corner having breakfast. I surely should have left word."

"No problem. Listen, Billy, I'd like to have you help me out on this, if that's all right with you."

"Anything I can do, Mr. Finley. It's why I came. I'd like to go crazy if I was just sittin' around."

"Terrific. Can you get over here right away? And do me a favor. Bring any letters that mention a woman named Kris Stanford."

"I met her once," he said. "I didn't much like her. I felt like she was always fillin' Peggy Lynn's head with sick ideas."

"Just bring the letters," I said and hung up the phone.

I walked out of the office and was preparing my speech for Charley Davidson about why the piece on the mayor would have to wait. Marty and Natalie were standing by Delores's desk. Natalie's face was the color of ice. She was holding a piece of wire copy in her hand.

Marty just looked like business.

"What's up?" I asked.

"No use in rushing over to see Kris Stanford, sport," he said. "The police just found her body. Somebody stuck an ice pick in the back of her neck."

CHAPTER

4

ACCORDING to the wire, they had found Kris
Stanford's body in Peggy Lynn's brownstone on the
Upper East Side.

There were two patrol cars parked in front when we
pulled up in Marty's ancient blue van. A couple of uniformed cops were managing a small crowd of people who
seemed intent on auditioning for the six o'clock news. The
brownstone was situated between York and First on Seventy-fourth. It didn't look like much from the outside, but
a lot of Manhattan palaces don't. I figured the inside
probably cost more than Elizabeth Taylor.

There was a dry-cleaning store on one side, and an
Original Ray's Pizza on the other. Next to the Original
Ray's was a parking garage. The crowd was milling in
front of the dry cleaner's. On the curb in front of the
parking garage a black man in an overcoat sat playing a
saxophone, oblivious of the gripping drama of crime. The

54

black man was playing "I Can't Get Started." It wasn't Bunny Berigan but it sounded pretty good.

Mick Dunphy was standing at the top of the steps, leaning against Peggy Lynn's front door. On the lower steps was a gaggle of cameras and microphones and reporters. When Marty and Natalie got our equipment out of the back of the van, they muscled their way near Dunphy. I usually waited until the rush-hour traffic thinned before I tried to talk to him. I just assumed he was still spicing the monologue with a lot of "allegeds" and "perpetrators." Natalie could handle all that. It made her feel like Police Woman.

I walked down the street toward the man playing the sax and sat down next to him, moving a brown Bloomingdale's shopping bag filled with old newspapers out of the way. He didn't seem to notice as he moved into the second verse. He was wearing an old high-topped black Converse sneaker, minus the laces, on one foot; he had a work boot on the other. His toes stuck out from the front of the work boot. His age seemed to be somewhere between sixty and Bellevue. He smelled like last week.

Sometimes you play hunches. Most of the time they only win you enough losing two-dollar tickets to wallpaper the Pentagon. And every once in a while you get lucky. I took out two Marlboros and offered the old man one. He looked at me with rheumy eyes for a fat minute, still playing the sax. Then he carefully put the sax on the curb and took the cigarette, which I lit for him. He took a drag that required more than the regulation number of lungs and coughed a cough I could understand, something out of a Sousa march.

I said, "You play real good."

The black man laughed. It was a tired sound that ran out of gas and died somewhere in his throat.

"You the heat?" He had a high-pitched, child's voice;

a don't-know-nuthin'-'bout-birthin'-no-babies-Miz-Scarlett voice. "Already tol' the cops I din' see *no*body."

I said, "I'm the jazz critic from the *Times,*" and smiled at him.

This time he laughed for real. My sense of humor clearly touched his bag-person soul. I pondered that while the two of us sat there smoking. Me and my new best friend. I looked over my shoulder. Dunphy was still talking. Sometimes when there are reporters around, you need a warrant to get Mick Dunphy to stop talking. His lung capacity suddenly rivals a deep-sea diver's.

"If you ain' a cop, then what?"

"Reporter, sort of. TV. You been sitting here all morning?"

"Maybe. An' maybe I been sleepin' over there. Nice over there." He pointed with his right hand toward a deserted playground across the street. I noticed that near the elbow there was a hole in the overcoat you could fit all of Mickey's Mouseketeers through.

I took out a twenty and stuck it in his right front pocket. His eyes followed the twenty the whole trip.

"You sure you didn't see anything?"

He said, "You won' tell the cops? Cops always be roustin' me, Jim."

I shook my head and shot a glance at the two uniformed cops. They were talking to a blonde in a tank top who made Dolly Parton look like a boy.

"Saw somebody, Jim. Saw somebody for sure." He took out the twenty and smoothed it lovingly against the front of the coat. "Early he come. Real early. Fancy li'l red car. He got out like Peter Pan, no bigger than a midget. Noticed the car right off, Jim. Differen' than all the other ones be pullin' up sometimes, people gettin' out, lookin' like the Lord himself some of them. I like this li'l red car best of all." He coughed again. "Anyway, Peter Pan go skippin' up them steps like the devil chasin' him for sure. Don' stay long."

I was losing him. I said, "Peter Pan?"

The old man dropped his voice to a whisper.

"Look like a homo, Jim. You hear me?"

"Homo," I said. "You remember anything else about what he looked like?"

He took off his stocking cap. His white hair, what was left of it, was in a crew cut. Or maybe just had retired. He passed a shaky hand over it.

"Short hair, like mine. Pointy li'l beard too. Nice car that was. Not like the big ones. But real nice, know?" He closed his eyes and started humming some blues thing, rocking from side to side.

"That all?"

"Tired a talkin'. Gon' play somethin' now, Jim. Somethin' you wanna hear maybe?"

I figured the "Tonight Show" theme was out of the question so I said "One O'Clock Jump" and tucked two more Marlboros and a pack of matches in with the twenty.

"Like you, Jim. Don' be tellin' the heat 'bout Peter Pan."

The crowd around Dunphy was breaking up. The spectators were leaving, too. The ones in front of the dry-cleaning store walked away in groups of twos and threes, occasionally looking back at the brownstone and pointing. They were probably hoping for a terrorist bombing later on; Rather might show up for that.

Dunphy was still leaning against the oak door, smoking a Lucky, talking to Natalie. Marty was sitting next to them, holding the gray minicam in his lap like it was a sleeping baby.

"Chatting with your public?" Mick Dunphy asked, waving a meaty hand at the saxophone player.

"He's voting a straight Republican ticket," I said. "Wants the welfare rolls cleaned up." I lit another cigarette of my own. "So what do you got?"

Dunphy took a silk handkerchief out of his breast pocket and made a dainty pass with it across his forehead. The day was starting to heat up. August had only tricked us for a little while.

"The maid found her about nine. Door was unlocked, but no sign of forced entry we could see. Whoever it was, she opened the door. She was on the living room rug, in front of the television set. The doc says she was dead before she hit the ground. Says whoever did it must have been one strong mother. It went in all the way up to the handle."

I checked out Natalie, who looked as if she were trying to swallow her lips.

I said, "Anything taken?"

"I don't think so," Dunphy said. "The lab boys are still dusting inside, but the place looks very clean, except for where the dead person was. Whoever did it got right to business and left. She must have known him, because she let him in, but from what I've been hearing, Kris Stanford hadn't been letting anybody into the joint lately."

"Did any of the neighbors see anything fascinating this morning?"

"We've got some of the boys doing a census up and down the block. If we're lucky, maybe we'll come up with something before the day's out."

I was thinking about Peter Pan in a red sports car, but I wanted to chase that one down myself. I'm usually a good citizen but I try not to be a fanatic about it. Somebody must have seen the car, if there really was one. I just wanted a head start on Dunphy.

"Weren't you guys supposed to be watching this house?" Marty said.

Dunphy snorted like a bull getting ready to go after one of those El Cordobas.

"The geniuses downtown pulled up the stake yesterday, without even telling me. Thought we were wasting quote manpower unquote. Jesus Fucking Christ. This is the safest city in the world considering we don't have any law enforcement."

I said, "Can I quote you?"

"Go have a heart attack, asshole," Dunphy said.

"You gonna say there's a connection between this and Peggy Lynn's disappearance?" I asked.

"I'm gonna dance around that one," he said, finally giving us a blast of the wise-guy grin. He hooked a thumb at Marty. "Then when Smokey the Bear comes in for one of his close-ups, you're gonna force me into it, you relentless bastard."

Natalie handed me the microphone with the Channel A logo on it. I straightened my tie and got into position next to Dunphy. Marty stood on the street, camera on his shoulder, shooting up slightly. Natalie was next to him with a headset on, fiddling with the dials on the sound equipment; the piece looked like one of those oversized tape players Japan exports directly to Harlem. The bigger operations can afford a camera guy and a sound guy. Not Channel A, a nonunion shop where versatility is encouraged. Marty often does both, unless Natalie is around, or Dwan.

"You got any blush?" Dunphy said.

Natalie said, "Sound."

Marty said, "Rolling tape."

The sax man was playing what sounded like "The Star-Spangled Banner." I tried to appear more sincere than the Reverend Endicott.

"This is Peter Finley," I started.

It had always worked well in the past, relatively speaking.

WHEN we finished the stand-up with Dunphy, I gave the cassette to Natalie and told her to take a cab back to the office. She and Dwan could put the bit together for the six-thirty news, about three minutes worth. I told her that Marty and I were stopping at O'Rourkes for lunch before we made our afternoon rounds. Down the street, toward First, I saw two of Dunphy's plainclothes guys ring a doorbell.

Natalie wanted to know what afternoon rounds meant.

I said, "We're going to pay a call on Seth Parker."

We were standing near the back of the van. Marty was inside, rummaging around for a clean cassette. He had been in there awhile. The back of Marty's van usually looks like the last days of Saigon.

"What do you have to see Seth Parker about?" Natalie asked.

"Because I've got to start somewhere on this thing, and my gut tells me Seth Parker might be the place to start. He seemed to hate Peggy Lynn as much as anybody. Ex-husbands usually get to carry the flag and lead the parade."

Natalie stuck out her jaw and gave me a cold look that indicated she'd hit me upside the head with a frying pan if she had one handy.

"Why can't I go with you two?"

"Because I get to play boss once in a while, and I say you can't. You go back to the office and edit the piece with Dwan. Billy Lynn will be waiting there for me. You wanted to meet Billy Lynn, right? Introduce yourself and make nice with him."

Natalie said, "You're not telling me something, you bastard."

"I might not be," I said. "Now run along. If you're good, I promise I'll fill you in later."

She stuffed the cassette into her purse, wheeled on her heels, walked away toward York. I had a feeling she hadn't delivered her exit line. She hadn't. She stopped at twenty paces. There was an old woman in a housecoat coming up behind her, walking a poodle. Natalie nearly took her out with the purse.

"You know," Natalie said for the neighborhood, "one of these days I'm going to tell you guys to piss off when you treat me like your goddamn kid sister." Natalie snapped, "I'm gonna level with you, Finley: Annette Fucking Funicello I'm not."

The woman with the dog looked like she'd been stabbed in the kidney. Natalie didn't wait for an answer. She knew Annette Funicello was going to be tough to top. I smiled until I saw her get into a Checker at the corner.

As the van crawled downtown toward O'Rourkes, I told Marty about my conversation with the old man, about Peter Pan and a red sports car. I told him that the old man's description of Peter Pan sounded to me like Seth Parker, even if the old man was crazier than betting on basketball games.

Marty said, "That's not a lot to go on, sport. New York's the headquarters for fruits like he thought he saw. And Mr. Sax isn't your basic reliable source. He sounds as dippy as my ex-wife, is what he sounds like."

"I know that. But if Seth Parker was married to Peggy Lynn, he sure as hell knew Kris Stanford. They were joined at the hip. If Seth had some unfinished business with Peggy Lynn, maybe he thought he could take it up with Kris. Maybe Peggy Lynn did have something on him he wanted to bury once and for all. Maybe it's nothing.

But it's time for us to start our engines. That much I know."

"We gonna find out about a red sports car?"

"As soon as we get to O'Rourkes."

"Then we visit Seth Parker?"

"Like the Welcome Wagon lady."

Marty said, "Long shot."

"I know. I watch a lot of television."

There was an empty parking space in front of O'Rourkes, at Fiftieth and Second, when we pulled up. There was a fire hydrant too. But the van had press plates. We locked it up and went in. Once the van was locked, Marty never worried about his equipment. He had installed his own alarm system; breaking in was harder than escaping from Attica. As an added crime deterrent, Marty had a big bumper sticker in back. It read: THEY'LL TAKE MY GUN AWAY WHEN THEY PRY IT FROM MY COLD, DEAD FINGERS.

Even at one o'clock, with stockbrokers and ad agency degenerates swarming the bar area like killer bees, O'Rourkes is everything a bar should be. It is dark for one thing. There is always some kind of sports event on one of the three televisions, but the sound is never on. They pour drinks that are drinks. When the front room gets crowded and begins to resemble the fall of France in 1940, you can sit and hide in a booth in the back room. O'Rourkes also has the best juke box in New York City, with everything from the Beatles to Billie Holiday to Willie and Waylon. You can listen to Cagney singing from *Yankee Doodle Dandy,* and you can listen to the entire score from *Guys and Dolls.* At its best—and I had seen it at its best a lot—O'Rourkes was a grand mixture of sports people and pols and network moguls and writers and pretty ladies and bookies and bust-outs; even a few shady fellows in sunglasses about whom I had never inquired.

O'Rourkes is what Toots Shor's used to be only better. It even has cable.

Jeannie Bogardus Finley did not like O'Rourkes; she referred to it acidly as "the frat house." My ongoing internship there was one of the many reasons why the post office had received her change-of-address card in February.

"It's your damn Alamo, Peter, you just can't see it because you don't want to," she had said during one of our more recent arguments. "It's where you make your last stand against being a real adult. And I'll be damned if I'm going to keep trying to storm the walls."

I remember saying something like "Um."

Jeannie was one of those people who talked as well as she wrote, angry or funny or sad. When she hit you with a line like that all you could do was ask for a standing eight count. I won arguments from her as often as I beat Andrew Jackson Finley in chess, which was never.

Jimmy O'Rourke was sitting in the back room, first table, inside right, sipping his first Canadian Club and ginger ale of the day. He called it his prom drink. The prom drinks had kept him out of law school. On the shelf in back of him was a two-foot-high statue of Babe Ruth. When O'Rourke got drunk enough watching baseball, he called the statue "George Herman," as in George Herman Ruth. O'Rourke was the greatest Yankee fan in all of New York. There were various Yankee memorabilia and photographs all over the back room, like you'd find in a shrine. O'Rourke and I had met in college. He had been to the last twenty-five Yankee home openers in succession. In 1973, to keep his streak alive, he had gone AWOL from Fort Dix, where he was a guest of the United States Army at the time. It was his favorite Yankee story. Right before a Lieutenant Maybee threw him into the stockade, he told

O'Rourke, "You're the kind of man who would turn his back on his troops in battle."

"Begging your pardon, sir," O'Rourke replied. "But only if the Yanks were in the Series."

It got him eight days.

In what passed for his adult years only chronologically, O'Rourke had worked in public relations for NBC, then CBS, making connections, getting enough scratch together to do what he had always wanted to do, run a saloon. And along the way he had lived the sort of New York life that Runyon would not have dared invent, setting North American records in gambling and stewardesses and Canadian Club. He had been married three times that we knew about. If you watch old movies, you would know he is a dead ringer for the young Frank McHugh. Tight mop of curly black hair. Pug nose. Blue eyes. Broad, square face. It was still the face of an altar boy. Despite the fact that we were always at war about the Red Sox and Yankees, he was my best friend, next to Marty.

"Scribe," he said brightly as Marty and I walked in. "Where do I go to view the remains of your raggedy-ass baseball team?"

"Cleveland, according to the schedule. How much do I owe you for the weekend?"

"Let's see," O'Rourke said. "Three-game series. Fifty a game. Double or nothing if somebody lost the first two. Aw shucks, I'm too well-bred to add it up for you."

I said, "Put it on my tab, okay?"

O'Rourke said, "I will do just that when the bus boys show up. They're the only ones who can lift it."

He went back to reading the box scores in the *Times* as Marty and I set up headquarters at the last booth in the back. Marty groaned and eased himself in in stages. The waitress was a perky little redhead named Becky. I happened to know she was currently living under a Jimmy O'Rourke grant at his apartment. If she was nineteen, I was Secretary of the Navy. Marty ordered a cheeseburger with everything and a beer from Becky. I ordered coffee and a telephone. The regulars could hook up the telephone at back room tables. O'Rourke was a hopeless romantic that way; he thought phones at the table made his joint resemble the Stork Club.

"Might as well find out what kind of car Seth Parker has before we mosey over there. I'm going to call Parker's office. Try to talk a little jive with whatever secretary I get. I'm going to tell the secretary that Mistuh Parker, his car be fixed, mon. The little red Porsche, mon. And Mistuh Parker, he can pick up the sucker when he be ready. You know, mon?"

"That really sucks," Marty said. "And what if it isn't a Porsche?"

"I'll accept a red anything."

"There must be an easier, more legit way to go about this. And without your dumb accent."

"Probably."

Becky came back with beer, coffee, black telephone. I hooked the phone into the plug. Marty drank down almost all of his beer and nearly grinned at me.

Drinking during the day makes him zany.

I got the number from information. They gave me the address too, which was 1515 Broadway. I dialed the number. The English woman who answered said that Mr. Parker was out to lunch. Her voice made me picture Margaret Thatcher. I went into my act. When I got to the part about the red Porsche, she cut me off like a New York cabbie.

"Mr. Parker's red automobile is a Lamborghini, sir," Margaret Thatcher said. Her *r*s came from a blender. "If that is the one you have repaired, I shall tell him it is ready. Good day." She hung up then. I didn't even get to ask her to tea.

"Bingo," I said to Marty. "Lamborghini. Red."

He was peeling the label off the Budweiser and staring around the corner at the kitchen. He knew his cheeseburger was in there somewhere.

I lit a Marlboro, waited a minute, dialed the number again. I was Peter Finley this time, so I used his voice. Margaret Thatcher told me Parker was out to lunch. I asked when he would be back. She said, "I expect him within the hour, at half-two." I told her to tell Mr. Parker that Mr. Finley would be paying him a visit at half-two. She sounded stricken, as though the pound had dropped again.

"Mr. Parker has an extremely busy afternoon," she said. "I couldn't possibly make an appointment without consulting with him first. Out of the question, absolutely."

She ran the last words all together.

I said, "Just tell him it's about Peggy Lynn Brady and Kris Stanford. And then you have a real nice day, sweet cakes."

Marty was finishing his beer and studying a photograph of O'Rourke standing between Mickey Mantle and Willie Mays at the old stadium. O'Rourke looked as if he'd died and gone to heaven in the picture, but it didn't mean too much to Marty. Marty was hungry.

"This mean I don't get to have any dessert?" he asked, frowning at O'Rourkes' wall.

I took a sip of my coffee, and made a list in my head of what I had so far.

I had Peggy Lynn Brady, missing and presumed dead. I had a husband nobody knew about in my office. I had a brand-new corpse. I had a saxophone player and a red Lamborghini and Peter Pan for a suspect.

In certain primitive countries, I was probably considered to be on a roll.

CHAPTER
5

SETH PARKER'S office was on the seventh floor.
The directory in the lobby told us that. It also told us there
were a lot of theatrical heavyweights on the menu at 1515
Broadway, which is at the corner of Forty-fifth.

"I've always wanted to stroll through *Variety*," Marty
said.

The guard in the lobby told us to take a right at David
Merrick's suite of offices when we got to seven. We did
that. The door we were looking for was the one that said
Gypsy Productions. It was Parker's company, named
after the gypsies in the chorus. Or the ones in his soul. The
door opened into a spacious reception area that had a lot
of stainless steel and even more glass. The furniture, chairs
and couches and lamps, was all black. A huge window
opened out on Shubert Alley. The walls were decorated
with posters from Parker's hits. There was a black-and-
white poster from *Tracy*, which was his remake of *The
Philadelphia Story*, an adaptation that made me rethink

my position on capital punishment. There were smaller
posters from *The Nation Sings,* the one about Carrie Nation, and from *Rockettes and Roll,* the black revue about
Radio City Music Hall, and from *Village,* an inspired
tribute to the street people of Greenwich Village.

Parker was standing next to his secretary's desk when
we walked in. It was obvious immediately that something
had been going on between Parker and the secretary, probably not a preliminary discussion about her Christmas
bonus. The secretary looked like a nanny, or maybe Miss
Moneypenny from the James Bond movies. Moneypenny
had elegant features and red hair the color of a bloody
Mary, heavy on the vodka. She was coming apart. Sniffling
into a doily. Staring down hard at the Rolodex in front of
her on the desk.

". . . gullible, overpaid, supercilious Limey bitch" was
the part I caught.

I looked at Parker more closely. The saxophone player's
description fit. He *was* short, a Broadway doll. Small
head, button eyes the color of coal, bushy black eyebrows
pushing together in the crowded room above the eyes, toy
goatee the same color as everything else. His face was one
of those charcoal sketches from a courtroom artist. Whit-
ish pallor. His outfit went nicely with him and had been
de rigueur in his business since Bob Fosse got hot. Black
cord Levi's. Black military-style shirt that was opened up
in a way the fashion magazines would call daring. Black
ankle boots.

Marty whispered, "Barbie's bigger than him."

I cleared my throat to end Parker's floor show with
Moneypenny and Parker turned our way. When he saw
the minicam, I thought he might bite one of us on the leg.

"You must be the witty Mr. Finley," he said, trying for
a hard-guy look. "Who's the gorilla with the hardware?"

In a voice you could have scraped off the floor Marty said, "Gorilla?"

But he let the insult slide for a moment and so did I, mostly because Parker's voice caught me by surprise. I had been expecting something out of the girls' glee club. What I got instead was deep and full and resonant, a voice from inside a bass drum. Before I got a chance to rebut, Parker gave the big drum another whack.

"I don't know what kind of silly game you're trying to run here, Mr. Finley." He spat my name out this time like it was puppy chow. "But I am not amused. Quite the contrary. You have upset my secretary. You cut short a backers' luncheon at Four Seasons. You obviously misrepresented yourself with that fairy tale about my car. But congratulate yourself, Mr. Finley. You *have* succeeded in hastening my return. That is where we stand. What we are going to do now is step briefly—very briefly—into my office. Then you are going to spin your little yarn about my ex-wife and Kris Stanford. And then you will be on your way before you . . . *obliterate* my afternoon entirely. I am a busy man. The news may have reached your terribly quaint station that my new show goes into previews at the Mark Hellinger next week."

It hadn't taken Seth Parker long to annoy me.

I said, "I read the trades, Seth. Your show is called *Dancing Shoes.* It stars an ex-drunk singer who can't dance, and a dancer who couldn't sing even before the face-lifts. You are a little worried about that, and *Dancing Shoes* in general, because you need a hit. You need a hit bad. Your last two shows should have been reviewed by the Tidy Bowl man. Open, flush, close. You have played the Kennedy Center in Washington with this one and the Orpheum in Boston, and already it looks like you're going for three bombs in a row. I was in Boston. Kevin Kelly wrote something about you in the *Globe* that could eat paint off the side of a car. We're talking battery acid. You do not need any bad publicity right now. So don't give me any shit in front of the help, unless you want me to ask all my questions right here. Also, if you insult my friend Marty Pearl again, I will urge him strongly to lift you up by your ears."

I just figured that someone has to break the ice at the mixers or nobody dances.

Parker finally said, "In there." He threw a hostile nod at his open office door, then pranced in ahead of us with the unmistakable carriage and movements of a dancer. Marty and I followed him, slightly less gracefully, like we were moving some scenery.

"Must have been the first fox terrier ever to win a Tony award," Marty murmured.

I leaned over and gave Moneypenny a pat on the cheek on my way by her desk. I could tell she was warming up to me.

As we walked into Parker's office I whispered to Marty, "Just sound, fuck pictures."

I interpreted his grunt as the sort of total understanding known only to the Greek philosophers.

THE office had a desk, another blue couch, a bookcase filled with books about the theater, another one filled with rows of video cassettes, a television with a video recorder on top of it, and a stereo setup that took up half a wall and looked like it belonged in Paul McCartney's den. Above the stereo was a large LeRoy Neiman sketch of Parker that made me want to giggle. It was just more of Neiman's fast food. There were three Tony awards sitting on the desk.

Sitting on the blue couch was a blond young man. If the blond were a place he would have been Maui.

Parker was already sitting behind the desk, fitting an unfiltered Camel into a cigarette holder that might have been made of ebony. When he finished he pointed the holder toward the blond. "This is David Ellison," he said. "He is my executive assistant and can hear anything you have to say."

Marty and I sat down in two leather chairs across from Parker. David was to our right. He looked at me. I looked at him.

I said, "Hi, David."

David was wearing a dark purple T-shirt that said CATS on the front. He was also wearing tight designer jeans and Adidas sneakers. Even sitting down David was a big boy. He looked as if he could bench press the Gershwin Theatre if he had a mind to do it.

He didn't say anything back to me but I was pretty sure I saw a ripple in his pectorals.

"We will not record any of this conversation, nor film any of it," Parker said. "Is that understood?"

"Perfectly," I said, and lit up a Marlboro.

"Yo," Marty said.

"Would you mind telling me what this is all about, Mr. Finley?" Parker said.

There are always a number of ways you can go about it. That is what they tell you in the journalism courses. You can establish some friendly rapport. That was out of the question unless Parker was going to have a personality transplant. You can ask four or five innocent questions before you hit him with the one you wanted to ask all along. I didn't have the time for that, and neither did Parker.

Sometimes you have to use the direct approach. My father had always compared my direct approach to the old joke about Irish foreplay. In the joke, Irish foreplay consists of: "Brace yourself, Bridget."

I said, "Somebody stuck an ice pick in Kris Stanford this morning. She's dead. It happened at Peggy Lynn's brownstone. We just came from there. I have an eyewitness who will swear he saw you pull up to that very same brownstone early this morning in your little red car, go in, stay awhile, come out, go away. She was either dead when you left, or alive. But she was in there. I thought we might chat about that, unless you care to hear my thoughts about the sad state of musical comedy."

I looked over at David, grinned and winked.

Parker was either genuinely surprised, or one hell of a little Method actor. His mouth dropped open. The cigarette holder froze halfway to his lips. What color he did have in his face disappeared.

"Kris . . . dead?"

"Dead. You hadn't heard?"

The cigarette holder made a shaky route to the ashtray, like traveling through choppy air.

"No . . . I mean I've been busy all day since . . . Who says I was there in the morning?"

I took a drag on my Marlboro. And lied. "One of my people."

Parker's eyes moved over to David. The eyes said something. David crossed his arms over CATS and slowly shook his head.

There is no accounting for the language of love.

Parker said to me, "Do the police . . ." His words disappeared into the mist of whatever the question was going to be.

"No. Not yet anyway," I said. "They were asking questions around the neighborhood when I left, but it's not a busy street. And you were there early."

"Are you going to tell them?"

I leaned back so I could see Marty better. The camera was in his lap. It is a Sony Betacam, a camera and recorder all in one unit. It is state of the art, and battleship gray. It uses professional half-inch cassettes instead of the three-quarter-inch ones we had to use in the old days. You can use attach-to-the-lapel ECM-50 mikes with it or a shotgun mike that extends out of the front for use on the street. It weighs about thirty pounds. Marty uses Lowell Omni lights with it, anywhere between 400 and 600 wattage. It always takes very nice pictures for him. Marty can focus the sucker in a race riot.

"I don't know if I'm going to tell them," I said to Parker. "It'll depend on whether you can answer some questions for me."

Parker chewed on that one and tried to compose himself. It was a big job now that his suave had spilled over the rug.

He said, "You don't think I . . . murdered Kris Stanford?"

"As a matter of fact, I don't. Even if you had a reason, I don't think you're dumb enough to waltz in during the Phil Donahue hour and kill her. You have a flashy car that people could remember. You parked it out front, plain as day. You would have had to worry about the neighbors seeing, noticing, remembering. It's a busy time of the day. People go to work. They walk dogs. Nah, you're a born director. You would have staged it a lot better, picked one hell of a better time. Also—big also—Kris Stanford was six feet tall if she was an inch. You're not big enough to ice-pick her at the angle she got ice-picked unless you shinnied up her leg to do it. And I gotta believe that since she was close to Peggy Lynn, she wouldn't turn her back on you for a minute. Dave here is big enough to have snuffed her, as part of his vast duties as executive assistant, but my guy says you went in alone. So that leaves Dave out. Alas and alack."

Out of the corner of my eye I saw David Ellison lean forward a little on the couch.

"Hey," he said.

I turned to him, sweet as you please.

"Shut up, David. I'm working here."

The direct approach. I wanted Parker to see P. Finley as a hard guy who would toss him to the cops if he didn't open up.

Parker said, "What do you want from me?"

"I'm not here about Kris Stanford, at least not directly. I'm working on the disappearance of your ex-wife. I'm convinced she was murdered too. I am told there was a repertory company of people with motives. You might be one of them. Talk to me, Seth."

"I was out of town the night she turned up missing, Mr. Finley. I told the police that already."

"Where?"

"Boston."

"Your show?"

"Yes."

"Had you seen her lately?"

Parker chuckled. The sound was like warm running water.

"I'm not sure how much you know of our marital history, Mr. Finley, but ours was not a happy union. And ours what not what you would call an amicable divorce. I hadn't spoken to her in years."

The phone rang a couple of times. He ignored it until it stopped.

I said, "I know about the divorce. The tabloids were ready to turn your marriage into a field trip. Then you settled. The word was big, and quiet. From your side of the field. Why did you settle, Mr. Parker?"

"My lawyers thought that made sense ultimately, from a public relations perspective."

I leaned over to the desk and picked up a Tony award. I said, "Bullshit."

"I beg your pardon."

"I don't believe you. Thus sprang the bullshit."

"That is not my problem, Mr. Finley."

"Yeah, it is," I said blandly. "Because I'm *your* problem right now. What you've told me so far I could get out of the newspaper morgue. You didn't want me to waste your time? Don't waste mine. Divorce cases like yours don't get dropped unless somebody has something dirty on somebody else. I think you were the somebody else. I feel we should now reason together about all that, or I'm going to call Mick Dunphy over at homicide and describe your morning. And by this evening you are going to be bigger on the news than a garbage strike."

Nobody said anything. David sat on the couch. Marty sat in his chair. The minicam sat on Marty. I lit another cigarette and gazed over at the Neiman. The Neiman didn't say anything either. The phone rang again and Parker ignored it again. I figured Seth Parker was doing what I would have been doing if I were in his ankle boots. He was weighing options. Thinking about things. The show. The bad publicity. Investors. His recent track record. Me. The police. Maybe the nuclear freeze.

Finally he said, "Why should I trust you, Mr. Finley?"

"Because it's better than trusting tomorrow's *New York Post*. And because I'm not after you. I'm after you only insofar as you relate to Peggy Lynn. There are things about her I need to know. And I'll find them out eventually, whether you tell me or not. I'm just looking for the shortest distance between two points."

There was another silence, a smaller one than before. Parker shot a hole in it by turning to David.

"Could you excuse us please, David?"

He looked wounded, a golden retriever with heartbreak, and said, "Seth. No."

I was beginning to speculate about the scope of David's vocabulary.

"Please," Parker said. "Just wait outside. And tell Miss Pence I do not wish to be disturbed."

David got up, but he wasn't happy about being told to shoo. He was nearly Marty's size, I noted. Bimbos come in all sizes. He closed the door behind him.

Parker said, "Does Mr. Pearl have to hear this?"

"Yes."

I casually looked down at the Sony. Marty had his arm casually draped over the red "on" button, his hand covering the tape window. I wondered how much tape he had left. I knew I wasn't playing by the Marquis of Queensberry rules with Seth Parker, but I wanted to have a present for Dunphy if he got testy about me withholding evidence in a homicide.

I said to Parker, "Tell me all of it."

He told me.

It was not something out of the Harlequin Romance series.

PEGGY LYNN had not yet made her big network splash when Parker met her one night at Elaine's. She was still working for Channel 2, and free-lancing sports pieces for cable whenever she could. Everyone around New York knew she was going places, but Peggy Lynn wanted more. Peggy Lynn wanted famous. Television wasn't fast enough for her. She was running with actresses; she liked what she saw. So Parker was perfect for her. He had just come off back-to-back Tonys for *Rockettes and Roll* and *Village*. He had three plays running on Broadway at the same time. Michael Bennett? Who was that?

From the way he told it, she went after him the same way she went after me, but on a much grander scale. He never had a chance.

Parker: "If erections were brains, we'd all be Einstein, wouldn't we?"

I didn't interject that we'd pledged at the same fraternity. Maybe he knew. He didn't say.

A whirlwind courtship. A Vegas wedding that made *People*. For about six months, they were the Prince Charles and Lady Di of the fan magazines and rags, king and queen of the supermarket check-out stands. They guested on all the local talk shows and hosted big parties. Now everybody knew who Peggy Lynn was.

In addition to her television work, she started taking singing and acting lessons and got passing grades in both. Barely, according to Parker. But no one confused the singing voice with Streisand's, or the acting with Streep's.

Except Peggy Lynn.

She told Parker she wanted to star in *The Nation Sings*.

Parker: "I didn't know whether to laugh or cry. But she was serious. God, was she serious. Before I knew it, I was reading in Liz Smith and Suzy that Peggy Lynn was going to star in the show. I knew the stork hadn't brought those items. They came from Peggy Lynn. But what was I going to do? Call my own wife a liar?"

He tested her, and tested her. And then he tested her. The backers and his own production staff thought he'd lost his mind. He went as far as he could with it, then told her no go. There were fights. Big fights.

In his telling, Peggy Lynn did not accept the news the way she would a singing telegram.

Parker: "That is when I began my sordid little journey into the netherworld, Mr. Finley."

They stayed together, but the marriage broke wide open. Parker had always, he said, thrown parties that were not of a kind covered on the society pages. There was cocaine. Colorful couplings and groupings usually found only on a jumping night at Plato's Retreat. Now there were more parties. A lot more dope. Peggy Lynn began to embrace all of it, in a big way. She paired off indiscriminately. So did Parker.

Parker: "I no longer gave a damn."

He did not say whether or not he was bisexual when he entered the marriage. I didn't ask.

Eventually he ended up with a young male dancer at one of the parties. They drifted into an affair. Peggy Lynn knew about it. Could not have cared less. Parker asked for a divorce. She laughed at him.

She still found it useful being Mrs. Seth Parker.

The dancer kept pressuring Parker to divorce Peggy Lynn.

Parker, though in love with him, kept putting him off.

One afternoon Parker showed up at the dancer's apartment. The kid was dead. Suicide. Sleeping pills.

There was a long note, made out to Parker. He took the note, called the police anonymously, left without anyone seeing him. He went home and kept rereading the letter until he passed out drunk.

Parker: "I have told no one about this, Mr. Finley. Perhaps I have wanted to. Perhaps I am relieved."

He moved out of his apartment, turned it over to Peggy Lynn, and threw himself into rehearsals for *The Nation Sings*. During that period two things happened: Peggy Lynn was hired by Global Broadcasting, after turning down NBC and ABC; *she* sued *Parker* for divorce.

Parker: "I was, shall we say, astounded at her nerve. She had, of course, fucked more of my friends than I had friends."

He was determined to fight the divorce but he never got the chance.

Peggy Lynn showed up at the office one afternoon. She reached into her purse.

The suicide note had been Xeroxed.

She told him there were others. Bragged they were part of her "files." Said she would use the Xeroxed letter gladly if he forced her to.

They were divorced quietly. She kept the apartment. He gave her a huge settlement.

When she disappeared, he didn't much care whether she was missing or dead. He was rooting for dead. But he was still worried about the files. That is why he had gone to see Kris Stanford. She told him that Peggy Lynn bragged to her about the files too, but she, Stanford, didn't have them. Wouldn't say who did. Parker and Kris Stanford argued briefly.

Then he left.

Parker: "I haven't killed anybody, Mr. Finley."

I told him I believed him.

That didn't seem to mean much to him, one way or another.

WHEN he finished, Seth Parker didn't look at Marty or me. He buzzed Miss Pence and told her to send David back in.

Parker said, "Now you know what you wanted to know. Happy? I have no further interest in your investigation. I am sorry Kris Stanford is dead. I do not care what happened to my ex-wife. What I have told you, I have told you to protect myself at a delicate time for me. I hope you will act accordingly, with some semblance of ethics. Should you ever come across the Xerox copy of that letter, I would hope that you will destroy it."

David opened the door and walked through it before I got a chance to answer.

It was then that Marty and I got a little unlucky.

When the tape runs out on the Sony, the machine makes a whining sound. It did that. In the quiet office, the Sony suddenly sounded like an air raid siren.

I stared at it. So did Marty, who fumbled with the stop switch and said, "Fuck." Parker put it together.

"You've been taping this, you son of a bitch," Parker hissed. Then he snapped: "Get the tape, David."

Parliamentary procedure broke down about that time.

David made a lunge for Marty, who was at a disadvantage because he was still sitting down, and David was coming from behind. I moved quickly and got to David before he got to Marty. I tried to get my arms around him. No soap. It was like trying to hug the Chrysler Building. He shucked me off with one arm. I ended up on the couch.

Marty would have been able to handle David fine, but by the time I hit the couch he had one hand on the Sony and one hand holding off Seth Parker, who had bounded around the desk. Parker was making little growling sounds, and looked more than half crazy.

I noticed he was trying to bite the hand Marty was using to hold him.

I went for David. He looked even bigger than he did before, and I didn't want it to last long. He threw a clumsy right. It clipped me over the eye but I slipped most of it. The couch was behind me. I didn't have much room to manuever, so before things got out of hand I hit him a quick slap on the right ear with the heel of my left hand. It stunned him just long enough. I set myself as best I could and threw a tight little combination, left hook then right hook, at his midsection. David's tummy was probably a thing of wonder at the Nautilus gym, but the shots went all the way through him and he went down into a tight curl, making sick sounds as he tried to catch his breath.

I turned around, since David was done. Marty was in front of the desk. He now had the Sony comfortably under one arm and Seth Parker under the other. Parker's feet were off the ground.

"Now be nice," Marty said.

My eye was beginning to sting where David caught me. I was also winded, which irritated me.

Marty sat Parker down in the chair I had been sitting in. He was hyperventilating. I felt bad for him and lousy for me. He gives me his guts on a china dish and I double-cross him. Then I beat up his boyfriend. I knew what Parker was thinking, and I knew I couldn't do a damn thing about it.

I said, "I'm not going to explain this to you now. We're leaving. I don't have any plan to use this tape, but I do need it. I am going to take it to my apartment and leave it there, unless my investigation about Peggy Lynn brings me back to it. I told you before to trust me. Do it whether you want to or not."

I stepped over David and picked up the minicam. The door was open. We walked past Miss Pence, who was looking at the scene in the office like it was goats having sex. Journalism is hard.

At the elevator Marty cheered me up some, but not much.

He said, "Which book do you think David liked better? *The Iliad* or *The Odyssey*?"

CHAPTER

6

CHARLEY DAVIDSON was in the middle of the newsroom yelling into a telephone like electricity hadn't been invented when he spotted Marty and me walking in at a little past five. The decibel level was something normally reserved for Mrs. Davidson. He called her his first wife. Charley's vest was unbuttoned, his sleeves rolled up, bow tie dangling better than a participle from his collar. His reading glasses were about to slide off the bald head. His face was red.

He reminded me, as always, of a popular television commercial: The Pillsbury Dough Boy in heat.

He was Seth Parker's size, just rounder.

He was also the best newsman, print or television—Charley had done both—I had ever known.

He wasn't happy to see me. He was trying to get the six-thirty news together and he didn't have the finished Stanford piece. I had done an open-and-close in front of the brownstone, but I needed to lay down some voice over the rest of it.

Charley said, "You stop right there, Mr. Fucking Television."

The room got quiet, considering the hectic time of day. Charley and I had played the scene before, but the cast of Channel A never seemed to tire of it. I gave him a crisp two-fingered salute and wondered how the person at the other end of the line liked the part about Mr. Fucking Television. I assumed it wasn't Cardinal O'Connor, but you could never tell with Charley.

I said, "Hi, boss."

"I mean it, Finley, you son of a bitch. You and I have some things to talk about. I vote we start with professionalism, or the lack thereof around here."

His voice had gone up an octave. He slammed down the receiver. A copy girl approached him with a script. He glared her back to the Columbia School of Journalism.

I knew I was late. I knew I had a lot to tell him and he was going to like what I had. But I was still feeling like a member of the great unwashed because of the vaudeville in Parker's office. And talking to C. Davidson when he's really angry is like playing in traffic.

"Be back in five, boss," I said. "Hey, we've got a show to put on here."

He started to say something as I moved by him, but Marty had put a soothing hand on his shoulder, drawing his fire.

I heard Marty say, "Why don't we put the show on ourselves, Charley? My dad's got a barn. And I think Natalie can play the piano."

I walked past my office and saw Natalie sitting Indian style on the floor in front of Billy Lynn, who was wearing the same suit as the day before. I rapped my knuckle on the window, mouthed an "I'll be right back," then headed

for the tape room and Dwan. I was still trying to decide
whether or not to let Billy listen to the Parker tape, which
I knew was going to hit him the way a bucket of sludge
would.

Dwan Bagley was sitting at the controls wearing an
Ellesse tennis warmup that was all pink and blue, fastfor-
warding the tape through my interview with Dunphy on
one of the screens. He hit stop and looked down at one of
those tricky runners' watches that can give you your splits
and tell you what time it is in Nepal.

"White trash," he said, "you is late. Even for you."

He was right. When I had to work the six-thirty, I was
usually back at Channel A by four. But the festivities at
Parker's office had boxed me into a familiar deadline
corner.

"Dwan," I said, trying a smile. "Suck."

I grunted and sat down in front of the microphone to
his right. If Dwan noticed the robin's egg over my eye, he
didn't let on. There wasn't time, and he was used to me
playing hurt.

I said, "Love your outfit, Dwan. Who are you playing
in the Open final? Good witch or bad witch?"

He took off his sunglasses, replacing them with a headset.

"Got a script?"

"The great ones don't need scripts."

Dwan adjusted some dials that were as understandable
to me as the Latin Mass.

He said, "Gimme a voice check then."

I did that.

Dwan said, "We pick up the network feed of the interview Kris Stanford did the day after Peggy Lynn Brady
took her powder. I'm only using a quick bite. You got
about fifteen seconds to set it up."

I lit a Marlboro and Dwan and I made what passes for magic at Channel A.

WE congregated in Charley's office after the news.

Charley was in the rocking chair his wife had given him the year after he won the Pulitzer at the *Baltimore Sun*. From the looks of the chair, I had always figured he copped the Pulitzer for covering all that difficulty at Fort Sumter.

Natalie sat smoking on the floor; she liked the floor. Billy was next to her, sitting in a straight-backed chair against the wall. His posture made it look like the electric chair. He was holding a fat manila envelope in his hands. Above Billy's head was a replica of Charley's last front page from when he was managing editor in Baltimore, the day after Nixon resigned. It read: CALIFORNIA, HERE HE COMES!

I was leaning against the window behind Charley, watching the last of the rush hour traffic on Fifty-seventh. Marty was gone. It was his night with his son. They were on their way to the movies.

Other than the muted car horns down below, the only sound in the room was Charley rooting around in the bowl of his pipe with the cap of a Bic.

I had just played the Parker tape.

It was Billy who spoke finally.

I had warned him about what was on the tape. He said he wanted to hear, said he didn't come all the way to New York City to hide. He said it was the truth he was after, nothin' more.

Now he said, "That man is a devil, Mr. Finley."

I looked at him. He was giving the manila envelope a workout, kneading it hard, clenching and unclenching the big hands. His eyes were a little wider than usual, a little too bright and unfocused. The skin was stretched tight against the hard lines of his face. But that was it. I had watched him while he listened to Parker tell his story, and he had mostly taken it like a champ. They built them sturdy in Guertin.

Quietly I said, "How so, Billy? I didn't much like what Parker told me, but I sort of believed him."

He answered me in a patient voice, like he was explaining the Book of Genesis or something at Sunday School.

"It's all there in the letters, Mr. Finley. You'll see. Oh, parts of what he said are true. The parts about those parties and him being, well, the way he is with men. Peggy Lynn tells about that. He was the one who pushed her to try for that play of his. He's the one who promised her Broadway. But it didn't mean so much to her when she failed. It was television she wanted, from the time she left home. The rest of it, about the boy and the suicide note, it's just one of his shows, nothin' more. He was lookin' for your sympathy, so's to throw you off. He's a devil, nothin' more, and that's why Peggy Lynn had to divorce him finally."

I started to say something. He wasn't finished.

He said, "I stopped bein' a boy a long time ago. I knew Peggy Lynn as well as anybody on this earth, and I know all the bad ways New York changed her. But what that man said about the drugs and the sex and the blackmail is all filth and lies. And I'm sorry to run on like this."

Natalie reached up and took his hand. "You didn't run on," she said.

Charley had the pipe going. I usually thought pipes were phony; him they fit. I very much wanted a cold beer. There is very little you can say to a man like Billy about his dreams. I reached over and ejected the tape from Charley's machine.

Maybe the answers would come when we figured out

the killing. That's the way Miss Marple always handled it.

"So where the Christ do we go from here?" Charley said. He had a way of not letting things turn into episodes of "The Waltons." During the news I had told him all of it, and he stopped being mad at me. Charley started hanging around newspapers when he was fifteen years old, running copy and fetching coffee at the New York *Mirror.* He had been a journalism junkie ever since. He liked what I had. Liked that I was ahead of the cops by a couple of furlongs.

I said, "I'm going to keep blundering along in my own inimitable way. My dad's been hanging around the station all day. He'll know if Dunphy turns up anything. I want to know if anyone else saw Parker go into the building this morning. Tomorrow Marty and I are going to go over to GBC and see a guy named Sam Cummings. Natalie says he was Peggy Lynn's trusty sidekick there. I want to talk to someone who didn't think she was the wicked witch of the West Side."

"What about those files Parker talked about?" Charley said.

"I'm going to see if Cummings knows anything about them, and where they might be."

"So you think they exist?"

"Who the hell knows? I'm looking for original smut, or the Cliff Notes."

Charley said, "If Cummings is her pal, think he'll want to help?"

"I intend to use trickery and deceit, same as I did with Parker. Be unethical. Lie a lot. Pull his hair. Same old stuff. It's why my body is running out of parts."

Natalie was leaning forward.

"And what am I supposed to be doing?"

"You're going to skulk around GBC. Find out what you can find out about Thomas Harrold, and how this sale to Endicott might have affected the operation over there. You're the best, sweetie. People will tell you things they won't tell the cops. Collect a bunch of theories. We've been accidentally lucky so far, but we got to keep moving. Someone is running around killing people."

I had forgotten about Billy Lynn. When I looked at him he was looking at me. There was no song in his heart.

He said, "You believe that man don't you, Mr. Finley? You believe Peggy was a . . . a . . . ?"

"I don't know what I believe, Billy. But whoever killed your wife had a good reason, and I want to know what it is. I've got one suspect now, Parker. Parker has a motive, and the motive is revenge. Payback. He does have an alibi for the night she disappeared, but maybe Peggy wasn't killed that night. I don't know. But at least we're in the game now. Parker is a start. He's at the front of the line. Just because I don't think he killed Kris Stanford doesn't make him clean with me. My basic posture for this one is to not trust anybody involved, whether they're breathing or not. Present company excluded. I like you, I really do, but don't turn into a wilting flower on me."

"Do you still want the letters, sir?"

"You betcha. I'm going to read them tonight. There may be things in there you didn't think were important, but which might mean something to me."

He smiled. "Peggy joked about you to me. I remember her sayin' once that you're the type who does the crosswords in pen."

I smiled back. "Are those all of the letters?"

He looked down at the envelope.

"Yes sir. All I could find."

He handed me the envelope. I stuck it into the valise along with the Parker tape.

"Are you sure you want to stay in New York, Billy?" He stood up.

"I'm staying, sir," he said quietly. "I want to see this all the way through. When it's done, one way or another, I'll go home and get on with the rest of my life. I just want to see justice."

I told him that was fine with me. To Natalie I said, "In your free time, check out Parker's story about that suicide, best as you can." I winked at her. "Then dry clean my office."

"Television is my life," she said. "I will count the seconds until your next command." Her legs were still crossed but she got herself into a standing position without bracing her hands on the floor. I used to be able to do that before my knee became a double agent.

Natalie and Billy walked out of the office. I started to follow them.

Charley said, "Stay in touch, Peter. Call your old boss once in a while. You know how I pine in your absences."

I turned around. He was rocking in the old chair, feet never quite touching the ground, his face wreathed in Borkum Riff, thinking boss's thoughts. Behind him, night was coming early, nudging the twilight into the Hudson.

From the newsroom a phone rang twice, then stopped.

"This one is mine, Charley. I can feel it."

"Then make sure you're the one who guesses the secret word. If you don't, I can't think of a goddamn reason in the world why I should put up with your bullshit."

I grinned at him. He sighed. It was one from the heart. The last time I'd heard a sigh like that was in the Houston airport. Some blue-haired woman wearing enough diamonds to sink the *Lusitania* had just been told by a ticket agent that there was no first class to West Palm.

Charley said, "Now get your ass out of here. I want a few moments of serenity before my wife beats the shit out of me with a pot roast."

I left him sitting there.

Little big man.

CHAPTER
7

I WALKED Billy east to the Holiday Inn and told him I would call him in the morning. He said that would be fine. I could have told him I was going to stick up Maxwell's Plum and he would have told me that was fine too. He shook my hand. His grip made my hand feel like it was caught in a garbage disposal. I watched him disappear through the revolving doors and wondered how he spent his evenings. Did he flip through the Good Book? Watch "The Cosby Show"? Order in Chinese? Had he ever seen Wade Boggs hit?

Idly I wondered how he ever got mixed up with Peggy Lynn Brady, who seemed to have had all of the qualities of a dog except loyalty.

I considered walking across town, thought better of it, hailed a cab, stopped at the Hole in the Wall deli on Fifty-eighth and First, picked up a couple of brisket sandwiches from Stan and Ziggy, went home. The window washers had been in finally. I could see Queens out the

terrace doors again. I opened a Coors, washed down three
aspirin with it, opened another Coors, and put on the tape
from Lena Horne's remarkable one-woman Broadway
show. The orchestra carried her out of the big speakers
and into the living room and suddenly her voice was moving into "Stormy Weather" like fog blowing in. She had
to be sixty-five if she was a day but when she sang "Stormy
Weather" like that she still made me want to offer her
yachts and the Riviera. By the time she moved into the
heart of the song, it was as if the room was filled with
smoke.

I sat down on my couch, drank the beer, and listened
to her. I made short work of the first brisket sandwich. I
was actually starting to feel better.

The Yankees-Tigers game would be on television soon
but I was in no mood for the Yankees. They were starting
to roll, and there wasn't a damn thing I could do about
it. The Red Sox were in Chicago, but Manhattan Cable
didn't pick up the feed from the Boston UHF channel
anymore. I considered it a terrible step backward for civilization.

I decided on the Mets.

The message light was blinking on the number hooked
into the answering service. I debated whether to have
another Coors or call Gina and get the messages. Another
mid-life crisis. I wanted to go through Peggy Lynn's letters. If I kept drinking they would make as much sense to
me as W2 forms. I dialed the service.

I said to Gina, "Did Paramount Pictures call?"

She giggled.

"Yeah, honey," she said. "Twice. Said they'll double
any offer Warner Brothers makes."

"Gina," I said. "You are overqualified."

"I know. Want the real messages?"

I said, "Uh-huh."

"We have a Micky Dunphy. Said he watched the news and he should have your job. Also said you shot him from his bad side. Your dad called and said he would call tomorrow. Said he didn't want any shit about *La Bohème* when he did. Also a man named Parker called. Mentioned something about wanting a tape from you."

"Parker pissed?"

"Sounded like a prick, if you'll pardon my French, honey."

"No Jeannie?"

"No Jeannie. Hey, can I ask you something?"

"Shoot."

"I asked your daddy about this *La Bohème* shit and he said he went with somebody named Muffin. That a real name?"

"Of course not, woman. It's a nickname. Her real name is Pebble."

That was it. I hung up. I walked over to the stereo and flipped the Lena tape. Decided to have a third Coors. The beer and I went out to the terrace. I sat down in the director's chair I kept out there and stared out at the river.

My terrace is one of the best places in Manhattan, right there with O'Rourkes and the back room at P. J. Clarke's and the lobby of the *Daily News* with its huge globe and the Garden when the Knicks were playing the Celtics and the tennis courts in Central Park and the front steps of the Metropolitan Museum and the bar at the Algonquin, where the big guys used to hang out. My terrace was right there with all those places, high up and facing east and cool as Miles Davis, even on summer nights. Jeannie and I would order pizza and open a bottle of red wine, lay out a comforter and put one of the speakers near the open door. We would feel like the city was a set designed for the two of us. That was before the live bouts began to be something Don King should have been promoting.

The bridge was to my right and looked fine in the night. It was a good old bridge. Paul Simon was smart to write a song about it. Below and to the right was Roosevelt Island and its high rises playing a drab shortstop between Manhattan and Queens. For maybe the thousandth time I wondered why in the world anyone would want to live there. One of Finley's Rules was this: Never live in a place you have to take a tram to get to. If I wanted to go home by high wire, I would have become one of the Flying Wallendas and worn those funny tights.

Beyond Roosevelt, on the other side of the river in Long Island City, the lights were on at East River Tennis Club. People were still playing. I had dated one of the women pros there when I first moved to New York from Boston. She was an enthusiastic little thing, and I was always a sucker for tennis dresses in what Fitzgerald would have called my younger and more vulnerable years. But one night at a cocktail party when Jack Daniel's encouraged me to give one of my journalism seminars, she had disappeared with a tennis player who happened to be ranked third in the entire world. I never saw her again.

Another Open was coming up. By now she had probably latched on to some dirty-haired Swede with one hell of a two-fisted backhand. I didn't hold grudges. I hoped the Swede was seeded.

Doctor Coors and Nurse Excedrin had finally taken care of my headache. I still should have felt lousy, about Seth Parker, about the look on Billy's face when the tape was playing, and Kris Stanford's dead ass, maybe even the wreckage of whatever dreams Peggy Lynn had brought to New York from Guertin, before she became a scheming little tramp. But I didn't. And knew why. I was in the middle of it again, after a drifting time. The pieces to the story were a mess, lying around like a jigsaw I'd dumped out of a box. I'd randomly hooked a few of them together with early speed and luck. Maybe more would come together tomorrow if I could get to Sam Cummings. You're supposed to do the corners first with a puzzle. Maybe tomorrow I'd get a corner. So I was excited. Already people had been hurt just by knowing Peggy Lynn Brady. And here I was smiling. This is the problem with my job. You care about the people, but not as much as you do about whether the story is good or not.

I had tried to explain this to Jeannie more times than I cared to remember. But it was like all those times when I tried to get her to see the same beauty in baseball I saw, the timelessness of it, the confrontations between pitcher and batter coming one after another, more than a hundred times a game, and all its crazy symmetry. She was a journalist too, and a better writer of sentences than I would ever be. But her talent came from her great heart. She would do a story on some day care center in Harlem, and each night she would take the pain and hopelessness of those lives home with her and go to a hurting place I could not reach. Jeannie always wanted happy endings.

I just wanted endings.

"People think you're championing them, but they're wrong," Jeannie said one night at Antolotti's after her fourth white wine spritzer. "You're just stealing bits and pieces of them, all for the greater good of Peter Finley."

Jeannie freely admitted that the fourth white wine was always a definite trouble spot in our marriage. Once she got past four it was like someone had shot the Archduke Ferdinand. War was inevitable. I got four belts in me and I just wanted to run through the score of *Singin' in the Rain.* Ah, sweet mystery of booze.

"They think you are fighting for them out of some sense of justice or fair play, and to a degree you are," she said. "But you're always apart. You're wondering how this or that will look, how it will fit, whether a particular piece of business will make a good sound bite or bridge or ending. Maybe that's why you're good, because you keep your vision glib and detached. But you will never be as good as you could be, because you don't give a good goddamn about your subjects, not deep down. I've never seen anyone who loved this sort of life more than you do, Peter. You love the excitement of it, the occasional danger, and the finding out, and the rehashing of it in saloons afterward. You like whatever fame it has brought you. But in the end it is all a juvenile game to you. You deal with life-and-death things like some postpubescent Tom Swift. Then you go to O'Rourkes with the boys. Then you tumble into bed with the former Jeannie Bogardus."

She was overstating, of course. Wives will do that to you now and again, and before you know it, wine and candlelight have turned into another holocaust. And yet there was a lot in what she said. I had always loved it. When I was twenty years old and working the police beat nights for the *Boston Post,* there wasn't any of it I didn't think was terrific. I always thought I was stealing money. I would go to a victim's home in Southie in the middle of the night and sometimes bring the news of death with me. That was never a trip to the beach. But the moment the father or mother or wife would start to talk I was writing the story, taking pictures with my eyes, making sure I would have the sights and sounds right when I got back to the office and Gellis, the night city man, would be looking over my shoulder. Get in. Get out. Get it down in six hundred words. I fancied myself as Hildy Johnson from *The Front Page.*

Baby, get me rewrite.

Somebody once said that journalism was history in a hurry. I'd always liked the definition. Jeannie wanted me to bleed, but there was never enough time for that. When I defended myself to her, I said that more good had come

out of what I did than bad. I knew I had never righted as
many wrongs as Jack Finley. His world was more cut and
dry, black and white. Good and evil were more clear-cut.
He spent a lifetime making his moral decisions on the run.
Maybe I needed more time. Maybe he would always be the
better of us. There were a lot of reasons I never became
a cop. The best was this: Jack Finley had been a cop. That
had been taken care of for the Finley family. The subject
never came up between my father and me. It was just
understood.

I did what I did. I was glad Billy Lynn had shown up.
It was like I'd told Charley: The story belonged to me
now.

The wind had picked up while my mind wandered,
scattering my terrace thoughts in a random way that
suited them. I could feel rain in the air. I should have felt
more death. I walked back into the living room and replaced the Lena tape with one of my favorites. Astaire. I'd
cut it myself. The first song was "I Guess I'll Have to
Change My Plans." I pictured him doing it in *The Band
Wagon,* in tie and tails and hat and cane, the soft shoe
executed in perfect concert with Jack Buchanan.

I decided I would read the letters in the morning. I also
decided it was a civilized enough hour for a man to fix
himself a civilized Jack Daniel's and splash. I was at the
bar working all that out when the doorbell rang.

Jeannie was standing there when I opened the door.

Some days, I have found, are more eventful than others.

SHE was wearing a simple blue blazer and a button-down
white shirt open at the collar and a pair of blue jeans that
fit her amazing legs the way Mr. Levi Strauss, or the Lord
himself, intended them to fit legs like hers. She had on her
favorite Tony Lama boots, and they nearly brought her to

eye level with me, her estranged husband. Her hair was in a Jeannie cut, short with just a hint of natural curls, pushed casually back and to the sides. No perms for her ever, no blow dries, just a shake when she came out of the shower and then a quick pass with a brush. The brown eyes were tilted just slightly upward, northeast and northwest at the edges, sloe-eyed is the way the fashion magazines would describe her. The eyes were merely deep enough and wide enough to save your life. The complexion, as always, made the expression "peaches and cream" seem like kid stuff, as though every other face that thought it was something had been Simonized.

She was smiling at me. It belonged in the coming storm, something that crackled and grew brighter as I watched it. Jeannie Bogardus Finley.

"Ness told me to just come on up," she said. Ness was the doorman.

I smiled back at her. "Ness is a good and wise man," I said. "That is why his Christmas tip has to be carried back to Staten Island in a wheelbarrow."

We were still facing each other across the threshold.

"I've just come from a magazine party at Regine's," she said. "They had wine there. I am not going to London. It may rain, incidentally."

I thought it might be the wine talking, but I wasn't going to interrupt unless she pulled a knife on me.

Jeannie said, "I am furious with you, Peter Finley. I mean it. We're talking pissed off here."

It was definitely the wine. Pissed off was not part of the cold sober vocabulary.

I said, "Pissed off?"

"Ask me why." She was swaying just slightly.

"Why?"

"Well, I'll tell you then. Because I was standing around at this boring party for the magazine, and I was drinking many white wines, and I found myself finally talking to an ad guy with the personality of a maple tree. And then all of a sudden I missed you. Which, as any fool can see, explains the previous part about pissed off."

She took a step across the doorway, very carefully, not swaying now, measuring me with the eyes. She put her arms around my neck, then she kissed me. I don't know how the kissing manual says you're supposed to do it, but this one would do. I hadn't touched her since February. I kissed her back.

Jeannie did in fact taste like wine. The taste was not at all displeasing. Her hair smelled sweet and clean, like morning. I felt ridiculously giddy, like I'd asked her to wear my class ring and she'd said yes. I kept kissing her.

She came up for air first. I shook my head slightly to clear it. We were still standing in front of the open door. I freed my right hand from its resting place at the small of her back and shut the door. Astaire was singing about the continental. You maybe could have fit a Visa card between my nose and her nose. I put my right hand back in place. Her eyes were very wide, very curious. You had to be this close to notice one was lighter than the other, a deep butterscotch color.

I kissed her just above the butterscotch one and said, "This was all very pleasant, miss, but I think you've got the wrong apartment. You must want fifteen-B."

"Don't the Finleys live here?"

"Used to. I heard they broke up."

She put her hands on the sides of my face and brushed some of my hair back, then traced the pale scar over my right eye with a finger.

I kissed her again on the lips, with a follow-through more pronounced than before. If this was a dream, I planned to buy a co-op in it.

Jeannie said, "We will discuss the significance and ramifications of all this later." She had a little trouble with ramifications, like her tongue had lost its way.

"I'll submit to a spot quiz. Twenty questions. True or false. No essays. No multiple choice."

I could have sworn her eyes made a laughing sound.

She said, "Are the sheets clean?"

"Nope."

"Whatever," she said, and led the way toward the bedroom, holding on to my hand.

I followed her like she was Lassie and I was little Timmy.

"THIS doesn't mean I'm moving back in," Jeannie said afterward. "But I would very much like to go with you out to the beach house this weekend."

We were lying in the big bed, the room lit just enough by New York. The window was open and the breeze felt fine as we lay coverless on top of the spread. It hadn't rained yet. Night sounds, some great, some small, were the background music. Jeannie's head fit into the crook of my neck, hair a-tangle where it touched my cheek. There was a fine mist of perspiration where hair met forehead. I made a thorough effort to kiss the perspiration away, moving left to right. From the street I heard the honk of a car horn, then a wolf whistle, then a burst of girlish laughter. From the bureau I heard the little beep my watch gives on the hour. I didn't care much what hour it was.

Jeannie. Me. Here. Right now there was that universe, and the one that belonged to everybody else.

I said, "I can't go out to the house this weekend. I'm in the middle of something right now." I leaned forward and ran a hand over the smooth geography of her left leg, which was draped over my right one. "But in view of the just-concluded, uh, sonata, I vote that you indeed move back in. If it's still today, I vote for tomorrow."

She rolled away and propped herself up on an elbow. Jeannie was slender in clothes, the figure almost boyish. She was not slender out of clothes. I admired the lush expanse of her.

She no longer seemed drunk. As a sobering agent, I obviously had it all over black coffee.

Jeannie said, "The vote of the Massachusetts delegation is duly noted. But I'm not ready to come back, and I hope you don't push it, not tonight anyway."

I said, "Then why tonight?"

"Tonight was tonight. Maybe it was an impulse. I do miss you, a lot lately. I miss being with you, like this. I came over. You were here. Let it be. It changes things a little, but not enough. I'm going to have a nightcap. Can I get you something?"

"A guy could be persuaded to have a Hennessy. But are you sure you want one? Your vase seemed to be kind of full when you showed up, my flower."

She laughed and hopped out of the bed and moved to the door in a coltish prance. Jeannie was never embarrassed about things like nakedness.

"So you think I had too much to drink, huh?" she said over her shoulder, moving through the door. "Methinks that is an example of the sot calling his petal wacked."

She always did have a facility for puns. It is the tiniest of flaws. Maybe Olivier does knock-knock jokes.

We drank our drinks when she came back. Hennessy for me, Grand Marnier for her. I was hoping she didn't drink this way with Phillip the talking hairdo. She asked me just what it was I was working on that prevented me from taking her to the beach house. I told her all of it.

When I was done she said, "I don't think your performance with Mr. Parker is going to win you a Peabody Award, Peter. That seems to fall into the dirty tricks category, even for you."

"So does killing people."

"I thought you had retired from hitting and fighting and such, by the way."

"He was going after Marty, J.B."

"Marty can take care of himself."

"Maybe you had to be there."

"Maybe I did."

We sat there in silence, drinking. She was sitting at the other end of the bed, facing me, knees up, both hands on the brandy snifter.

"So who done it?" she asked finally.

"It had to be someone at GBC for Peggy Lynn, somebody she pushed too far with these phantom files. I have no idea how Kris Stanford fits, at least not yet. Maybe the letters will tell me something."

I lit a cigarette to change the subject. I am extremely versatile with cigarettes.

I said, "I wish I could go to the beach with you, I really do, J.B. But I've got to hang with this one. I feel like I owe that much to Billy. He looks at me like the court of last resort."

Jeannie sighed. I didn't especially like the sound of it.

"*You,* of course, Peter the Great, could not just take Billy over to Mick Dunphy's office and drop him like the stork?"

I was right about the sigh.

"No," I said.

"Who was it that said the one about people not learning from history being doomed to repeat it, Peter? Mickey Rooney?"

"Either him or Toynbee."

"How many wives did Toynbee have?"

I butted the cigarette out in the ashtray on the night-stand.

I said, "I don't know about anybody else. I'm still working on my first wife. Maybe she should understand me a little better by now. I do what I do the only way I know how. But I want my wife back because I need her."

Jeannie finished her drink, reached over me and placed it on the nightstand, then lay back down next to me.

"I know you need me, sailor. I've just got to figure out how much. Night."

She kissed me on the cheek and was asleep by the time I finished the Hennessy. And was gone when I woke up in the morning. I found the note on the kitchen table.

Mr. Finley. I'll be in touch. If you're going to smoke out the baddies, please be careful. Thanks, as they say, for the use of the room. Hey, it was fun being like a guy for a night. You know: Get drunk, get . . .

Love,
Mrs.
Finley

I concluded once again that any marriage counselor who doesn't drive a Rolls-Royce is brain dead.

CHAPTER
8

IT began to rain in the morning about the time I had to give the last rites to Mister Coffee.

There is this little note inside the little door at the top, where you pour the water in. The note politely asks that you clean Mister Coffee at least twice a month with white vinegar. The problem was that white vinegar had never been a staple in the Finley kitchen like, say, Fig Newtons. So the machine picked this morning to give a death rattle and expire. I didn't ever remember that happening with Joe DiMaggio. I had instant instead.

The storm was something magnificent, as New York storms are when they visit August. The wind played the overture. The rain sounded like the opening tap number from *42nd Street* before long; it happened a lot the day after I'd had the windows cleaned, one of those cosmic practical jokes that followed me around. Morning suddenly looked like midnight. I knew getting to work would be easy as swimming the English Channel, so I decided to work the phones some and ride the storm out. New York City is the capital of the known universe, but thirty minutes of hard rain can turn it into a paraplegic.

I called Sam Cummings at GBC. His secretary told me he wouldn't be in until the afternoon; the "Midnite" show had been in reruns since Peggy Lynn's disappearance. I left a message for him to call me.

It was just after ten. I called Jeannie to compliment her on the clear, sparkling line of her prose. A woman with a nasal Queens Boulevard accent told me Mrs. Finley would be in editorial meetings all day. I told Queens Boulevard to tell her Mr. Finley had called. She was singularly unimpressed.

There was no answer in Billy's room. I figured he was out to breakfast or had found the Manhattan chapter of Moral Majority. Or a branch of the Rev's church.

Natalie called me before I called her. I was going over the standings and box scores in the *Times*. Yankees had lost. Sox had won. I checked Wade Boggs's numbers for the Sox. He is my favorite player. Another two-for-four. Maybe there was hope yet.

"Don't go outside," Natalie said.

I told her I had no plans to do that anytime soon.

"It sure doesn't look like Kansas anymore, Toto," Natalie said. "Getting to work was a bitch."

"I'll remember that at merit badge time."

"Thomas Harrold is in Delaware meeting with Endicott's people," she said. "But I'm gonna hang around GBC anyway. Talk to some of the lesser lights on 'Midnite,' techs and makeup people and such. Maybe even try Johnny Brant. The way I hear it, flashing a little thigh has a way of loosening little Johnny's tongue."

I told her to unbutton things only if the situation got desperate. And to take Marty along with her.

Natalie said, "What's your deal?"

"I'm going to look over those letters, at least until we all stop sliding toward Jersey. Then go see Dunphy and maybe sleaze a look at some reports if he'll let me, or at least compare notes."

"Talk to you later, coach."

"Natalie?"

"Uh hum?"

"My Mister Coffee passed away."

"I'm very sorry, Peter. I'll send a note to Mrs. Coffee."

I dialed my father and got his recording, which told me he was on his way to Guertin, Alabama, to snoop and cajole.

"I intend to dress down and spit a lot," my father's voice said on the tape. They were going to love him around the cracker barrel.

I commenced reading the letters like they were part of my ten-thirty Lit class.

She had written some of them by hand, in a hasty, hurried scrawl. Not the Palmer Method. Some were type-written, in type that I recalled from my newspaper days. Looked like an old Royal. Pica. Some of them were simply chatty accounts of life in the big city, the people she was meeting, her world on the perimeter of the spotlight, then inside the spotlight. Others were a subway stop after amazing, fitting into a category that could only be called Bad Potboiler, lurid and detailed and sad.

The rain came down. I smoked, drank instant coffee, occasionally took a note, and went through all of them.

The typewritten ones seemed more recent. "My Dearest Billy." Most of them began that way. She seemed to be crying out for his help, for the values she said she had left behind in Guertin.

"Whatever happened to me?" she wrote more than once. "I was happier when we were young."

In one, she told of being slapped around by Johnny

Brant. She mentioned it once in a brief handwritten note, then elaborated in a sequel.

"I wish sometimes you were around to protect me, my darling. People like Johnny Brant would never dare lay a hand on me if you were around."

They seemed pretty close for ex-husband and ex-wife. Maybe the poor slob thought she was going to come back to him someday.

Apparently, Billy had made some trips to New York. She wrote like he'd met Kris Stanford, who was portrayed as loyal, but a storm trooper. It was Stanford, according to the letters, who was always urging her to find out things about people, as a form of protection.

"Kris says I should always use, instead of being used," she wrote.

I had heard that song before.

"She is so posessive!" was the message in one. I noticed that in the scrawl, she had dropped an *s*. Later on, with the Royal, she told him: "I sometimes worry about Kris. She is so posessive. I am starting to feel uncomfortable having her under the same roof with me. Billy, she might be a *lesbian*! It has been so long since I saw her with a man."

I took a note on that one.

"My Dearest Billy. It was so much simpler when we were together."

"My Dearest Billy. I feel a million miles from Guertin."

"My Dearest Billy. Sometimes I feel like the devil is all around me."

"My Dearest Billy . . . I will not sleep with these people to get ahead, especially not now that there is a strong and good man in my life. Maybe I did do that with Seth. It was so sinful! God has made me see that now. The memory of him touching me makes my skin crawl!"

I looked for a date. There wasn't one. A strong and

good man. I thought: Harrold? She had only mentioned him in one other letter.

"I have learned from my mistakes, I truly have. I'm changing. No matter what happens with Thomas Harrold, I just can't bring myself to use the leverage I have against him. He doesn't deserve that, from me or anyone else. I was wrong to look for leverage in the first place. It was like slipping back into the past."

The parts about Parker were pretty much as Billy had said. It was Parker who promised Broadway, Parker who was the kink sexually, Parker who threatened to ruin *her* in the divorce. There wasn't anything in the letters about her ever blackmailing anybody. The mention of leverage with Harrold, leverage rejected, was the only hint. She just wrote one time and was single again.

Sam Cummings came across as her only true ally at GBC. But the letters about Cummings weren't dated either, so I couldn't tell if the position still held. Cummings was going to help her become boss lady at "Midnite."

"Sam seems to know what's right for me, most always," she wrote. "Kris had only steered me wrong, time and again."

She was going to get rid of Kris Stanford, that was plain enough.

And she was going to fix Johnny Brant.

"I can still feel his fist on my face, Billy."

The last letter, handwritten, was dated a couple of weeks before she disappeared.

She wrote, "I cannot tell you the name of my new man. What we have is private. But I am so happy. For the first time since Guertin, I feel like my house is clean."

It was noon by the time I finished. The rain had stopped. I went through the mess again, to see if there was anything I'd missed. I didn't know how much to believe, but I wanted to at least have her version of her life down cold, like multiplication tables.

Her house might have been clean at the end. I felt dirty. When I finished the second time I did the only sensible thing.

I went and took another shower.

CHAPTER
9

HE Global Broadcasting Company started out once upon a time as one of those super stations like Ted Turner's and slowly grew into a fourth major network, leaving Turner and WGN in Chicago and WOR in New York behind. Global's Arabs had more money than all of them. But after early speed faded and the novelty wore off and the ratings dropped and you began to need a plunger to inspect the Global stock, the Arabs cooled on the idea. Which is where Endicott came in.

Global's offices were located in the first high rise of the new Times Square redevelopment project, on Forty-second between Broadway and Eighth. Where once there had been peep show theaters and massage parlors and clip joints and every fast food in the known universe; where hookers and pimps had promenaded in brazen splendor like part of a Thanksgiving parade, all in Spandex and fur and gold, we now had the GBC Building, an instant New York landmark in shiny glass and lime rock. The geniuses from City and the geniuses from State had spent millions upon millions razing that section of Times Square and promising us that the sleaze would disappear cleaner than the Dodgers from Brooklyn. The sleaze had simply moved a few blocks west.

I figured that someday the pimps and porno kings would make their stand against the armies of decency somewhere near the entrance to the Lincoln Tunnel.

Loser had to pay the toll.

"Big deal," Marty Pearl said as he pulled the van right on Thirty-ninth Street, so as to come back around GBC and come east on Forty-second. "Now we got high-rent sex instead of street prices. Arab TV moguls instead of tits." Marty pronounced it A-rab, by the way.

I told him I loved sociology made simple for young adults.

It was Monday morning. I had a lunch date with Sam Cummings uptown later and nothing meaningful to do until then so I had decided to accompany Marty and Natalie and the minicam to their interview with Johnny Brant. Billy had stopped by Channel A at coffee wagon time and told us he wanted to come too. I told him to go check out the renovation of the Statue of Liberty, promising we'd show him the Brant tape later if Brant turned out to be more colorful with us than when he was asking Boy George for health and beauty tips on his own show.

"You don't need Peggy's letters to know about that man, Mr. Finley," Billy said. He was wearing the same blue suit he'd had on when I met him. "Johnny Brant is a smiling snake."

I said, "Billy, in television that just makes him another Girl Scout selling chocolate mints."

"He turned on her when she wouldn't have sex with him."

I reminded him I'd read the letters.

"Peggy said that he struck her."

"I know, Billy. I know."

He left, reluctantly, when he realized we weren't going to take him with us to the zoo.

We finished our coffee at A, then piled into the van and commenced the usual Monday morning crawl down Seventh Avenue. Natalie gave us the Brant dossier as we went. As usual, she was more thorough than a tax audit. She'd done everything except go on an archaeological dig through Brant's garbage.

Natalie began her report. "Brant started out as a sportswriter in Washington, D.C. Baseball writer. Covered the Senators before they moved to Texas. Did a morning radio show on the side for one of the smaller stations in D.C. His prose style left a little to be desired, but he had this voice that was, and is, sweeter than Aunt Jemima. And, as you probably know if you've ever seen him on the proverbial tube, he is good-looking in a 'Wheel of Fortune' sort of way."

Marty and I nodded. Even Brant's hair smiled.

Natalie continued. "Anyway, one day the Senators color announcer didn't show up. Sick. Brant knew the producer and the play-by-play guy—he used to lick their faces every time there was a rain delay, hoping to be their guest—so they took a chance and let him work the game that day. Destiny deal. His voice and lack of writing skill and lack of knowledge about baseball made him a natural for the job. They loved him. The color announcer stayed sick forever. Brant did baseball until the Senators moved, then started doing six and eleven sports at one of the independent stations, WNUR. And guess who the general manager was at station WNUR, class?"

I said, "Thomas Harrold." More casual than Perry Como. Not even looking back at her. We always made Natalie sit in back with the camera.

She said, "Thomas Harrold." She didn't hear me, then she heard, like the words were on a seven-second radio delay.

Natalie jabbed a finger into my rotator cuff area.

"How come you know that?"

"I read *People*, Nat. I read *US*. I buy *TV Guide* on Mondays. I watch 'Entertainment Tonight.' I even read *Variety*, when I can get a translator. Rona Barrett wants no part of my ass."

"You looked through my notes, you bastard."

"I do get a certain thrill going through your things, yes."

She said, "You want me to go on, or do you want me to throw it back to you and what you cribbed?"

Marty was in the process of running a bicycle up onto the sidewalk in front of the Sheraton Centre Hotel. In the van, Marty hunted down bicycles the way Pat Garrett tracked Billy the Kid. He said, "Please go on, honey. Educate the heathens. Throw open the windows of knowledge."

"C'mon, Nat," I chimed. She hated Nat the way I hated Pete. "You can't stop now. The story's had everything so far. I laughed, I cried . . ."

"One," she said. "Two . . . three . . . four . . ." She wasn't as angry as I thought because she stopped at four, then she told more about Brant.

Harrold tried him as a news anchor for a while, but it didn't take. He gave Brant a morning talk show, nine to ten, lots of blue-haired ladies in the audience. Shows about the mating habits of diabetic dwarfs and albino amputees, that sort of thing. That did take. Blue-haired ladies loved him. When Harrold went to GBC, Brant went with him. Made him the host of a weekend sports anthology. Then gave him "Midnite." Brant was the only host of the show the first two seasons it was on the air. Then Thomas

Harrold teamed up Johnny Brant and Peggy Lynn Brady.

"At which point," Natalie said, "the show became the Tet offensive. It was hate at first sight. People tell me Brant was an insecure little prick to begin with. When it became obvious that Peggy Lynn was the real star of the show, it was like he wanted to stick a gun in his mouth. The last two years the two of them kept smiling like always on the air and didn't speak word one when the little red light went off. Somebody'd come up to do a magazine piece on 'Midnite' and Brant would stipulate beforehand that he would talk about everything except Peggy Lynn. One of the associate directors told me that if Brant was walking through an airport and somebody would yell out 'Where's Peggy Lynn?'—which happened all the time— Brant would just snap. Lose it. Make a scene at the baggage claim, the ticket counter, wherever. When the rumors began that Peggy Lynn might become producer of the show, Brant went into total panic. Remember when he had to take three weeks off because of that so-called chemical imbalance?"

I vaguely remembered. It had been in the spring. I had assumed it was cocaine. So did everyone else in the industry. When you heard, in television or movies or sports, that somebody had the flu for more than three days, you wanted to check the urine samples.

Natalie said, "Well, the chemical imbalance was the blood pumping through Peggy Lynn's veins. Brant knew that if she took over, he was on the street."

Marty was making a right on Forty-second from Eighth without further bicycle incidents.

"How come Harrold didn't take care of his boy Johnny?" Marty asked.

"That's the way his boy Johnny thought the hand would be played," Natalie said. "He started camping out in Harrold's office. But Harrold knew that Peggy Lynn was the biggest thing GBC had, no matter who owned the network. He wasn't about to rock that particular dinghy. So Johnny was in definite danger of becoming a nonperson, friendship with Harrold or no friendship. Plus, there were still the rumors that Peggy Lynn either had something *on* Harrold, or something *going* on with Harrold, and could give his balls a squeeze anytime she wanted to."

I said, "What could be that big?" I asked that question a lot.

"Damned if I know," Natalie said. That was the answer I got a lot.

Marty parked the van behind four Rolls-Royces, all white. I assumed it was a board of directors meeting for all the guys named Ali and Haji and Sheikh who still owned the Global Broadcasting Company. I had always been surprised in the past that a regular network feature wasn't "This Week in Saudi Arabia."

I said to Natalie, "One last question from the studio audience: Was Johnny Brant scared enough of Peggy Lynn to get crazy?"

"Crazy, I dunno. But stupid, yes. The word I get is that deep down, without a prompter, Johnny Brant is so dumb you could valet park cars inside his head."

We all clambered out of the van. Marty suddenly lurched and grabbed his right shoulder.

"Damn, Natalie," he said through clenched teeth. "The old bursitis is acting up. Why don't you grab the cameras and lights?"

"IT'S no secret that Peggy Lynn and I had some creative differences around here," Johnny Brant was saying.

He was shooting for the Dan Rather look. Navy V-neck sweater and blue button-down shirt with the Brooks Brothers roll in it and burgundy knit tie. He was leaning forward, elbows on desk, chin resting on the back of his left hand. Unless I missed my guess, he had enough pancake on to feed a summer camp. He reminded me more of a game show host; or the master of ceremonies on "The Living God Live!" He had stay-in-place black hair. Some gray sprinkled here and there. Sugar on cereal. Killer caps on the teeth. I figured if I could come up with the cost of the Rolex smiling brightly at me from his left wrist, I would win the weekend in Acapulco.

I sat across the desk from him. Natalie sat next to me. Marty was in back. Lights had been adjusted, mikes had been attached to his sweater, my sports jacket. Marty hadn't started shooting yet, at Brant's request. I smoked and listened and thought: He's looking at me, so I must be the one he's trying to kid.

"Pete," he said.

Pete.

"I'm sure I don't have to tell you that one of the unfortunate aspects of our business is a collision, I guess that's the right word, between two strong-willed people, two talented pros who have to go out there five nights a week without a net and try to make some magic on that set."

"Damned unfortunate," I said gravely.

Johnny Brant said, "Exactly. That's what we had on 'Midnite.' But the key word really is pro. That's what Peggy Lynn and I both are . . . were? . . . through and through. And I'll be damned if the occasional sparks between us didn't provide for crackling good television."

Pause. Switch the position of the hands. Put the chin back in its resting place. Wistful, he seemed to be shooting for wistful.

"That's why I miss the old girl so much."

He swiveled around from the desk with a sudden jerk, like he was someone on a Nautilus machine trying to take the roll off the hips. He looked out toward the Hudson from his eighteenth-floor cockpit and sighed. Wistful it was. The sound busted through the window and fell toward Eighth. I wondered idly if a pedestrian had ever been killed by falling bullshit.

To the Hudson, Brant said, "I'm sure you've heard a lot of rumors about Peggy Lynn and me, Pete, but if I'm lying I'm dying. I never knew what a bond there was between us until she was gone. To wherever she is."

Brant had obviously spent the morning deciding how he was going to play this and decided that sensitive was the ticket. Heart on the sleeve. I remembered an old line of Jeannie's and smiled at the thought: "Let's be frank and earnest. You be Frank. I'll be Ernest."

I decided to be Frank and interrupt Brant's phony reverie before everyone on Team Finley got sick.

I said, "Johnny, what's say we tape before this turns into group therapy."

Marty got out of his chair and stood behind me, shooting over my right shoulder. Softly he said, "Speed."

Brant wheeled the chair back around and glared at me. "That's a little cold-blooded, isn't it, Finley?"

No more Pete.

"I've lost a colleague and you're sitting here doing schtick," Brant said solemnly.

He reached into his desk for a pipe and a leather tobacco pouch that had the Mark Cross emblem on it. Pipe. I should have seen it coming.

"Johnny," I said amiably, "I go all to pieces when somebody treats me like I've got stupid tattooed on my forehead. You have absolutely and positively lost a colleague. But don't act like it's keeping you up nights. You know and I know that Peggy Lynn was trying to get herself into position to take this show over and run your ass out on the street. I can walk out of this office and down to the newsroom and even the janitor will tell me that.

Now you can tell me the truth, or you can look like a dick when this piece airs and everyone even remotely associated with 'Midnite' makes you out to be a fucking liar. So please spare me all the do-do about how you miss the old girl, okay?"

Brant took it all, making little sucking noises on the pipe, applying his match to the bowl as he did. The smoke struggled out at first, then the whole thing took. I had to admit I had always hated the equipment and procedure, but I did love the smell.

Brant pointed at Marty with it.

"Shut that thing off for a second."

I looked over my shoulder and nodded at Marty.

"Do it," I said.

Brant took a deep breath and said, "She couldn't even type her own copy for the prompter. Couldn't even use a freaking typewriter. Can you believe it? She had her bitch goddess sidekick, the late great Miss Stanford, do it for her. Every time. We'd be getting ready to go on air, like five minutes to show, and Peggy Lynn would want to make a change in her opening, and she'd scribble it out, and then Stanford would try to decipher it, then type it. And Peggy Lynn Brady would smile at me and say 'So I can't type. So I'm not perfect.' No one has ever confused me with Ed Murrow, Finley. But Jesus God. There has never been anyone like this cunt in the history of television." He sighed again. "All she could do was look good and talk."

Brant seemed to notice Natalie for the first time.

"Sorry," he said.

He meant the cunt stuff. Natalie grinned at him. She knew the routine. She was good cop today. Cagney to my Lacey.

"No problem," she said to Johnny Brant. "When you are lucky enough to work with two Greek deckhands like

Mr. Finley and Mr. Pearl, you get to learn all the various words for all the various parts. You get to memorize them, in fact."

I said to Brant, "You want to try taping again?"

"Yeah, okay. But I've seen your work, Finley, and your, uh, interviewing technique. Don't pull my kidneys out through my ears, okay?"

Marty gave me speed again. Natalie made sure her chair was out of the shot. Brant kept the pipe in his hand. It had gone out. He didn't seem to mind. I was sure he only brought it out when a camera came to visit.

Brant gave Marty another voice check. So did I. Then I said, "There were rumors, before Peggy Lynn Brady's disappearance, that she was about to become executive producer of 'Midnite,' sole host. You heard them obviously."

"I heard them." He gave his head a little shake, like a man coming out of a shower. "I was frankly amazed. Now I would be the last person to discount Peggy's popularity with the viewers. I knew what the ratings were before she came aboard, and I was perfectly aware of how they jumped after she came aboard. But carry the show by herself? *Produce* the show? There was as much a chance of her doing that, even with help, as there was her playing shortstop for the Yankees. After ten years in the business, or whatever she had, the mechanics of television were still totally foreign to her. She never asked a question in her life that wasn't scripted for her. There was a teleprompter whichever way she turned because everyone was scared to death that she'd have to ad lib going into, coming out of, commercials even. Everything was done for her. I used to wonder just how much time she spent with the newspapers after she got done with the gossip columns. Her entire frame of reference seemed to stretch from Liz Smith to Suzy to Marilyn Beck. We had David Letterman on the show one night and he was doing some jokes about the arms talks between the U.S. and Russia. Right before we went to a break he did a line about Karl Marx. During the break Peggy Lynn turned to him, swear to God, and asked 'Which one of those funny little brothers was Karl?' "

I said, "You thought she was smile masquerading as host?"

Brant: "I'm not sure I would put it that way exactly. Let's just say that her lack of skills had not prevented her from becoming a huge star. Let's say we hid her weaknesses very, very well. We got good guests. I did the heavy lifting when it came to interviews. Peggy Lynn sat there and always looked wonderful and somehow asked the questions that appealed to Mr. and Mrs. America. After someone wrote them out for her."

"No love lost at all then?"

Brant smiled a smile that was all his caps and full of poison. We had a family cat in Boston who smiled that way. Ethel her name was. Bared her teeth same way. The look said: I'm going to scratch the back of your hand because I'm not big enough to go for your throat.

"You can't lose what you never had," Brant said.

"She didn't have many friends on the show?"

"Kris and Sam. They kept her covered like the Secret Service. One in front. One in back."

"If everything you say about her is true, why would anyone think about giving the show over to her?"

Brant sniffed. "Because she carried the best of all possible clout in the television business. She was on a hit show and her contract was up. If you've got those things going for you, someone upstairs will give you half of South America to stay. Especially if the hit show is the one a suffering network has. All you have to do is stand there and catch all the money they throw at you, and when they're done throwing the money, you go for the extras.

You say 'Twenty-four-hour-a-day limo' and they say okay. You get more time off. If you're on a roll and the president of the network is your pet—hypothetically speaking, of course—you can try to get rid of your co-host and take over the whole damn show."

"You say hypothetically, but you're obviously referring to Thomas Harrold, president of GBC. He and Peggy Lynn were close?"

"They were close, but that was normal in her situation."

"But you think he was about to give Peggy Lynn everything she wanted?"

Brant cocked an eyebrow and waved the pipe.

"Your information is as good as mine."

"But Thomas Harrold is the man given credit for helping make Johnny Brant a star. Why would he turn his back on you in someone else's contract negotiation?"

"You'll have to ask Mr. Harrold that."

"Did you?"

"You bet."

"Did he give you any answers that would fall into the satisfactory category?"

Cat smile again. Ethel used to purr when she did it.

"Mr. Harrold is a bottom liner. He was when he hired me in Washington. He was when he gave me 'Midnite.' He was when he brought Peggy Lynn to 'Midnite.' If she had not disappeared, he was apparently prepared to make another bottom line decision."

"Had he definitely made up his mind?"

"He said no."

"When you took ill last spring, what was the true nature of your illness?"

"Frankly, it was what I called Peggies."

I was jumping around now. It works sometimes. You stop circling. Get to the middle of the ring and open up like Marvelous Marvin Hagler.

"Are there people in this building who would have wanted to kill Peggy Lynn Brady?"

Brant eye-locked me. He knew the rules. He was in the business. We weren't going to stop tape now unless I said okay. No timeouts.

Carefully he said, "Having worked with her, having known her, I would say yes."

"You?"

"Absolutely not. No. If she had gotten this show, the ratings would have done that to her eventually. She would have brought new vistas to the expression dead air."

"Was the relationship between Thomas Harrold and Peggy Lynn strictly business?"

"Is the next question going to be about when I stopped beating my wife, Mr. Finley?"

I turned to Marty and said, "Hold it." He stopped tape. I said to Brant: "Was Harrold fucking around with her?"

Brant threw up his hands. It was probably the most honest emotion he'd offered up yet.

"I'll be damned if I know. You've heard the rumors obviously. I've heard them. But I never could pin them down. She was seeing someone at the end, though. You could tell. There was actually something softer about her, human, girlish. Something had changed her. But I just don't know if it was Harrold or not."

Brant shrugged.

"For the last year around here, no one could really figure out if she had any boy-girl life at all. She seemed to have no life away from the show. It was useless trying to find out anything from Kris. Every once in a while, I'd overhear them talking about a Friday night getaway, to a Hampton, I think, but that was about it. Maybe she had retired from screwing around."

I said, "It's hard to believe someone with her track record in that area was going through a trial celibacy."

I was leading him, remembering the good and strong man from her letters.

But Brant just whistled and said, "You got that right."

"I've heard here and there that you made a big try with her and struck out."

Brant said, "I don't know if you'd call it a big try. It was before she came on the show. I made the requisite pass. She turned me down. I tried again. She turned me down again. I spotted a trend. That was it. Looking back, I consider myself one of the chosen people. With apologies to Ms. Ferrare one more time, to get seriously involved with that woman you'd have to have a grudge against your dick."

I thought of the letters and said, "Did you ever hit her?"

Brant's eyes narrowed up into slits and he threw the pipe down on the desk, the tobacco spilling all over the glass top.

"Goddammit, I'm sick and tired of that story. That was one of her major fantasies. We had an argument about the show one day in my dressing room. It was a doozy. Yells and threats and curses. Nothing more. She tried to make a big exit and tripped over a footstool and clipped her forehead. You could have put the blood into a thimble, there was that little, but she got fucking hysterical and went running for Cummings, telling him I'd smacked her. The next thing I know my own producer has me up against the wall, threatening to kill me if I ever laid a hand on her again. We're a very close-knit team on 'Midnite,' boy. Like Kukla, Fran, and Ollie."

I let that sit for a moment, then said, "One last question: Could Peggy Lynn have had something on Harrold, something to blackmail him with?"

"Finley," Brant said, "I've wondered the same thing for a long time. But let me ask you something: What kind of leverage would be that strong? What can you have on the president of a network in this day and age that turns him into a fucking Muppet?"

I still didn't have an answer for that one. Marty turned off the lights. I shook hands with Brant and thanked him for his time while Marty packed up the lights and sound gear. It was like shaking hands with a tile fish. Brant was cold and he was sweating.

"Some days," he said, "I need my run in the park more than others. I do the reservoir this time every day, give myself a good hour between eleven and twelve. It's like therapy. Mind clearer. Dead of winter, heat of summer, rain and snow, I have to have that run. Wouldn't ever think of being able to do the show without it. It's ten miles of feeling like a human being."

We started to head for the door.

Brant called after us.

"Uh, Finley, while I'm running today, I don't have to worry about what this piece of yours might do to my already shaky career, do I?"

He was starting to wear me out. We were buddies again.

"Only if you lied to me, pal."

We just left him standing there, just another scared little product of television, making a half-million a year and afraid of his shadow, worried about what the fall would be like when the fall came, because it came for everybody. I wondered if he wore the makeup jogging.

No one spoke in the elevator. There was something nagging at me, something Brant had said that I knew was important, like a name you wanted to remember but couldn't. I made a mental note to go over the tape later with Dwan. On the street I told Marty and Natalie I would catch them at the office later, after lunch with Sam Cummings. They got into the van and left me on Forty-second.

I called Jeannie from a pay phone at the corner. Her

secretary at *Era* told me that Ms. Bogardus—she had always used her maiden name professionally, more to piss off her husband than to be a feminist—had gone to Chicago on business, and had not called from there with a phone number where she could be reached.

I slammed down the receiver and pondered for maybe the millionth time why a guy would love the Red Sox *and* Jeannie Bogardus (Finley) in the same lifetime.

CHAPTER
10

THE Summerhouse restaurant was in the low nineties on Madison, just south of the part of Manhattan where a lot of boutique restaurants have this terrible collision with Harlem. They serve pink butter at Summerhouse. It matches the walls. Still it is one of the best lunch places in town, with a lot of sun, a lot of flora and fauna, and hostesses and waitresses so pretty they make even your clothes hurt. There is also a big old antique carousel horse in the window.

The antique carousel horse had more personality than Sam Cummings, producer of "Midnite," friend of Peggy Lynn.

"If I knew about any files, I would tell you about files," Cummings was saying. "I don't. So I can't. I call lunch a wrap, okay?"

I looked up at the horse when Cummings said wrap. The horse seemed mildly amused by television talk.

We had been waltzing around the subject of Peggy

Lynn's files through the cute salad with buttermilk dressing and the fried chicken and the brownie cake I really didn't need. Now we were both having coffee. Sam Cummings was also having another Scotch. He fished some ice cubes out of the Scotch and stirred them into his coffee. It was the most enthusiasm I'd seen from him yet. Sam and I were having a failure to communicate that rivaled the ones I used to have in the backseat of a sixty-four Impala.

I took a sip of wine. When I drink Jack Daniel's at lunch, my afternoons usually require bypass surgery.

I said, "Sam, we've got to find a common language here. How about we try English? You keep saying that you and Peggy Lynn weren't running any power games at GBC. I hear different. I think she's dead, Sam. You were her best friend at the network. You might be able to help me find out who killed her. Talk to me."

Cummings slouched down a little further in his wicker chair. He seemed permanently locked in the slouch mode. All in all, he reminded me of a very sleepy sheep dog. His sandy hair was too long. Not fashionably long, just messy and uncut, falling almost to eyes that had gotten stuck about a quarter open. Unless I missed my guess, hair and shampoo were working on a trial separation. His shirt was a couple of sizes too big and spilled out of the front of his jeans. He was wearing ancient penny loafers and no socks and was smoking one Marlboro after another, hitting the ashtray with ashes about half the time.

This was not a neat person. Throughout lunch I had also noted he had the table manners of a pro wrestler.

"Nobody's proved she's dead yet," he said. Then he belched. The blonde hostess, Liz, was walking past the table when the belch came and she doubled up, like he'd hit her with it.

"She's dead, Sam. I say so. The cops say so, off the

record anyway. Somewhere along the line, I'm guessing here, she did something to somebody at GBC, and it was bad enough to get her dead. You two worked real close. You might know what she did, and who she did it to. I'm on your side. Gimme a break."

Cummings looked out the window at Madison.

"Peggy Lynn got to where she was because she had more talent than any of those fools at the network had ever seen," he said. "You must have seen her. She was the best. She was a little rough around the edges when she first came from local, but I worked with her, and I saw her grow. If people hated her, it's because they were jealous."

He slouched a little more. In a minute I was going to have to feed him the rest of his brownie cake under the table.

I said, "I hear that she and Brant weren't exactly Hansel and Gretel."

"Johnny Brant is an incompetent," he said, slurping more coffee. "Brant has the brains of a lamp shade. He hated Peggy Lynn because he couldn't get into her pants. Even when she started to soften around work, he wouldn't give her a chance."

"So she was going to dump Brant when she took over as executive producer?"

Cummings had a habit of dropping his head to the side when he wanted to indicate some interest in the conversation. He did that now, as he went through the business of lighting another cigarette.

"Where'd you hear that?"

"The network fairy told me. Any truth to it?"

"Peggy Lynn and I used to talk about what we'd change if she were ever in charge of the show. But it was just talk."

"How shook up do you think Brant would have gotten if he heard something like that, even if it was just a rumor?"

"Not shook up enough to kill, if that's what you're driving at. Brant always knows there's another place for him in television, if not network, then in local back in Washington."

Liz came to the table. Cummings stuck a finger in his coffee and said "More ice." She gave me a wicked look. I thought she might be getting it into her head to set Sam's hair on fire. He didn't see the look because he was wiping his finger on his jeans.

"What about Thomas Harrold?" I said. "How did he get along with our girl?"

"Okay. But just okay. It's a tight-asshole time for him, because of the sale. It was that way before, because of Peggy Lynn's new contract. We didn't see him as a problem in the long run. Peggy figured he'd be gone when Reverend Endicott took over."

"Why?"

The head drooped to the side again.

"Just figured."

"Tell me about the night Peggy Lynn disappeared," I said.

He shifted around in his dirty ensemble and recrossed his legs. The movement seemed to tire him.

"I went over this with the cops about fifty times."

"Humor me. I'm picking up the check."

"Okay. The show ended at eight-thirty, just like always. Peggy Lynn and I would usually stop for a drink after that. Then the limo would take her home. This night she said she couldn't have the drink. Said she had an appointment. That was fine with me. Kris and I had some work to do on the next week's formats. I asked her if the limo could drop me off at her place. She told me that the limo driver was gone, she was being picked up. I figured it was this new guy in her life, one she hadn't even told me or Kris about. I said good-bye to her at the front door and got into a cab and headed uptown. It was the last I saw her."

"You got any clue who the guy was?"

"Nope. It was the only big secret she kept from me. I didn't press her. I'm pretty sure Kris knew. Whoever it was, when Peggy wanted to entertain at home, she made Kris take a hotel room for the night. When I'd ask her where she was going some weekends, she'd look mysterious and say, 'Someplace with water.' "

"She own any homes other than the Connecticut place?"

"Nope."

"Could the guy have been Harrold?"

"Nope. He tried once, put a little pressure on her. She faded him good."

"Had anything been bothering her that you knew about?"

"Nope. Like I said, she seemed more at peace than she'd been in a long time."

"But Stanford knew who the lover was?"

"Yup."

I looked at the pink walls and at the carousel horse and at Sam Cummings. I was getting tired of playing yup and nope with him.

"You got any ideas about who might have wanted to kill Kris Stanford?"

He said, "Nope."

So I figured I would give him a little jolt from the letters.

"Some people think there wasn't a guy at all, that there might have been something a little dykey going on between Kris and Peggy Lynn. Got any theories about that?"

I'd hit the jackpot, in a manner of speaking.

He came across the table at me, shoving me back in my chair. He had me before I knew what was happening. The chair went over into the horse as cups and plates and things went clattering to the floor. My head would've clattered to the floor with them if it didn't catch what felt like a carousel hoof first. Cummings hadn't looked like much trouble in repose. But he got perky when you insulted his girl. I heard someone scream when I went down. It sounded like a noise coming from across the street. Cummings was all over me, knee in my chest, fist with my tie in it, his face very close to mine. I could see his eyes finally. They were green. In better circumstances I would have considered it a moral victory.

But I was just waiting for him to commence hitting me. I could smell the Scotch on his breath. What he said next would have been comical if I wasn't so sure that the back of my head was bleeding. It felt awfully toasty in the cowlick area.

"Take it back," he said in a growl.

His right fist was in the go position.

"Take it back."

Over Cummings's shoulder I could see one of the busboys make a move on him. I tried to move out from under when he did, but he pressed the knee harder. Cummings shifted around and gave the busboy a forearm shiver that had some mustard to it. The busboy went into a ficus tree. Cummings turned his attention back to me, grabbing more of my tie and rapping my head into the tiled floor. Hard.

"You called her a dyke. Take it back, Finley."

I was having trouble breathing, focusing. It had happened too fast.

"I take it back," I managed.

"Interview's over," he said and let go of me.

Cummings got up. I managed to lift my head, no small effort, watched him go. The busboy sat under the ficus tree. Liz had backed all the way into the dessert cart. The customers near us, most of them middle-aged women, sat stricken and wordless. They had probably come just for the pink butter.

When Cummings was on the street, Liz came over to me. She cradled my head in her lap, felt gingerly in back, gave a tiny gasp, and shouted for someone to call a doctor.

It sounded like a smashing idea to me.

"Floor show," I mumbled.

"No doubt about it, Finley," Liz said. "You got one hell of an interviewing technique."

That was the last thing I heard before I passed out.

CHAPTER

11

THEY took me over to Lenox Hill Hospital when I came to. A doctor who looked like a past president of the National Honor Society said I was going to need eight stitches. We became pals when I told him my name. Said he was a fan. I didn't catch his. It should have been Doctor Wasp. He was blond, blue-eyed, deep-voiced, square-shouldered, and one big son of a gun. I saw important things ahead for him in private practice.

From the smell of him he'd just come from major surgery on the Aqua Velva man.

"That's one heck of a nasty whack, fella," he said. "How'd it happen?"

I groaned. The nurse had finished snipping hair from around the cut. He was making the first stitch. It felt like he was using a corkscrew.

I said, "What?"

"I was just wondering what happened back there. A boom mike fall on you?"

The nurse stifled a giggle. Stitching humor.

"I fell off a fucking polo pony."

That pretty much ended the badinage.

When he finished up with his needlepoint, I filled out some insurance forms. The nurse told me my own doctor could take out the stitches in a couple of days, and that I should be careful showering until then. I told her I never showered alone, so I figured I'd be safe. Then I used a pay phone to call Mick Dunphy. I asked him if he wanted to meet me at O'Rourkes. It was the cocktail hour by then. If the downtown traffic wasn't bad, I could be there in fifteen minutes.

Dunphy told me to start my engines without him if he was late. He said he had a couple of more phone calls to make on the Stanford thing.

I said, "Got a lead?"

"If I do, pal, you got a scoop."

THE period between six o'clock and eight o'clock is known as The Desperate Hours to regulars at O'Rourkes. The less refined just call it "scum time." The stockbrokers and ad agency guys and lawyers and secretaries and publishing riffraff barricade themselves at the bar and hold yell practice. There is a lot of heady conversation about The Market. The top of the bar is a precision drill for martini glasses. A lot of Sinatra is played on the juke box, but nobody hears. When they do hear the music, the worst O'Rourkes sin, dancing in the front room, is committed frequently. Two glasses shatter on the half hour, and if by seven o'clock a gray suit isn't passed out in one of the grandstand seats from the old Yankee Stadium—they adorn the entrance—no one is having a good time at all.

Jimmy O'Rourke politely refers to the crowd as his

"day people." Seamus, the day bartender, refers to the six-to-eight group as "them."

Everything seemed to be normal when I walked in. A suit was sitting next to a middle-aged woman on the juke box, nibbling on her right ear like it was the smoked salmon appetizer. A vice-president from NBC whom I knew slightly already had his head communing with a glass table top under the Yankee team picture. Buster, the quirky little runner for O'Rourke's bookie, was sitting at a corner of the bar with an egg timer in front of him; when it went off every fifteen minutes, Buster would smoke a cigarette. It was his way of cutting down.

On the bench against the left-hand wall, a fat girl in a softball jersey that said KENNEDY'S on the front was crying softly, while a thinner girl in the same uniform shouted that someone or other was a rotten no good scumbag and they were both better off without him.

Home is what I called it.

"Don't get blind-sided," Seamus called in greeting as I made my way through the crush.

"Why would terrorists hijack TWAs when they could have this place," I said to Seamus. I figured if I could get to the back room with stitches still in I could maybe turn my day around. A man without goals has a terrible poverty of the spirit, I thought.

O'Rourke wasn't in yet. I asked his debutante waitress for a telephone, a Jack Daniel's, a glass of water, an aspirin bottle from Jimmy's private stock. She brought all of them. I called Natalie at the office. She wasn't there. Neither was Marty. I left a message for Natalie to meet me at O'Rourkes. She didn't know it yet, but Sam Cummings was going to be a project for her at some point.

I sipped some Jack. Dunphy walked in. My back was to the wall, but he saw the bandage in the mirror. Cop, I have found, is cop.

"Unless your marital situation has changed," he said, "I assume you didn't get that in the throes of carnal something or other."

I told him about my elegant lunch date with Sam Cummings. By the time I finished he had his first drink in front of him and there was a backup for me.

When I finished Dunphy said, "You want me to roust him a little bit for you?" He grinned. "Can't have these television hooligans beating up on their brethren, now can we?"

"Funny," I said. "But it would be like rousting a fire hydrant, Lieutenant. This is not a normal person. He grunted at me for an hour, then I just hint that someone, not even me, might have thought she was a lesbo princess and the next thing I know I'm getting worked over by a doctor who wants to write gags for Henny Youngman. I felt like a bozo."

"Good for you." The waitress brought him a pack of matches and he lit a Lucky. "My lighter is in the shop," he said in explanation. The waitress left. Dunphy looked at her like she was an ice cream sundae, two scoops of vanilla.

A suit staggered past us. He braced a hand on our table, spun off, ran into the cigarette machine, narrowly missed the wall telephone with his head, and fell into the men's room.

"You think Cummings might have had something to do with the Peggy Lynn deal?" Dunphy said, still looking at the men's room door.

"I don't know if he did it, but he certainly might know why it happened. The way I get it, there's a lot of dirt over there, and he was one of the ones doing the digging."

I told Dunphy a lot of what I'd found in the letters without telling him about the letters. That would have meant handing him Billy. I wasn't ready to do that. So I told about the problems Peggy Lynn had with Johnny Brant. I told him that there could have been something going on between Peggy Lynn and Harrold. I told him Peggy had a date the night she disappeared. I assumed he already knew the last, but I told anyway. The more I gave him the less he'd think I was holding back. We'd played these games before, but you never wanted to try to win all the cute awards with Mick Dunphy.

When I was done he said, "Would I be flattering your butt too much if I told you you'd done a whole hell of a lot better than some of my drones?"

"You make me blush, sir."

He lit another Lucky, cupping his hand around the match flame even though the wind wasn't blowing out in the back room, far as I could tell. A lot of Dunphy's mannerisms would be stagey if he wasn't Dunphy.

"So what's your next play?" he asked. "Seems like you need to talk to the top guy, Harrold, before the leaves turn color."

"I'd even like to talk to the Reverend Eugene Endicott, but he's off saving European souls."

"Makes sense." He waved for two more drinks. I looked out to the bar and saw O'Rourke talking to Seamus. The two girls in the softball uniforms brushed past O'Rourke but he didn't even look up. He must have been distracted.

I said to Dunphy, "What's happening with the Kris Stanford investigation?"

"It's bothering me 'cause it's so damned clean. Could be the worst kind, one where the killer just drops in from the moon. We got nothing from the house, nothing from the body. The ice pick you can get in any hardware store. My guys have been knocking on all the doors, and nobody saw anything out of the ordinary. One lady said a car could've pulled up but then again maybe not. Maybe it was a small car, or bigger. Big help."

I spilled some of my drink when he mentioned a car. Dunphy looked at me. I looked at him.

"Yes?" he mused.

"Bad hands."

"Anyway," he said, "I think whoever did it didn't decide until he got there for sure. And he must have done it quick. There isn't a print in the place, not that that would do us any good necessarily. The guy just walked in, did it, walked out the back door and through an alley that goes to Seventy-third. Went and had lunch or some fucking thing. Just fell out of a tree and landed on his feet. And the dead girl, she had been keeping to herself, so I am not exactly overloaded with tips or theories or leads. I know there's got to be a way this is connected to Peggy Lynn. We don't teach any courses in coincidences. But right now I'm going to stick with Stanford, because at least there I have a corpus delicious."

"Corpus delicious," I said. "You've been spending too much time with me, Mick."

We sat there and drank. The tables around us began to fill up with an early dinner crowd. The back room amp for the juke box was turned down low. The lights dimmed. Little John Henderson, who doubles as waiter and host at night, climbed up on a chair and put the Mets game on the corner television.

"You don't think it might just be a random crazy?" I asked after a while.

Dunphy ran a hand through his thick shock of hair, then patted the hair when he was done.

"It might be a crazy, but I don't think it's random anymore."

Somewhere, Kris Stanford's killer was walking around, on his way to dinner or a show or to get pizza. Somewhere Peggy Lynn was probably dead too. Dunphy and I sat in our booth at our saloon at twilight like characters in some

Pinter play, not knowing whether the action was going backward or forward. Maybe we were the play within the play.

When I get philosophical, I'm either getting loaded, or just horny.

I said, "Mick, why do you keep doing this?"

"You mean, other than the well-known fact that I am the Babe Freaking Ruth of homicide detectives, now that your old man is emeritus?"

"I mean, when you're in the middle of quicksand like this, and the faster you move the more helpless you feel, don't you feel like turning the whole deal over to someone else?"

Dunphy smiled like he'd found a pearl in an oyster.

"Never," he said. "I am still the master of the game, Peter. I am law and order, with some style. Sometimes I really can't tell why you like to play cops and robbers as much as you do. I know you like the flash of it sometimes, and the challenge, because you get both without having to go through a lot of shit. You like to smoke out the bad guys because it proves to you you're as clever as you think you are. It's a little more complicated with me. People who think they can get away with it all insult me, they really do. Maybe they think all cops are like Pat O'Brien in the old movies, walking the beat and saying 'Top of the mornin' to ya, Mrs. O'Riley.' I want to get out there and let them know they're dealing with *me*. This'll probably make you laugh, friend, but when they fuck around they're messing up *my* city, that's the way I look at it. Every time I take a little flotsam and jetsam off the street, I think I got the best job in the world. And still good seats at Giants games."

"Like my father."

"Quick," Dunphy said approvingly. "You always been this quick?"

"When the sun goes down."

"Don't despair, we'll get this all worked out. Always do."

I lit a cigarette.

"Jeannie thinks it's a game for me too."

"That is why Jeannie Finley is your best part. Her and your old man. They'll both get you through puberty yet."

I chuckled. "So you're going to stay with Stanford and I'm going to stay with Peggy Lynn."

"Like that, yeah."

My head was starting to hurt again. But I was in no rush to go anywhere. I was about to address the great dilemma for the man who reads *Playboy*—go home or get truly shitfaced—when Little John came over and told Dunphy there was a phone call for him.

"You can take it at the bar, Lieutenant," John said. "I assume yer armed."

Dunphy got up.

"Wanna look at a menu?" John said to me.

"Shit no," I said.

"Thought not."

Dunphy was away a long time. When he got back, his face said the call wasn't about getting a date for the Policeman's Ball. He threw a twenty on the table, downed the last of his drink, looked hard at me and said, "Let's go."

"Don't tell me. We're double dating at the drive-in."

Mick Dunphy grabbed his cigarettes off the table, me by the arm.

"Call your teammates," he said. "They just called me from Seth Parker's office. Somebody stuck another ice pick. In him."

CHAPTER

12

MICK DUNPHY was about to move into a second hour of what would have sounded a great deal like full pitch Byzantine-Gregorian chanting if it hadn't been for all the fucks.

I assumed it was a second hour. I didn't even want to glance at my Timex because I was afraid Mick might take it off my wrist and floss his teeth with it.

It was after two in the morning, I knew that much. We were in Mick's downstairs office at the 17th Precinct, which is on Fifty-first between Third and Lex. In more sociable times I had always liked the office, which made mine at Channel A look like the broom closet at a men's shelter.

It was carpeted, for one thing. The desk was a venerable and imposing rolltop monster and seemed to be made of redwood. There were elegantly framed pictures all over the walls, all of them signed by celebrities standing with Mick Dunphy. There was Mick with Frank Gifford and

Alex Webster, when they were still with the Giants. Mick with a couple of famous Jacks, Dempsey and Kennedy. Mick with Sinatra. Mick with what seemed like just about every New York City mayor back to Jimmy Walker. There was Mick with Marilyn Monroe at the back room at Clarke's. One of his hands was under the table. Marilyn was smiling. I figured he was checking her for a concealed weapon.

There was an antique cappuccino machine. It was on one of the three gray filing cabinets against the wall to the right of the rolltop. It was what Mick called his ego wall, the one with all the plaques and medals and commendations; they seemed to indicate Mick had solved everything except Amelia Earhart. Next to the filing cabinet was a portable Trinitron color set. It was attached to a video recorder.

The first time I saw the office I said to Dunphy, "You take my apartment. I'll live here. Just tell me where you've got the Jacuzzi."

There were also two leather armchairs on the suspect side of the rolltop. I was squirming in one at the moment. Marty Pearl was slouched in the other.

Mick's presentation—which had now dwindled down to mostly pacing with a splash of yelling—was about our visit to Seth Parker's office the day before.

"Actually, Finley," he was saying, poking the air with a Lucky, "you have won all the asshole nominations this time. Writing, directing, acting, you're the Woody Allen of assholes. Remind me to ask your old man next time I see him just how many times you fell out of your fucking highchair when you were a baby. Because you have gotta have a brain which at this point in time looks like a fucking zucchini surprise."

I leaned forward and said, "Mick . . ."

Dunphy pounded the cabinet closest to mine and made

the cappuccino machine wiggle suggestively. His name fell
out of the air a few feet in front of my mouth, like I hadn't
used enough club.

"Don't 'Mick' me!" he snapped. "Goddammit, you are
the *dumbest* white man. We are talking about a homicide
investigation here, Finley. Read my fucking lips. We are
talking about withholding evidence. You and fucking
Tonto there. So now I've got two stiffs instead of one."

Dunphy wasn't through.

"You don't tell me that Parker went to Kris Stanford's.
You don't tell me about the trip to Parker's office, the tape
of yours with all the goodies on it. Maybe by now it has
occurred to your dead Irish brain that if you had, Parker
might not be in the archives now. Jesus Christ, you are one
arrogant fuck."

There was a lot in what he said. I had run sneakers on
him before. It was part of our game and we both knew it.
But no one had ended up dead before because of the game.

When we'd shown up at 1515 Broadway from
O'Rourkes, the NYPD program was in full swing. The
cops had set up some blue barriers in front of the building,
clearing the sidewalk from the crowd. Traffic was backed
up to White Plains. Some rap dancers across the street
from 1515 were working up a number to the erratic
rhythm of the car horns. Reporters and photographers
were pushing through the crowd, trying to get past the
cops and the barriers. Blue lights flashed on the top of the
cop cars. Red lights on the police ambulance. Television
cameras. Flash cameras. Some of the movies in the neighborhood were letting out. The movie people made the
whole attendance figure grow.

I felt sick.

Trust me, I'd said to Seth Parker.

Dunphy put a hammerlock on my arm and got me
through the wave of uniforms. A reporter I knew from

Cable News yelled something at Dunphy from behind the
barriers as we were approaching the revolving doors at
1515. Dunphy stopped, walked back, glared at Cable
News and said, "Die."

The people in the lobby were mostly official. There was
a stretcher near the elevator bank. I knew what was under
the sheet. Marty was off to the side, blending into the
woodwork, shooting it all. I don't know how he does it.
He just gets there, first. Natalie was talking to the Medical
Examiner, a chipmunk of a man named Feeney.

Dunphy went about the business of taking charge. I
walked over to Marty.

"Do we make the eleven-thirty, sport?" he said. Channel A goes a half hour later than the regular stations.

I said, "Yeah."

Marty gave me a long look. "You tell Mick yet about
yesterday with Parker?"

"First chance I get."

"What do you think he'll do?"

I said, "Probably keep it simple. Arrest us."

Marty told me what he knew, in his terse way. A secu-
rity man had gotten suspicious making his early rounds.
He knew the cleaning woman had to have finished in
Parker's office, but there was a light on. There was more
than a light when he got inside. There was Parker. Neat.
No sign of a scuffle. No forced entry. No David. Just the
body. Somebody was going to keep doing it until he got
it right. Somebody had gotten in before the building
closed, hid, waited. An invisible somebody.

I saw Mick Dunphy get into an elevator with two uniforms. I took the microphone from Marty and motioned
for Natalie not to let Feeney wander off. You put a microphone near Feeney and he'll begin to talk like he's seen
God.

I did a fast stand-up, then interviewed Feeney, who did

another audition for Celebrity Coroner.

When Dunphy came back down from Parker's office, I told him everything. His look tossed me away like an umbrella he'd bought on the street.

"My office," he spat. "Soon as you're off the fucking air."

WHEN Dunphy finally calmed down in his office, we did it all by the numbers. Marty and I recited our accounts of the Parker visit into a tape recorder. A stenographer backed up the tape recorder. The statements were transcribed. We signed them. Dunphy had asked the right questions in the right places. He made me describe the old sax player; said the sax player would have to be picked up, if anyone could find him. He wanted to know David's last name. I started to say Adorable, thought better of it, remembered it was Ellison. Dunphy wanted to know where the tape was. I told him my apartment.

It was way past four in the morning when we finished. The painkillers had worn off long ago. My stitches felt like they were reproducing.

Dunphy sat behind his desk, feet up. I hadn't asked about going home, he hadn't said anything about going home. The smart money had us watching the sunrise together. A burst of male bonding.

Mick finally said, "Here is the bottom line: You fucked up. And you owe me one, boy. I don't know when I'll call it in, but you owe me a big one."

I said, "Check."

He leaned forward a little bit and rubbed some dirt off the toe of a Bally with a finger and said, "I want to hear that tape in the morning. Here. And I want to ask you one last question. Have you told me all of it?"

I thought about Billy Lynn and said, "Yes."

Born to lie.

He looked over at Marty.

"You back him up on that?"

Marty's answer was a snort.

Dunphy grinned for the first time.

"Okay," he said. "Dumb question. Now the two of you get the hell out of here. I'm going to Clarke's for a close-down cocktail. Make sure you don't. I'm sick of looking at you."

We left like it was the last day of school. Marty's van was parked near the corner of Third. We walked east toward it. Neither one of us spoke. By the time we did, we were halfway through a conversation. You get a wavelength like this only a few times in your life, with friend or lover. It saves a lot of time, a lot of useless chatter. I am told there are actually six living males who are able to communicate the same way with their wives.

Marty said, "We just go back to the singing Lynn family now, right?"

"Billy's still the only hole card we've got. Somehow it's all connected, the letters and Stanford and Parker. But I've got to level, murder is making my ass real tired."

"Better your ass than your neck, the way you've been going the last couple of days."

I looked at my friend in the mix of streetlights and night and bar signs and even summer stars. We get clear skies sometimes in Manhattan.

"Louie . . ." I began.

"We done stepped into a pile of pukey," Marty finished.

I took off my sports jacket and slung it over my shoulder; New York is the only place in the world where the temperature seems to rise fifteen degrees in the middle of the night. Fifty-first was still and humid. We approached a bar called Lancelot. Gay joint. Two male hookers who had come straight from a Calvin Klein underwear ad were standing in front, lounging against a wrought-iron railing with unlit cigarettes in their hands. The window behind them said something about a "Fire Island Patio." Lancelot 1 started to make the requisite move at me and ask for a light. Lancelot 1A took a look at Marty and put a restraining hand on his business associate's arm. 1A apparently decided that Marty might want to play devil's advocate in a debate about gay liberation. They let us pass.

When we got to the van, Marty asked if I wanted to stop at O'Rourkes for a hubcap. We never used nightcap, because we knew there was no such thing. The real nightcap process for us was assembling a car, drink by drink by drink; the last part of the process was the hubcap.

"Not tonight. Home, James."

Marty put the key in the ignition and looked sideways at me.

"Don't get the guilts," he said in a soft voice that always seemed so incongruous coming from the big man. "Whoever got to Parker was going to get to him, one way or another. If it wasn't today it would've been tomorrow. Or next week. We've got a serious loon running around, and he's got real big balls, son."

The engine turned over and he put the van in gear and we made the uptown left onto Third.

I said, "Shit, I could've told Mick. I don't feel bad about keeping Billy in the bullpen, but I damn well could have told him about Seth Parker. Maybe Mick's right. Maybe I am an arrogant fuck."

"Well, of course you are," Marty said. "All part of your killer, pardon the expression, charm. It's why those of us who've been blessed as your supplicants worship you so."

"Don't try any of that slick talk with me. I'm not inviting you up to my apartment. God, you big city guys are all alike."

He spat the tip of a cigar out the window and said, "Prig."

As we crossed Fifty-third Street Marty had to do a triple salchow double toe loop to avoid a gypsy cab driver. We nearly landed in the front window of Conran's. Marty did it all one-handed. He was lighting the cigar.

I said, "I'll meet you at Dunphy's in the morning. We'll drop the tape in his lap and figure out where to go next. I want to touch base with Billy. And I expect to hear from my dad. He left for Guertin this morning."

Marty pulled over at Fifty-ninth, near Bloomingdale's. I walked the rest of the way from there, past the Fifty-ninth Street Army-Navy Store, my favorite place to buy clothes in the city, past the Roosevelt Island tram stop, past T. J. Tucker, a new hangaround owned by an old friend; past the doorway at Fifty-ninth and First where The Shrink had her office. Jeannie had made me go. There had been only one visit. After fifteen minutes The Shrink, an angular woman in her forties who smoked unfiltered Gitanes and had an early Beatles haircut, told me I was clearly trying to prolong an ideal of adolescence, and that the effort was foolish and romantic and doomed.

I told her I could get the same advice from a bartender named Seamus, and watch ball games at the same time. I paid for the hour in cash and went and did just that with Seamus. Jeannie hadn't taken it well. But by then we had reached a point where Jeannie wasn't taking "good morning" all that well if I was the one saying it. There are all sorts of murder.

I walked through the night toward York, taking my sweet time. You are somehow fearless in these moments, sober or full of whiskey, no matter what the hour, moving in the night with drunks and hookers and bartenders going home from work and the garbage trucks out and cabs, empty now after dodging you so artfully in the daylight; and the unsteady men who are making the unsteady walk toward one more saloon, hoping to find the willing nubile thing they have searched mightily for since the cocktail hour the day before. And you always believe that just once, in the middle of the night, you will meet her on the street—*her*—and she will smile at you and say, "Where the hell have you *been*?" I had always believed that and never met her, not on Fifty-ninth Street, or anywhere else, in the time before dawn. But it was a fine New York dream. . . .

It was Ness's night off; his replacement at the door was an ex-light-heavyweight named Lenny Morrissey. Lenny was a light-heavy when he was fighting anyway. That was about twenty years ago. It looked like he hadn't missed a meal since. In his ill-fitting, dark green doorman's uniform, belly doomed to never meet belt, he always reminded me of Oliver Hardy, minus the funny hat. All the features in his scarred face seemed to have rushed to the center for a quick huddle. Button eyes. Ruined nose. Lips permanently swollen. Lenny had no chin. He had checked it somewhere along the way, and it had become just another piece of lost luggage.

When I walked in he was reading a boxing magazine at the concierge pulpit and listening to a transistor radio. I heard the disc jockey say, "This is Milkman's Matinee." That meant it was WNEW, the most civilized radio station in America, and one of the oldest. Just standards and big bands and show tunes.

"Mornin' Mr. F," Lenny said. "Pretty late, even for you. You been havin' a soda pop somewhere?"

I faked a short little jab to his shin. Lenny blocked it easily with his right hand and had his own left patting me on the ear in a boxer's instant. I was out of his league. When you have the moves, you have the moves.

I said, "Lenny, I feel like I just went fifteen with Sugar Ray, and I mean the real one."

"Was only one," Lenny said.

I headed for the elevator. Lenny called after me.

"By the way, Mr. F. Your daddy's up there. He come in a little while ago."

He must have postponed going to Alabama. On late nights in the city, Jack Finley sometimes stayed with me instead of driving back to Forest Hills. Sometimes he even brought a guest, if I was out of town. At sixty-three, my father has hormones stronger than the Marines.

The elevator door opened. I got in and managed to press the right button for my floor. The door closed. I kept thinking about Seth Parker, and what it was like in the end. Did he know? Did he see it coming? Did he hear music? Did he have a chance? Did he try to negotiate? Or did the final blackness come all of a sudden?

A little windup doll of a man, gone to meet the dead lover, away from Peggy Lynn at last. Maybe.

I started to fumble with key and lock when I got to my door but then the door was opening and my father was standing there in the foyer, too stiffly.

"Sorry, sonny," he said softly.

Jack Finley was not alone.

Seth Parker's friend David was behind him in the foyer and to his left. David looked like a disco at closing time. The legs were planted but he was weaving slightly, alone in a slow, rhythmless dance. His eyes were sparklers. Beads of sweat were working into a perfect wave on his forehead. His kamikaze smile was locked forever in madness. What was coming out of the corners of his mouth was sweat, or spit, or both.

Any fool could see that David was the one with the gun.

CHAPTER
13

THE foyer in my apartment sprays into the living room. David motioned us that way with the gun. His hand wavered a bit. The smile was still locked in place and the eyes were jumping all around now. I stared at the gun, which looked like a toy in David Ellison's hand. It might have been a .22 but I wasn't sure. I know as much about handguns as I do the mating habits of quail. My mother wouldn't let my father even show me one when I was growing up. I just figured David's worked fine or he wouldn't have brought it.

I thought of the line from the opening of *Dirty Harry* when Eastwood pointed a much bigger gun at the punk and said, "Do you feel lucky today?"

I decided I hadn't felt lucky since they abolished the draft.

My father must have put on the stereo before David came. Johnny Mercer was fooling around with "Moon River." The terrace door was open slightly and the leaves

of my big old marsagiana tree—Jeannie called it "that
deformed rubber thing"—whipped noiselessly against
each other. My father moved toward the sofa. He was
wearing his monogrammed blue robe. He kept his hands
where David could see them and he looked at me. His look
was made of brick and it said: Don't be a hero, boy.
There's a cop here and the cop is still me.

He sat down at one end of the sofa. I moved around and
sat at the other end. The coffee table was its usual toxic
waste dump: *Time* and *Newsweek* jockeying for position
with *New York* and *GQ* and *People* and *The Sporting
News.* Irwin Shaw's autographed copy of *Five Decades,*
his short story collection for all time, which told of girls
in their summer dresses and eighty-yard runs. Dan Jen-
kins's *Life Its Ownself.* An ashtray with cigarette butts
crawling out of it. The remote control switcher for the
cassette machine. The most recent Emmy. A single cassette. I dwelled on the rubble because the alternative was
the gun.

David stood across the table from us. He wore a white
Lacoste shirt and army fatigue slacks that had pockets
everywhere and high-topped red sneakers.

He said, "The gun has lots of bullets in it, I think." He
was delighted with the news; a kid at a spelling bee.

I looked at him and said, "What do you want here,
David?"

"Oh, you know what I want. You know I want that
cassette, you smart fucking bastard. You know that's what
I want, because you're not going to hurt Seth with it
anymore. You're going to give it to me, then you're going
to watch while I maybe kill your daddy. What fun!"

I figured he had taken some pills. The uppers were
winning.

I shifted my weight on the couch, for lack of anything

better to do. David locked both hands on the little gun and focused it on me.

"Do something smart, Finley," he said. "Be cute. Please. Give me a reason to do you first."

I stayed in place like an anchorman's hair.

"David," I said, "I didn't kill Seth. You know better than that. The cassette didn't kill Seth. But I'm going to find out who did, if we can just talk. Maybe you can help me."

Next to me, my father's breath became harsh. David looked at him, then back at me.

David said, "Everything was fine until you came around. You and your buddy and all that business in the office. Yeah, I know you didn't do it, but you started something, you know you did, I don't know what exactly, but someone came along to finish it. Now somebody has to pay, that's all. You cost me everything. *Everything!* So I vote you and the old-timer here pay. What do you think about that, old-timer?"

Jack Finley's breath was labored now and his face was the color of a plum.

"Do what you have to do, kid," he said to David. The words came hard. He put a trembling hand to his chest and closed his eyes.

"What's the matter with him?" David asked suspiciously. "He tries anything, I'll use this thing, I mean it." The voice was girlish.

"Just relax," I said. "He gets these attacks sometimes. It's why he had to leave the cops. They come and go. Jesus God, David, don't get edgy. I'll get the tape and we'll talk about it, okay? There are things you might know that could help me out. You might even know the one who did it. Just don't get crazy on me."

"Oh, we'll talk. We'll talk and talk and talk. Good

golly, Miss Molly, where are the cameras and tape record-
ers when you really need them?"

"How did you find out about Seth?" I said quietly.

"Why, on the radio! The all-news station. Isn't that the
way everybody finds out about everything?"

The music from the stereo had stopped. I heard a tugboat blast on the river. From the street came the messy
roar of a garbage truck loading. Morning already.

David said, "The cassette. Now. Chat's over."

I pointed down at the coffee table. "That's the tape right
there, as a matter of fact. It's yours. Just leave my father
out of this and we'll settle however you want."

I reached down for the cassette.

"Careful now," David said.

"Careful," I repeated. "I'm just showing you where it
is. No big deal."

David bent over for the cassette just as Jack Finley
groaned and pitched forward all over the coffee table.
David wheeled at him with the gun. I grabbed the Emmy
with my left hand and as I was grabbing it, thrust the globe
part and the wings part right into David's balls. He made
a sound like Jeanette MacDonald singing "Indian Love
Call" to Nelson Eddy and staggered backward, trying to
grab his crotch with one hand and aim the gun with the
other. Jack Finley, all sixty-three years of him, just kept
rolling across the table, scattering the books and magazines, and took David down with a rolling block the way
a free safety would.

"Get the gun, sonny," my father called from the rug.

I was right there. David couldn't raise the gun anymore
because I was standing on it.

My father got up, smoothed his hair out, and tied his
robe back up in front where it had come open, while David
writhed in the fetal position, making hen sounds. I handed
the gun to my father like it was contaminated. He turned

it over in his hands and said, "Who makes these things nowadays? Ralph Lauren?"

I walked over to the wall phone between the den and the kitchen and dialed 911.

Jack Finley kept an eye on David, who rocked back and forth on the rug and held on firmly and lovingly to body parts that Marty usually referred to as Vernon and his ear muffs.

"Peter," my father said, "I don't think I ever told you how I burst with fatherly pride when you won your last Emmy."

I put my hand over the receiver; they are sometimes a little tardy picking up at 911.

I said, "I'd like to thank the academy."

"What was that cassette you were giving him anyway?" my father asked.

"I'm pretty sure it was the Chuckles the Clown episode from 'The Mary Tyler Moore Show,'" I said.

FIFTEEN minutes later Lenny showed up with a couple of uniforms. My father took them into the kitchen after they handcuffed David and laid it out for them in cop shorthand. The taller uniform, who looked like Mickey Mantle and spoke fluent Flatbush, asked me if I wanted to press charges. I looked at David, handcuffed and beaten and quite mad, and said no.

"But you should probably take him over to the station and give Mick Dunphy a wake-up call," I said. "David and Mick should really get to know each other."

Mickey Mantle said, "You really get him in the jewels with that statue?"

I gave him my hard-guy look. "Television isn't for pansies, fella."

They took David.

My father flipped the Mercer record and went to fix us a couple of bloody Marys. Breakfast of champions at the Finley house. It was almost eight o'clock in the morning. I felt like I'd slept in the bathtub.

I noticed Lenny lingering in the foyer, nervously cracking knuckles in those dead boxer's hands like he was waiting for someone to read the judges' cards. He kept blinking eyes that seemed full of resin.

"I don't know how he gets up here, Mr. F," he said. "But I'm going downstairs and have me a chat with the guard at the service entrance. The guy with the gun must have told some story to get up the back way. Aw, shit."

"No problem, Lenny. Really." I took him by the shoulder and walked him out into the hall. "That's why I still live with a cop at my age. It beats a nightlight all to hell, don't you think?"

Lenny shuffled off to the elevators. When I came back into the living room my father was waiting for me. He started to say something, but I cut him short.

"What was all that business before? Andrew Jackson Finley has a coronary?"

"Goodness no. I go into full spasm when I do a coronary. That was just a mild angina attack. 'Oh God, where are my nitro tablets?' Like that. It's subtle, but effective, I must say." He laughed softly, like the tinkle of piano keys. "God, when you're good, you're good."

I said, "I thought you were going to Guertin today."

"I got back late. Came straight here from the airport. I've been trying to reach you all day. Where in the world have you been?"

I told him where I'd been. Summerhouse, Lenox Hill, 1515 Broadway, the 17th Precinct. "This day will live in goddamned infamy," I said.

"Your day is about to get worse, Peter. Billy Lynn lied to you."

He sat down in the sofa, leaned back, and closed his eyes. Somewhere in his head a tape was being rewound. I had seen him do it hundreds of times before, back on the cloth divan in Southie late at night, when he was trying to talk his way through some complicated case, find something he'd missed by telling it to me. It was after my mother was gone. I'd keep fixing him cups of strong tea and be an audience of one for the best bedtime stories in all of Boston. My position was that Jack Finley always kicked the shit out of *Treasure Island.*

"Guertin, Alabama," he said, eyes still closed. "It will never be confused with Beverly Hills. It is, in fact, a Seven-eleven store that just seemed to spread. Main Street is perhaps one hundred yards long. There are three churches on the street, one Baptist, one Presbyterian, one known as the Guertin Alliance of the Living God, which is an offshoot of that Reverend Endicott's church. That one is Billy's church of choice. The only hotel in town is the Guertin Arms. Eight rooms, two floors. I was told by the desk clerk that Robert E. Lee once slept there. I assume he only stayed one night, if the Guertin Arms was as short on facilities in the last century as it is in this one. And I was only there long enough to shower and drop my bag. The movie theater, the Rialto, has been empty for years; they play bingo there on Tuesday night, a civic event of some import. A diner near the Baptist church, across from the general store—Taylor's Kitchen it is called—offers the best food in town and the best conversation."

I wanted him to move it along, but you couldn't rush him. He had to do it at his own speed, even when it was important.

"I talked to people at Taylor's Kitchen. And at Guertin's bank. And at the churches. According to the townsfolk, Peter, Peggy Lynn was never married to Billy. Peggy Lynn's mother married Billy's father. If she was anything, you would have to call her his stepsister."

My voice dropped to ground zero. "Say that again."

"Billy's own mother died in childbirth. When he was in high school, his late father—a Bible-thumping preacher of some legend in Guertin, Alabama—married a woman from Texas named Cecily Denton. Cecily had a daughter a few years younger than Billy. Cute little scamp named Peggy. A heartbreaker even then."

I found myself standing in front of the couch.

"Jesus Christ," I said. "They were brother and sister, not husband and wife?"

"Again, only by marriage, Peter."

"They weren't sweethearts?"

"Not that anyone in the little town ever saw."

"Marriage certificate?"

"No. I called the county clerk."

"They just grew up in the same house with Mama and the preacher?"

"For about four years. Peggy's mother apparently tired of the marriage and the Bible-thumping, so the two of them—Cecily and her daughter—moved to Birmingham the year after Billy graduated from high school. The next anyone in Guertin knew, Peggy Lynn was winning the Miss Alabama beauty contest. Brady was her real father's name. She must have liked Lynn. I guess it's a rule that beauty contest winners have three names."

I walked out onto the terrace and stared at Queens. My head felt like the spin cycle. Natalie had gone through all the files on Peggy Lynn Brady, again and again and again. There had been a lot about the mother, an oft-married Auntie Mame character, dead now, who had trundled her way through Texas and New Mexico and Louisiana and Virginia, finally Alabama. In the clips, Peggy Lynn had always talked a lot about her mother and father, real father, who had been a Texas oil wildcatter. The Guertin parts of the bio, the Alabama parts, had been sketchy and brief. One line here, two lines there. I figured that's where Billy must have been hiding, since I believed him.

"Not many people back home knew about us," Billy Lynn had said to me, dripping all that sincerity.

"We ran away young," Billy Lynn had said.

I had believed him.

My father had come out to stand beside me.

"Is any of it true?" I said. "Does he run the general store? Does he own the gas station? Was he a farmer once? Dammit, Pap, I bought everything the son of a bitch said. Peggy's clips never bothered me. Everyone rewrites their life story once they get famous or whatever. Then somebody else comes along to rewrite the rewrites. It's what I did with Tony Altamero."

He put a hand on my shoulder.

"Billy does own and run the general store. There is a gas station in town that belongs to him. He wasn't much of a farmer. He is a deacon at the Guertin Alliance church. He lives alone outside town, in the same house he and Peggy Lynn grew up in. He has always lived alone, and has never left Guertin. He has never been married, not to Peggy Lynn or anyone else. In a town of fairly holy rollers, he is viewed to be one of the holiest."

I threw a cigarette down, mashed it good, and kicked it into the terrace drain. "Why did he lie to me, Pap? And what is he doing here?"

"Maybe he thought you would help him more if he touched up his story a bit," my father said.

"And maybe he has his own ice pick collection."

I went inside and asked information for the number of the Holiday Inn on West Fifty-seventh. I got it and called Billy's room. He wasn't in.

"I'll shower first," my father said, disappearing toward my bathroom.

CHAPTER
14

I T took us a long time to hail a taxi on York. My father finally stepped in the middle of the street and waved a twenty-dollar bill at an off-duty old yellow Checker—the eighties version of Claudette Colbert hiking up her skirt. The cab stopped, we got in and headed west.

"He was out the morning Kris Stanford got it," I said, nervously playing with my tie. "I couldn't reach him the afternoon Seth Parker got it."

"It still doesn't prove anything," Jack Finley said. "He is a scared country man out of his element. Maybe he thought he had to impress you."

At the Holiday Inn the pretty young cheerleader at the front desk said Mr. Lynn had been out all morning.

"Would you gentlemen care to leave a message?" she asked breathlessly. Her name tag identified her as Sandi.

Sandi said, "I'll make sure he gets the message as *soon* as he gets back."

I told the cheerleader we would think about that for a

minute, then said, "But I sure hope you guys beat State on Saturday."

She looked at me blankly. They don't teach you comeback lines in hotel management.

My father and I sat down on a plastic sofa across from the front desk, next to a round glass table featuring a vase with plastic Holiday Inn flowers. I fished the last Marlboro out of my pack and lit it. It wasn't noon yet. I was going for a record. I was a lousy judge of character, but I had always been straight-A in smoking.

Jack Finley said, "Do we both wait here for him? Does one of us wait? And where do you think the lad might be? Field those in any order you want to."

I smoked and inspected the lobby scene instead. A large group of elderly men and women were milling near the front doors, waiting to board the tour bus we'd seen out front. They should have been wearing name tags that read "Midwest."

A blonde with hair the color of buttered popcorn got out of an elevator, checked herself in a compact mirror, patted the popcorn lovingly, smoothed out the front of her Levi's skirt, and headed for the street. If she wasn't a hooker, she had ignored all her aptitude tests.

"You're the cop," I said wearily. "Say something profound, cop-wise."

"Could Billy have done it, killed the girl and Parker?" my father asked softly. "Because if he did, it would explain a lot, sonny. It would mostly explain why Mick Dunphy has no leads. The worst nightmare of all in a business such as this is the one who just drops in from another planet. And Mr. Billy Lynn has done just that. Because clearly Mick Dunphy does not know he exists, or that he is here."

He waved some of my smoke away from his face. He never complained about my smoking. He just waved.

I said, "Pap, I'll be good and goddamned if I know. I

don't think so. I had this feel about him, you know? I felt like I had to protect the son of a bitch and find him some answers he could take home with him. I watched his face when he listened to the Seth Parker tape and it was like I wanted to die. Now I find out he's lied to me from the starting blocks. But does lying make him a killer? Has he been walking around burning people every couple of days, all the time he was wringing his big hands and saying 'Lordy, Lordy, Lordy'?"

My father reached over and put a hand on my knee. Then he winked. It was the same sort of sly wink he usually offered before heading out to terrorize the Muffins of the world with the old soft shoe.

He said, "Idle hands are the devil's workshop, Peter."

I was watching the tour group head for the sidewalk. "What?"

"Idle hands are the devil's workshop."

I just looked at him.

"Wonderful," I said. "Why didn't I think of that? I guess you know it's going all over town that a stitch in time saves nine."

He patted my knee again.

"Let's go have a look-see at Billy's room," Jack Finley said.

"Jesus, Pap," I said. "Miss Button Cute over there isn't going to give us the key."

My father bounced up out of his plastic chair. Whole special delivery package of mischief, wrapped in a seersucker suit.

"Who said anything about a key?"

"I suppose you play poker with the house detective here."

"Nope." He impatiently pulled me up by the arm.

I said, "Are we by chance talking about breaking and entering here, retired Chief of Dicks Finley?"

"Goodness no, sonny," he said, heading off toward the elevator banks. "We're talking about a field trip."

THE maid, a heavyset Puerto Rican woman who was going to have to be air-lifted out of her tight-fitting uniform, never stood a chance once she showed up on the eleventh floor.

My father had me wait around the corner from 1116, Billy's room, while he went and talked to her. I stuck my head out and watched. He was already patting the pockets of the seersucker jacket, hunting for the imaginary key. She looked up from emptying a wastebasket into the Hefty trash bag attached to her cart. Bored, she shook her head slowly. He got down on his haunches and made a helpless gesture with his hands. I couldn't hear what he was saying, but saw him offer one of those Jack Finley grins that made the whole world feel young and safe. The maid finally smiled back. My father touched her on the shoulder. Said something. She began to giggle. It was over. As she let him into 1116 she stuck an extra stack of clean towels in his arms. She looked back over her shoulder at him as she pushed the cart away down the hall.

Jack Finley waved and blew her a kiss.

If Julio Iglesias was in town somewhere, I was pretty sure it was a date.

As soon as she let herself into her next room I pushed open the door to 1116. Jack Finley was already taking a look at the clothes closet.

He said, "Take the bureau, Peter."

I looked around. It was standard issue Holiday Inn. Lots of blue. More yellow. That long chain hanging from ceiling to curtain rod, one for the life of me I'd never been able to figure out, unless you were traveling with a chimpanzee. Twin beds. Color television set in the corner.

Room service menu on top of it, plus what I had always assumed was the Holiday Inn yearbook but had never opened. I had been staying in rooms like it my entire life.

There was a small round table next to the television set.

The typewriter was on the table. An old black Royal typewriter. An elegant antique, the kind they don't make anymore but still belongs on all rolltop desks everywhere, and in every black-and-white newspaper movie ever made. There was a stack of white bond paper next to it.

I felt very tired all of a sudden.

Jack Finley called out, from inside the closet, "Nothing in here except two white shirts and a blue suit."

I was riveted on the typewriter as I rummaged through a cluttered closet of my own. Occasionally the closet was useful as a brain. Inside it somewhere, maybe behind all the empty Jack Daniel's bottles, was an important thought if I could find the little rascal.

Typewriter. The back of my neck felt very hot.

Jack Finley was peering underneath the other bed. I heard him say, "I'm still not sure what we're looking for here, but it's quite clear that somebody is not helping with the chores."

I walked to the Royal, slid a piece of white paper into the carriage and rolled it toward me, very careful, very precise. I put my fingers to the keys and typed out two words:

"Dearest Billy."

They looked just the way I knew they would. I had seen plenty of Dearest Billy, read the words over and over again in the same distinctive Royal pica that was on the paper in front of me.

In the letters.

From across the room my father was chattering something about a suitcase. I was hearing something else, something that had been gnawing at me, the line from Johnny

Brant I'd meant to find before the Finley decathlon began the day before. I knew there had been something he'd said that did not fit, something I should have heard and didn't.

I could hear it now. I could see Brant.

He had leaned across his desk and said, "She couldn't even type her own copy for the prompter. Couldn't even use a typewriter. Can you believe it?"

Peggy Lynn Brady couldn't type.

Not copy for the teleprompter.

And not letters to Billy.

I ran a couple of lines of dialogue inside my head.

"And if she couldn't type letters to him, what does that mean, Mr. Finley? And remember, you're under oath here."

"It means he wrote them to himself."

He wrote the letters to himself.

The handwritten letters in the collected works had been the short ones, the chatty ones. The real ones. Peggy Lynn could have been writing them to an aunt. The typewritten ones had been different altogether. They had been about all the villains in her life, all the sickness around her. About all the people who had changed her, used her, tried to ruin her. The ones she had called evil. Ones she had to get.

Those were the letters to her dearest Billy.

I hadn't seen it. Two sets.

I said to the Royal, quietly, "You killed them all. You played me for a sucker while you killed them. You crazy, twisted, lying fucker."

Jack Finley was next to me, looking at the two words on the paper.

"What are you saying, Peter?"

I started to pace then, an expectant daddy pace. Twins on the way. The words came out in a babble. The voice was too high, too girlish, to be my own.

I said, "Pap, it's got to be some kind of obsessive deal, some madness born a long time ago, something like that. Maybe she drove him crazy from the time they were both kids, living in the same house. Maybe she gave him a taste once or twice, then took it away. Or maybe guilt, it could have been guilt, 'cause she was like his sister. I don't know. But the guy is some holy-rolling loon, I know that now. It's got to fall that way. Somewhere along the line something snapped, and he waited and waited, then came up here to get her. Avenging angel or like that. Jesus Christ, it was all right there in the letters. He even brought the fucking typewriter. Maybe he wrote some letters after he got here. He probably got Peggy Lynn before he got Stanford and Parker. Now he's out to get them all. We've got to find him. He's out there somewhere, and there's no way the sucker is finished. There's got to be something in this room to help us. There's got to be!"

I was shouting.

The room was starting to move on me. I sat down on the bed again, got a cigarette out, tried to light it, couldn't, hands shaking too much. Jack Finley took the matches out of my hands and lit the cigarette for me. He said, "Slower, much slower."

I took a deep drag, coughed, took another one. I still couldn't catch my breath. My father went away and came back with a glass of water. I drank some.

My father said, "Why in the world did he need you?"

"Because the normal part of him remembered what she told him about me. He said it in my office. I'm good. I'm the kind who does crosswords in fucking pen, he said. He didn't know anyone else. He wanted vengeance so he couldn't go to the cops. He was so sure that somebody close to her killed her. It's got to be a split personality deal. I think he came up here and in his scrambled egg of a brain he thought I could help him find out who did it, then he could kill the someone before the cops got there. But then he must have gotten impatient, wigged out completely, figured if he could ace everyone around here, he'd get the killer by process of elimination. Maybe he really wanted to kill them all anyway and getting up here just touched all that off. Shit, I don't know. All I *do* know is that I let him do it. We've got to find him *now,* Pap, 'cause he wrote those loony tune letters, and he's got to be the one. And if he is the one, he ain't done yet. If I don't know who did it, neither does he."

I walked over to the Royal, grabbed the paper, crumpled it up into a mean ball and flung it across the room. I could feel myself sweating.

I could feel dead bodies in the room.

"He must have carried it with him all these years, love and hate and all of it mixed up. And he just created this fantasy world for himself, writing the letters, following her life, staying in touch just enough, making the letters fit the way he wanted things to be. He obviously stayed in touch with her, convincing himself all the way that she'd come back to him, come home to Alabama. Then she disappeared and, I don't know, he became God's law or something. Vengeance is mine, sayeth the loon."

We went back to work. My father unlatched the sorry-looking blue suitcase and began sorting through underwear and socks. I went through the drawers of the bureau. They were empty. The nightstand was next. Phone books in the top drawer, white pages and yellow. King James Bible in the bottom drawer. Next to the phone on top of the nightstand was what looked to be Billy's own Bible, leather bound and worn. I wondered how many miles it had on it. I picked it up and threw it at the television set.

When it hit, the piece of paper came out.

I fetched it. It was a primitive diagram, a map, like something a second-grader would do in drawing class and get a C. A big circle dominated it, with trees sketched here and there, a house on one side of the circle, wavy lines and the word "water" in the middle of the circle.

And at the bottom of the map, in very small script, were the letters *jb*. Next to them Billy had written "Wednesday."

Johnny Brant. Wednesday.

Had to be.

"I can still feel his hand on my face, Billy." That one had been handwritten. It had been real. He hadn't had to make it up. But if Billy thought Brant had ever slugged his precious princess, it was plenty enough to make him want to get Brant. Like he'd gotten Kris Stanford. And Parker.

Johnny Brant. Wednesday.

I picked up the phone, dialed nine for outside, then dialed information. I got the number for Global. I asked for Brant's office, got his secretary finally.

"He just left in his running clothes," she said. "He . . ." I slammed down the receiver.

"What time is it?" I said to my father.

He looked at his watch.

"Little before eleven. Why? What was on that paper, Peter?"

I was heading for the door.

I said, "Call Mick. Tell him to meet me at the Ninetieth Street entrance to the Central Park reservoir. Tell him to bring help. Then call Marty and Natalie at the office and tell them the same thing, and to bring the gear."

"What is this, Peter?" Jack Finley snapped.

I opened the door to 1116.

"It's Johnny Brant and it's Wednesday," I said, out of breath. "Brant runs every day around this time. The reservoir. Like clockwork, he told me. I think Billy's actually going to try and take him there."

CHAPTER
15

ANOTHER rainstorm had hit while we were inside. It looked bigger and brassier than the one a few days before and had turned the afternoon the color of coal. The doorman, buffeted by wind and wet but still smiling like the Good Humor man, was holding a toy umbrella in one hand and opening a cab door for a black couple as I came out the revolving door in a dead run. I shoved him out of the way. His umbrella flipped up and he said, "Hey there." I was already into the cab and telling the driver it was a twenty-dollar ride as I slammed the door. The Finleys were throwing twenties at cabbies like cabbies were belly dancers. I gave him the address and told him to cut through the park at Eighty-sixth. Brant said he always started at Ninetieth. It was a habit. I hoped it was a habit he'd be able to continue.

When we got to Eighty-sixth I threw the money into the tray, got out, and started running the rest of the way, uptown on Fifth, into the teeth of the day. The rain beat down in a strident roar. Ethel Merman of a storm. The temperature had dropped at least fifteen degrees since I'd left the apartment a few hours ago. The back of my head was pounding to the rhythm of the rain. Was that a song? I'd forgotten about the stitches. But then I'd been busy the last twenty-four hours or so, what with Cummings kicking the shit out of me and Seth Parker getting whacked and Mick Dunphy screaming and the waltz around the dance floor with David.

And Billy.

I wanted Billy first, if it wasn't too late.

Being stupid for me was like having a second job, I decided. When I died, St. Peter was going to say "You Finley?" and I was going to say, Yeah, and he was going to say "Jesus, you should pardon the expression, you were one dumb son of a bitch, weren't you?"

I nearly tripped as I sprinted into the Park entrance on Ninetieth and up the steps past the monument to a World War I hero named John Purroy Mitchel. Mitchel looked steadfast as always, the kind of lug who wouldn't let you down. Wouldn't screw up like me. He'd probably spreadeagled the grenade like Cagney in *Fighting 69th*. Was it Cagney? I stopped at the top of the steps, leaned against a brick wall that had YUPPIE DEATH written across it. My clothes felt heavy as a suit of armor. There is designer running and serious running. I hadn't done any serious running in a long time.

My knees were already threatening a job action.

I squinted into the blanket of rain over the reservoir and tried to make my mind work. It was like trying to make a car battery turn over after it had been sitting in the garage for a month. A girl in a baby-blue Bill Rodgers outfit, hood pulled down to her eyes, scrambled past me and down the steps. The storm had finished her. It wasn't going to run off Brant, I was pretty sure. He was out there somewhere.

"It's like therapy," he'd said. "Dead of winter, heat of summer, rain and snow, I run."

Billy had drawn the map, so he'd already staked out the 1.6-mile oval. Maybe he'd even stood in the cherry trees and watched Brant go by, figuring how he'd do it. He was not just crazy. He had to be fearless. Maybe they were the same for him. He'd walked right through the front door and killed Kris Stanford. He'd figured out a time when he could do the same thing with Seth Parker at the office. A nondescript man in a blue suit, blending into the background. The worst kind, my dad had said, was the one who just falls to earth from another planet.

Now he was going to whack Johnny Brant if he could. And he'd gotten a break, a big one, with the storm. The girl in the Bill Rodgers suit was the only living soul I'd seen come by. It was just me and John Purroy Mitchel and he was no help.

Think.

I could wait for Brant to run by the monument. But if I waited he might never come by. Billy wasn't just going to jog along with him and stick in the ice pick—it had to be another ice pick; they'd sure done the trick so far—into the back of Brant's neck. He was going to wait somewhere, then jump out and take him fast. Brant said he ran ten miles. Six times around.

How many so far?

Had Billy taken him already?

Wait or not wait?

I couldn't wait. If Brant had just come by, he was ten to twelve minutes from running past the monument again. His pace had to be slow in this weather. I could barely see across the water. I could run one way and try to catch up with him. Go the other way and hope to run into him. I thought of the map. He'd sketched the main pump house off to my left and the smaller two across the water to the right, facing the tennis courts. *Think.* I ran right.

I went hard, pumping the arms, trying to ignore the fire bombs going off one after another in my chest, feeling the puddles underneath my sneakers, trying to see in the pouring rain. I kept looking over my left shoulder, across the rez, hoping to catch a glimpse of Brant or someone, then looking to the right, into the bushes and cherry trees, hoping I saw Billy before he saw me. If he was in the trees.

I needed a break. I thought, Nobody stays in a slump like yours forever.

Where would Billy try to take him? I knew the oval. When Jeannie and I lived at Eighty-ninth and Park, there was the summer when we'd both tried to quit smoking, had run the rez every morning before work. There had even been some brave talk about trying for the New York Marathon. I hated the running but loved being with her in the mornings so I did it. I'd even joke sometimes about sneaking into one of the pump houses for a quickie, before the maintenance men got there. Jeannie didn't go for it, not even in the smallest house, which had been condemned by the Water Supply Commission and never restored. Jeannie believed that public sex, even semi-public sex, was for farm animals.

Billy had to have a spot. He had to know that even with the temperature where it had been lately, near 100, the runners were still out there during this time of day, out there with Brant, chasing the perfect cardiovascular systems or thinner thighs or flatter tummies or lungs so big you could open a Wendy's inside them. Billy had to know it wasn't just going to be him and Brant, one on one. He had to have the right place. A place where he could jump out, take him, use the ice pick, do it.

Where?

I looked down to get the rain out of my eyes. My sneakers, covered with mud, kept making slapping sounds as they hit. They felt like lead weights.

Maybe two hundred yards away, around and to my left, I could see the pump houses. I stopped near a sign on the chain-link fence that read THE WATER IN THIS RESERVOIR IS YOUR DRINKING WATER. I had to catch my breath or throw up. Caught my breath first.

The rain came harder and with it more wind. Then I saw someone, all the way down at the far end of the oval, near the main pump house. Brant? I had to assume yes. No other way to go. I still hadn't seen another runner. We were half a mile apart, across our very own New York City drinking water from each other.

Now where was Billy?

I scanned the rez in the rain. Stopped the scan.

Out loud I said, "Wouldn't he be in the deserted pump house if he is anywhere, asshole?"

It would be perfect. It had been sitting there since I couldn't remember when, boarded up, while the water supply guys and the city planners fretted about it and ran feasibility studies and tried to decide just what to do about a bunch of bricks that was no bigger than an outhouse. Kids kept getting into it, tearing down the boards at night, smoking dope and doing other creative things when they were stoned enough and brave enough and horny enough. The cops couldn't run them off and couldn't post a twenty-four-hour watch.

Billy could wait at the pump house even on a good day; the rez was always crowded, but not like the bridle path, that big five-mile circle. He could wait in the entrance, on the turn. Why not, the way his grisly luck was going? Billy was strong enough. He could have Brant inside before Brant could fight him or scream.

I started running again. I was closer to the house than

Brant, but he was coming faster. All I could hear was the storm. No sirens yet. I wanted very much to be right about all of it because if I was I had a chance.

It was a race to the finish line but we were coming from different directions. Brant was running with his head down. It was him for sure. Same silly red baseball cap he'd slapped on his head in the office. Like he was posing.

He was maybe fifty yards from me now.

I screamed his name, trying to beat the howl of the storm.

Nothing.

I screamed again, a high-pitched Beverly Sills scream. "Brant!"

He stopped, saw me, tilted his head to the side. Curious. The baseball cap matched the red rain outfit.

"Brant, get the fuck out of here!" I was shooing him with my arms, flapping them like a duck. "Go back the other way!"

He just stared at me.

He yelled back, "Finley, that you?"

Then I saw Billy in the doorway. Blue suit. White shirt. Just like the first day, all the days, when he was pulling heartstrings. He had a pair of silly-looking red sneakers on his feet and was looking down the track at Brant. Brant still wasn't moving. Billy had an ice pick.

Billy put it all together and turned in my direction a beat late, like he'd missed his cue out in the wings. I hit him on the run from the blind side, trying to chop at his right hand as I went into him. We bounced off the door frame and came rolling down into the slop off the tiny stoop, rolling into the middle of the track. I briefly had a grip on his right wrist but he threw me off and then we were kneeling, facing each other in the filth, chests heaving.

I glanced to my right. Brant was gone.

I blinked mud out of my eyes and gasped, "It's over, Billy. I know all about it. Give me that thing."

He spit mud out of his mouth.

"You are not part of this!" It came out in a preacher's wail, a sound to match all the elements. "YOU ARE NOT A PART OF THIS! Do not stand in the way of God's will."

I kept my eyes on the ice pick. I didn't want to look at Billy's eyes. They weren't going to help. I'd seen eyes like them only once before, when I'd interviewed Manson in prison.

"Give it up, Billy. You don't want to hurt me."

He screamed, "Don't you see? It's his *time*!" He yanked his head to the left, looking for Brant. But Brant was gone. I went for the ice pick again, chopping upward at the wrist with both hands. I got it this time. The pick flipped back up over Billy's head. He reached back and tried to grab it out of the air; I put my hands together again and clubbed him across the face, sending him sprawling on his side. But as I went for him again, I slipped in the mud and landed face first, not getting my hands out to break the fall. I swallowed enough mud to make me gag, tried to keep rolling as I did, away from Billy. I couldn't see. My eyes burned with the mud.

Billy didn't waste any time. He stood up and kicked me once near the ear, then again. If I hadn't been choking so badly I would have gone out. Dreamily I went over on my back and tried to clean out my eyes. From somewhere, maybe Suffolk County, I could hear Billy's voice.

"I thought you could help me," he said, the words coming from my right, through the wrong end of a megaphone, filtered way down. "The police would have laughed at me, shoved me out of the way, if I tried to find out myself. She always used to go on and on about how clever you were, like some TV private detective." He made a sound that was like laughter. "But then it was so easy. Call up Miss Kris Stanford, go see her, rid the world of her poison. Wait for the right time with Mr. Seth Parker. *So* easy. They had all soiled her, don't you see now? They stole her goodness, kept her from coming back to me. And it was our destiny to be together. Our *destiny*. SHE DID NOT HAVE TO DIE!"

The voice was coming closer. I tried to turn my head toward him. It wouldn't go. I stared straight up into the rain. I felt like I was drowning in quicksand.

"How do you know?" I managed to say. I could just hear my own words. "That she's dead. How?"

"The Stanford woman told me, the first time I saw her. She had figured it out. She was scared that he would get her too."

"Who?"

He wasn't listening. Not to me anyway.

"Peggy never should have gone away. *Never!* It should always have been like it was when we were young. You can see that, can't you? We could have shared things. We belonged together. *In that house.*" He was wailing again, louder than before. Sermon in the slop. "SHE DID NOT BELONG TO THEM! I have to see God's will. The woman first. Then Parker. Then Brant. I will save the murderer for last, make him wait and wonder. *But I will come for him.*"

I could see him raise the ice pick. I thought I heard something—shout? another voice?—in the distance. Billy looked off.

I tried to raise an arm. Any arm. It was like trying to lift refrigerators. Billy looked down at me, sadly.

"Who?" I croaked again. He'd said murderer.

"I'm so sorry, Mr. Finley."

I heard the gunshot over the sound of the storm as Billy Lynn groaned and looked sadder than before and the mud on the front of his white shirt began to turn red and he pitched over me. I managed to move my head away from the ice pick as it fell out of his hand and then they were pulling him off me and there was Mick Dunphy, gun in hand, trench coat belted tight against the rain.

He said, "You all right, fuckhead?"

CHAPTER
16

THE ball was headed for right field between Bill Buckner and Barrett, the little second baseman. The crowd, stretched out along the bar at Van's like railbirds, cheered. Eddie Murray was doing it to me again. It was going to be tied. But then here was Buckner flicking down the right hand, glove hand, stopping the ball in the dirt like a street cleaner stabbing litter. His momentum was carrying him toward second but he managed to plant the right foot, spin around, back to the plate, until he came around and was facing first again. His throw got to first as Stanley, the relief pitcher, got there, one step ahead of Murray. Red Sox 3, Orioles 2. We had tied them for third. A week away from September, we were only four behind the Yankees.

I saw it as a reaffirmation of a Supreme Being.

I nodded triumphantly at Walter, the bartender. He was a big, slow-moving man with a crew cut and the face of a drill instructor, but the heart of Uncle Remus.

179

"Walter," I said. "Whiskey and fresh horses for my men."

Walter frowned. He had been pouring drinks for me since I'd gotten to Bridgehampton the previous Thursday, the day after Mick Dunphy shot Billy through the heart with the first bullet and killed him. Walter's look said his arm was tired and he needed help from the bullpen.

I saw the hesitation and said, "Walter, you are my friend and I don't mean to speak harshly to you. But if you don't get me a fresh cocktail, I'll kill you."

I turned over the box of Marlboros on the bar in front of me and the last cigarette fell out. I lit it. Walter slid the new old-fashioned in front of me. I was using the fruit in them as a hedge against scurvy. I drank some of the old-fashioned. Walter watched me and said, "How long you plan to keep this up?"

"Until we have victory in Europe over the stinking Jerries." It came out too loudly.

At the end of the bar, near the video game, two potato farmers looked up from a conversation with Susan, the real-estate woman from next door. They looked down at me like I'd announced the crop was in.

Walter just shrugged. He was good at it. He was good at shrugging and pouring and giving me shit. I was good at other things. Marital discord. Drinking. Hangovers. Smoking. Helping get people killed in triplicate.

At Van's bar, I decided that it was this diversification of skills that separated civilized man from the savages.

I shared the insight with Walter.

"Thank you," he said and went over to answer the telephone.

My life needed order, I decided. Or overhauling. Or a wrecking crew. I had been drinking for ten days straight. I had started the night after Billy. I had done my stand-up with Marty and Natalie right there at the reservoir; they had arrived fifteen minutes after Dunphy. I hadn't even bothered to clean myself up. Just stood there in the rain and told how I'd kept Billy a secret from the cops, and what the results had been.

The close was: "People will call me a hero for saving a life, Johnny Brant's life, today. But there comes the time when stupidity and arrogance make even a brave effort shallow and self-serving. I took the law into my own hands, not knowing I was using those hands to set loose a maniac. To celebrate what happened here today is to celebrate a fool. Being a wise guy catches up with you eventually. And a guy should be wise enough to know that. This is Peter Finley."

Mick took me with him to the station and I gave him my statement. When I was done, he started screaming about how this time he was really fucking going to throw me in jail. I got up and said, "Send the arresting officer to O'Rourkes. I'll be unarmed." I drank with Jimmy until six in the morning, then went home with him and slept on his couch, then rented a Budget in the afternoon and drove to the house in Bridgehampton. The house was half a mile from Van's on Hildreth Lane, two miles from the ocean.

The Van's geography was more important than the ocean geography.

I settled into a routine almost immediately: Walk to the beach in the morning, bring radio. Walk back to Van's about one. Pound a couple of bloody Marys and a few beers around a cheeseburger. Walk home, watch soap operas until they put me to sleep. Wake up about six, clean up, walk back to Van's. Watch baseball, eat dinner if I remember, chat with the regulars, drink until I can't drink any more, walk home. Pass out. Get up in the morning and repeat the procedure.

Summer camp for a deadbeat.

The phone had been unplugged the moment I walked

into the house the first day. I would hook it up in the morning, call SportsPhone and get the scores I'd forgotten from the night before, then the jack would come out of the wall again. Maybe once a day I would remember that I never did find out what happened to Peggy Lynn Brady. But as soon as I got to Van's and put myself into custody of Walter, or Bobby Black, the day bartender, and they would pour something and push it with God's help in my direction, the thoughts about Peggy Lynn would pass.

If I thought about her I had to think about all of it.

When people called Van's looking for me, the bartenders faded them, under orders from me. The callers were told I had gone over to Montauk for the night. Or I had bought a boat over in Hampton Bays and was living on it. Or I had bought a boutique in Sag Harbor and had moved in with a landscape painter. Or I was busy collecting seashells.

Pretty soon people stopped calling Van's.

I looked up at the clock. Fifteen minutes to the Mets-Dodgers. The game would run at least two and a half hours. Using the cover of passionate baseball fan, I could keep drinking until at least two in the morning. West Coast baseball, as a sleep deterrent, was better than birth control.

I said, "Walter, I think I will make that always tricky transition to Hennessy."

Jeannie Bogardus Finley said, "Walter, give Mr. Finley something to sign."

I turned around. It was her. It was as if Van's had suddenly emptied out. She looked the way college girls are supposed to look on summer nights. Jeannie just kept going through life and life kept backlighting her.

"She was the one what called a little while ago," said Walter. "I told her you were here. I figured you're a drunk these days, but you ain't Alzheimered yet."

I said, "That's very perceptive of you, Walter," and kept staring at Jeannie, who was smiling at me. She wore a pink sweatshirt over some kind of polo shirt, white. The collar of the white shirt was turned up in the preppy way. On Jeannie an upturned collar just looked like it made perfect sense. She was also wearing baggy white tennis shorts. Even in the semidarkness of Van's you could not miss the tan on the legs. They not only won the gold medal for tanning, there was no silver or bronze.

I felt like I had resumed radio contact with the planet earth for the first time since the reservoir.

"Hi," I said finally.

"Hi, yourself. Pay the man."

I paid the man.

JEANNIE said, "This isn't like you. You've always played hurt in the past."

We walked up Church Lane in the velvety late-summer stillness of Bridgehampton night. The ocean was still too far away to cause much commotion. So it was the crickets and mostly nothing. Sometimes nothing is better.

"It's different this time, J.B.," I said. "The differentest of all. People died this time."

I thought about taking her hand and didn't. Even when she was on a mercy mission she was harder to read than *Paradise Lost*.

Instead I said, "What are you doing here, by the way?"

"Dumb question. You want to keep acting like a sap, or do you want to talk about it?"

"I want to talk about it." We got to Hildreth and took a left. Home was to the right. I wanted to head toward the water, on Ocean Road. A hint of land fog had begun to drift in, from the northeast; it was like a whispered threat of rain in the morning.

"I've talked to Mick and Charley," she said. "I had a drink with Marty last night. They're all worried about you, Peter. They've all tried to call."

I said, "Mick is not worried about me. The last time I saw Mick, he wanted to put me in a cell where I would be raped by someone nicknamed Lucille."

"Mick is your friend. He gets annoyed when you think you're smarter than he is, but he is your friend. You got taken in by Billy Lynn. You thought you were helping a helpless, which is usually one of your best things. You were wrong. But he is better off dead."

I stopped and lit a cigarette, cupping my hands around the match as we started to feel the breeze snaking down Ocean from the water.

I said, "I know he is better off dead. I know that even if I had been quick as quick can be, I wasn't going to stop him from doing Kris Stanford. Damn, J.B., it's Seth Parker I keep thinking about. The way I tricked him with the Betacam. The stupid fight in the office. I told the little bastard to trust me and then I all but hand delivered him to Billy. I shoulda seen that the letters were phony. I shoulda had my dad check Billy out sooner or something. My instincts are usually better than that."

Bridgehampton Country Club, the tiny nine-hole track for snobs, was to our left now. A jeep came barreling toward us, caught us in its lights, turned on the high beams, kept charging ahead in the direction of Route 27, known as Montauk Highway to the natives. I heard a dog bark. I could hear rock 'n' roll music from one of the houses set back from the road. Jeannie took the cigarette out of my hand, took a drag, handed it back. Fifty yards ahead I could make out a rabbit scurrying into the weeds.

I said, "I love you."

We kept walking toward the Atlantic in silence. The fog got heavier but it didn't matter, because the moon had

come out from behind night clouds and was putting on a
show. I turned and looked at Jeannie. Didn't need even the
moon. Her eyes were a luminous presence, all I needed to
find my way. She had a leather handbag, shapeless and
expensive, slung over her shoulder.

She looked back at me, reached into the bag, and came
out with a bottle of Hennessy.

"You're only sweet talking me because I brought the
hooch, big boy."

I heard a laugh and realized it came from me. I thought,
the sound needs practice.

"Where did you get that?"

"Walter. While you were settling up. I figured if you're
going to drink, you might as well do it with a drop-dead
looker."

"He give you snifters too?"

"Hey, Finley. We aren't going to a state dinner. It's
dark out. We're going to the beach. You're going to say
things like, 'Why ask for the moon when we have the
stars,' hokey stuff like that. You'll probably make a pass
and then we'll take it from there, if the local constabulary
doesn't roust us."

Now I took her hand.

I said, "You're right. Fuck snifters."

JEANNIE said, "In the words of the philosopher Otter in
Animal House, 'So you fucked up. You trusted him.'"

She drank some of the Hennessy out of the bottle. The
moon lit the waves, but not in a showy way. The sound
of the waves was all start and stop, build and catch, crash
and roll back and away. No subtlety to the fog now.
Wuthering Heights time. I waited for Cathy and Heath-
cliff to sprint by, slug some of the Hennessy, beat it toward
Wainscott. I slugged some of the Hennessy myself. Jack

Finley had told me once that watching the ocean made him believe in God.

It had always made me believe in me.

I said, "J.B., it's like all the comic book stuff finally caught up with me. I said it on the broadcast that night. In the end being a wise guy just means you are terminally dumb, and it doesn't matter how fucking good your intentions are."

She gave my knee a healthy rap with a knuckle.

"Let's not forget to give Mr. Ego the credit he deserves here."

I pulled my arm tighter around her. I had already given her my O'Rourkes windbreaker. We sat, legs dangling over the side of a dock to the left of Ocean Road. The dock belonged to old friends named Krumpe.

"Okay there was ego too. Always is. No crime. But that's not the problem. The problem is that I would have kept right on with my college hijinks approach to the goddamn job if they all didn't start dying on me. I looked into Billy's eyes. And before that, without some luck and some pretty slick business from my dad, that guy David would have pulled the trigger, and Billy would still be out there and Brant would be dead and God knows who else. Jesus, I don't know. Shit. I never intended for all this to get into the job description. What I'm trying to say is all of a sudden it stopped being a game. I feel like I not only breezed into being a full-out grown-up but kept right on going into asshole."

Jeannie let out a long, slow whistle through her teeth. She was great at it. I always admired the skill. Whistling like that is very underrated.

Then she said, "I love you too." She edged to her right on the dock and faced me full. Her eyes were bright as cat eyes, only deeper, softer. She kissed me. I kissed her back. And for a long while we didn't bother much with the ocean business or the moon business or the brandy business. I felt like someone with a life preserver around him.

We stopped kissing after what felt like six or seven days. I was sure there had been a time change in there too, but I couldn't figure out which way. Spring ahead. Kiss back.

I tried to catch my breath discreetly, the way you did when you were fifteen. "What," I said, "brought that on? Me and the night and the music?"

"There's no music, goose."

"What then?"

She shifted back again, pretzling her legs underneath her and then getting them organized comfortably. The wind played with her hair but did not muss it. Like the wind was saying: Hello, old friend. Jeannie took both my hands and squeezed.

"I didn't want to say the growing-up part. Too trite. And more than a little mean-spirited."

"Thank you. I must point out, however, that you frequently strike a different pose during the fights."

"Shut up, Peter. This is important."

I shut up. My mouth closing must have sounded like prison doors.

She made another quick hit on the Hennessy. Jeannie could make swigging out of a bottle look as elegant as sipping tea with the pinky extended. She went on.

"Your problem is that you don't listen to your heart enough, Peter. And it is really what you do the best, even if you do insist on keeping that part of you locked up. I don't know. Most of the time it's like you force yourself to believe that you're still twenty years old and making a run on the girls' dorms, and that afterward everybody is going to tap a keg. But you're more than that—I think so anyway—more than all the glib dialogue. You should hear yourself tonight. It's like you've slowed down to a speed you haven't seen in a long time. The pace is the beat of your heart almost. Your words are resonating with that rhythm. Is any of this making sense? I think it is, but then again, the Hennessy might be making a speech."

"You are making perfect sense, I'm afraid."

She always did, even when I did not want to admit it. Even when we were apart. She could pare down big cumbersome ideas into chunks you could pick up, one by one, without breaking into a sweat.

She stood up on the dock and took one last look at the ocean.

"I need to get warm."

I stood up myself.

"Now you're talking," I said.

We walked back toward the village and home faster than we had walked away.

Almost as fast as it took us to get undressed and get into the big bed in the ground floor bedroom in the house on Hildreth. The ocean breeze that had been at our backs followed us into the bedroom and ruffled the white curtains that faced east in the night.

There should be prizes for that sort of speed, that late at night.

IT was when we were walking back to the house from the Candy Kitchen early the next morning that Jeannie said, "I'm taking the six o'clock jitney back to the city. I want you to come with me. It's time for you to get back to work. That which is not used atrophies and dies."

"If you want to go step by step with me through the last eight hours, I think I've got physical proof to the contrary."

Jeannie sniffed. "Very funny," she said. "That is one part of you that I never worry about, Peter. They will shut the coffin lid and it will be begging for another chance."

I said, "You're too kind."

"Who said anything about kind?"

The traffic was already in a slow, midmorning mess on Route 27 as the cars inched patiently toward the ocean. I was ready for the beach myself: A T-shirt that read WHOEVER HAS THE MOST MONEY AT THE END OF THE WORLD, WINS; my Red Sox cap and tennis shorts. Ancient Topsiders. No sunglasses. Sometimes I like to squint. Machos me out at the beach.

Jeannie wore what looked to be a pink halter but was actually the best part of her two-piece, and the same baggy shorts from the night before, a pair of my sunglasses, and sandals. The black hair glistened. She looked radiant.

"I'm not ready to go back to work."

"Yeah, you are. The longest you were ever away from this job you say you're not ready to go back to was on our honeymoon. And the honeymoon wasn't even as long as this furlough. *And*"—she was poking me in the arm with a finger and her voice was rising; I thought she might really be getting hot—"even on our goddamn honeymoon you racked up nearly a thousand dollars in calls to the States from Switzerland and Austria."

"It was that year."

"I know what year it was. It was the year we got married, which is why we went on a honeymoon. The sequence is fairly straightforward."

"It was also the year the Sox blew the fourteen-game lead and lost to the Yankees in the playoff game."

"Oh, I remember. Wasn't that the year when little Corky hit that home run or something?"

She did this on purpose. She knew perfectly well that the Finley List of the ten worst days in the history of the known universe started with October 2, 1978, when Bucky Dent hit the three-run homer off Mike Torrez and beat me out of the American League pennant.

"Not Corky," I said. "Bucky. Bucky Dent."

"Corky. Bucky. Whatever. The point I'm making is that you can't stand being away from everybody. After a week, you always want to go looking for some kind of action somewhere. So go look. Six o'clock jitney. Book it, soldier. You still haven't found out what happened to Peggy Lynn."

"I know that."

"So come back and find the finding out out. Is that how that song went?"

"No. And no."

I reached into the pocket of the tennis shorts and found my pack of Marlboros. Jeannie flicked them out of my hand.

"No cigarettes until you say you'll come back."

We were in the back parking lot of the IGA supermarket, maybe seventy-five yards from my front door.

I said, "J.B., you're being silly. I can walk right into the store and buy some."

"Actually, you can't. I have the money. I have the house keys. And besides, I think you might want these."

She pushed the red-and-white box underneath the waistband of her shorts slowly, until it disappeared. Then she ran for the house.

I ran after her.

In a little while, after I managed to trap her in the bedroom and retrieve the Marlboros after a by-the-book strip search that worked into something else, I told Jeannie that we did not have to take the jitney since I had a rental car. We were back in bed.

"I have not seen such a vehicle parked here."

"I left it at Van's when I arrived. I'm a good citizen. They aren't going to get Peter Finley for driving while intoxicated."

"I love this country," Jeannie said.

I wasn't crazy about the jitney anyway. It is a boutique bus that runs from Manhattan to the Hamptons. They serve designer mineral water on it and they have stewardesses. Plus, you can't smoke.

I took Jeannie's hand and kissed the fingers, one by one. I said, "Back to the old salt mine."

She turned and smiled up at me. "I'm glad."

I told her, "You're right. It's time to find out what happened to the little bitch."

CHAPTER
17

JIMMY O'ROURKE looked around my office at Channel A and said, "I always wondered what a roach motel looked like from the inside."

It was Monday afternoon, after Bridgehampton. I felt like I'd been hand washed and dried in the sun. Jeannie and I had eaten dinner at O'Rourkes the night before, and it had been over coffee—no brandy—that Jimmy reminded me that he had pretty good connections at GBC from his flack days at CBS.

"I cut some fairly dazzling figure-eights when they first came along, if I do say so myself," he said. "Spirit of cooperation between the networks, scribe. Welcome-wagon sort of thing for the new kid on the block."

Jeannie was in the ladies' room. I checked the ladies' room door.

I said, "If I'm reading you correctly, and I think I am, you fucked a lot of secretaries."

"More broadcast associates," he said seriously. Jimmy

O'Rourke discussed his mating habits the way he would his last good dental checkup. "Yeah, two B.A.'s. No, three. One secretary in business affairs. A news producer. And an anchorperson."

"Male or female?"

He just let that go by. Ball one.

"Any of them still there?" I said. There was a crash from the kitchen. O'Rourke hired mostly boat people as busboys. I saw that Jeannie had come out of the ladies' room and was talking to Little John. I wanted to put a bow around the conversation. I was fairly certain that Jeannie knew I had always been faithful. She was also aware of how many 4 A.M.s I had logged with O'Rourke. Bottom line: She did not see O'Rourke as an influence as positive as, say, Father Flanagan of Boys' Town.

O'Rourke said, "What?" I followed his eyes. He'd spotted a woman alone at the juke box. O'Rourke's radar was better than LaGuardia's.

"I was wondering if any of your ex's are still at Global."

He stared at the juke box and said idly, "Oh sure."

"You wanna help me out on this?"

"Fine," he said, getting up out of his chair, transfixed, straightening the Yankee tie as he moved toward the front room.

"My office, about eleven," I called after him.

O'Rourke could find out things even Natalie couldn't. As they say in baseball, he wasn't afraid to give up the body.

Now in my office I said to him, "Flight of heavenly transport last evening, sport?"

"Nah," O'Rourke said. "Rego Park. Pissed me off."

He didn't believe in going to Queens for sex except in emergencies: wars, floods, famines, that sort of thing.

He was wearing a cream-colored linen jacket, burgundy polo shirt, blue jeans, no socks. Topsiders. His face was shaved and talcumed and red. With O'Rourke there was no telling how much sleep there'd been, if any. Some people needed the morning as dress rehearsal. He just got right after the day, whenever it started.

He sipped a soft drink out of a Styrofoam cup and said, "Okay, what's our program?"

"I still can't get to Thomas Harrold," I said. "Remember what it was like in the old days, trying to get hold of Roone Arledge when he started out at ABC? Harrold's same way. A Howard Hughes deal. Reclusive chic. I would like it if you could somehow get close to someone who is close to Harrold. Or someone who might know office stuff that Natalie's contacts don't know, or won't tell. Did you know Harrold at all, before he left NBC to go to Washington?"

O'Rourke held up two fingers, an inch apart.

"He was always strictly six-forty-two," said O'Rourke. "Lurch, I think it was. We hardly ever saw him at Mike's, or any of the other after-school malt shops."

You either knew O'Rourke's verbal shorthand or you didn't. There was no glossary. Lurch was Larchmont. The 6:42 was the Larchmont train out of Grand Central. Mike's was Mike Manuche's, a restaurant not far from Network Row on West Fifty-second, gone now. The other malt shops for the television crowd were Rose, 21, Kee-Wah-Yen, Mercurio's; 21 mostly.

"He was never a hang-around like our guys at CBS or most of the NBCs," O'Rourke said. "One martini and then into the cabbola. Serious nonsmiler. Never real chatty. Never saw him shitfaced."

He lit a Winston, looked around in vain for an ashtray, dropped the match on the floor.

I said, "Well, I got to get to him somehow. I'm scrambling now. Everybody seems to think there might have been something going on between him and Peggy Lynn.

I'd just like to get a hint of what it was. Shit, I'd like to get a hint of anything. Natalie keeps calling Harrold's secretary and the secretary just keeps jacking her."

O'Rourke said, "Suppose I pick up something especially tasty. What's in it for me, outside of the usual honor and glory?"

"A guy could pay his bar bill at your store."

"Nah. You'll do that eventually. Catholic guilt."

"I could let you use the house in Bridgehampton."

"I have a key, scribe, remember?"

He'd never stopped calling me scribe, even after I quit newspapers.

"I could try to get Natalie to go out with you again."

O'Rourke made his right hand into a gun and made a motion like he was firing it at me. "Bingo," he said.

He stood up and smoothed out the linen jacket as best he could.

"I am on my way over to the Global Broadcasting Company to tell an old friend that I just happened to be in the neighborhood," he said.

He did his stiff-legged Cagney walk toward the door and began to whistle "Yankee Doodle Dandy." Natalie came bursting through the door. O'Rourke spun away from her and backed into the wall, hand over heart.

"I want you," he said. "I need you. I would give up night baseball just to lie naked beside you."

Natalie said, "What about day baseball, you old goat?"

"I won't beg, Ferrare," O'Rourke sniffed.

She hooked a thumb at the door.

"Scram," she said. "Gots to talk to the boss."

He kissed her lightly on the cheek, picked up "Yankee Doodle Dandy" where he'd left off, and Cagneyed out.

Natalie watched him go. "What was he doing here? He find out high school girls were getting a tour or something?"

"He thinks he might have some connections at GBC. I told him to go connect."

"And get what?" It must have been her gym day. Her hair was in a ponytail and she was wearing Keds with her long blue summer dress.

"Hmmm?"

"You heard me. Jimmy O'Rourke does nothing for nothing. Did you tell him you'd try to get me to go out with him, you weasel?"

I picked a pencil off the desk and aimed it at her like it was a dart.

"I might have."

She snorted. "Forget it. Forever forget it. If I was on a desert island with him, I'd swim for it."

"That would probably be wise, Natalie," I said solemnly. "But I must tell you that there are those women who warm to him occasionally and tell things out of school when he gets enough whiskey in them. Now, whatcha got, kiddo?"

Natalie grinned wickedly at me and came around to my side of the desk and stuck out her palm like she wanted me to slap her five.

"We've got an interview with Thomas Harrold, day after tomorrow," she said. "His office. Regulation interview. Lights, camera, action, et cetera. Go get him, tiger."

I jumped up and said, "Gimme some," meaning palm, and Natalie gave me a low five, then a high one.

OVER the next two days, before the Harrold interview, Team Finley spent more time around GBC than the coffee wagon. We even brought Dwan along; when things were slow around Channel A, he helped Marty out with sound and lights.

"It's not the money, it's the experience," Dwan said.

"Plus I like to watch white people sweat."

And it occurred to me once again, as we did one interview after another in the makeshift studio they set up for us in a corner of the newsroom, that if a guy talked to enough television people at the network level, no matter what their jobs were, he started to feel like Margaret Mead.

Even if a guy was television people himself.

I talked to a tall, stunning black woman with the improbable name of Charity Roussel. She was an associate producer in news who had started out as a secretary and made a brief stop as intern for Johnny Brant on "Midnite." Charity's white cable-stitched sweater dress was snug enough to make the front of her look like the Adirondacks. She had one of those semi-Mohawk New Wave Grace Jones haircuts and incredible cheekbones that looked like they were made of black marble.

Dwan volunteered to hook up the mike on Charity's white cable-stitched sweater dress.

Charity told me that Thomas Harrold and Peggy Lynn Brady had a major row in her dressing room the day before the disappearance. It was before we rolled tape. She asked that it be off the record. I told her that was fine.

"Only time I ever heard Mr. Harrold raise his voice," she said, her chewing gum occasionally making a sound that resembled a rear tire exploding. "Came right out and said he was running the network and her, not the other way around. Miz Brady, she said, 'We'll see about that' and then he stormed off."

When we started the actual interview, she gave me a lot of bland. When we were done, Dwan excused himself and tried to look casual as he trotted after her.

I next talked to a flack named Hindle who I knew from saloons. He'd worked for all three major networks in various p.r. jobs before landing at GBC. O'Rourke had been his assistant for a couple of years at CBS. It was at CBS that one of Hindle's bosses said, "I don't know what he does exactly, but whatever it is he's indispensable." Hindle had been a twenty-one-year-old war hero at Normandy as a kid second lieutenant; after he survived World War II, he figured he'd beat the game and commenced drinking and laughing and womanizing and had never stopped. He was known as "Kingfish" in the business and had a baritone that over the years had been slowly carved up by the dull knives of whiskey and tobacco. Everything about Hindle was plain worn out—complexion, mismatched clothes, hair that was gray and brown and gone—except his attitude. Hindle's attitude was still V-E Day.

He had even written his own epitaph without knowing it a couple of months earlier at O'Rourkes, when he decided to pick up a dinner tab for a table of eight. He handed the waiter, Little John, his credit card, then grabbed Little John by the arm before he could leave.

"Date it tomorrow," he growled from the bottom of a gravel pit.

Little John said sure, then asked why.

Hindle yelled, " 'Cause I used up today last night."

Hindle was retiring in two weeks. He said he would go ahead and talk on camera.

Under the glare of the lights his skin looked like the yellow brick road. I asked him if there had been anything funny going on around "Midnite" before Peggy Lynn's sudden exit.

He said, "At the end, this show was not the Good Ship Lollipop. Couldn't tell the teams without a scorecard. See, I had always thought that Peggy and Kris Stanford and Cummings were stronger than the Allied invasion force. Then a coupla days before Peggy Lynn scoots, or whatever, I walk onto the set and in front of everybody, she is telling Sam Cummings that if he ever speaks to her that way from the control room again, he is history."

That was the best of it. When the lights went off, Hindle loosened a paisley tie from a dark green collar.

"I need an old-fashioned," he said. "Hold the fruit. Hold the bitters."

I TALKED to the stage manager of "Midnite," a big, courtly man from Mississippi named LaMarr Stoddard. He had a shock of white hair, thick, black horn-rimmed glasses, and one of the most prodigious pot bellies I'd ever seen. If the Commies came, LaMarr's dress white shirt was going to provide emergency shelter for a lot of homeless.

The voice was small for such a big man. The first time he spoke, Dwan took off his headset and put up a hand.

"This gonna be a talkie or what?" he asked.

I asked LaMarr to speak up. He did.

He said: "I told the police this, but I shall repeat it for you. I usually made sure the limousine was here for Miss Peggy. And it was that night. But right before she was prepared to leave, she got a phone call, then proceeded to tell me that the driver could go along. That another car was being sent for her."

I asked, "She say who called, who was sending the car?"

"No, sir. But I assumed it was Mister Harrold. When Miss Peggy didn't use her own car, she was frequently picked up by Mister Harrold's car."

I thanked him. He rose imperiously and left.

I was getting bits and pieces but it wasn't enough. Not yet, anyway.

Johnny Brant was next. I wanted him again. He told me something about Thomas Harrold, off camera, in conversation, like he thought it was curious, but not important.

"He is such a buttoned-up guy you won't believe it,"

Brant said. We were in his office. "I've never seen him laugh out loud. That kind of guy. You talk to him and talk to him, and he fixes you with those gray eyes, and when you're done you realize he did all the listening and you did all the talking. I can't believe he started out in the business as an actor."

Brant had taken time off after the reservoir adventure and had just returned to "Midnite," which was ready to come off reruns. Brant had vacationed by going on every television and radio talk show in captivity to share his brush with death with the viewers and the listeners. He had even written a first-person account in the *Post*.

It was light reading. Johnny managed to skip the part where he turned and ran.

I said, "Harrold was an actor?" It wasn't in any of the bios or clips Natalie had produced from here and there.

Brant said, "He mentioned it just one time. Said it gave him insights into dealing with talent or something. According to him he knocked around in New York in his early twenties. Didn't get anywhere. Then he went to work in the mailroom at NBC, where he began one of those Horatio Alger stories we love so much."

Brant was a beauty. He pronounced Alger with a hard *g*.

"Was he in anything at all that I ever might have heard of?" I asked.

Brant shook his head.

"That's the weird part. Just out of curiosity I had him checked out by SAG and Actors Equity. Figured I'd see what kind of credits the boy had. Even if you use a stage name, they've also got your real name on file. And there was no record of Thomas Harrold being a member of either club."

"Maybe he never wanted to join," I said. "Or couldn't afford the dues in his proverbial salad days."

"Maybe," Brant said.

I took out a notebook anyway and scrawled "Harrold —actor?" in it. I would ask the boss man about it.

Brant waited until I put the notebook away then said, "Listen, Pete, I'd like to chat with you longer, but I gotta run."

I idly asked where. He was wearing the same red running outfit he'd worn at the rez.

"Gotta meet with an editor from Random House. This is the craziest thing. They want me to do a book about the whole Peggy Lynn–Billy Lynn thing."

I then tried to talk to Sam Cummings. I had seen him watching us from across the newsroom a few times. Glaring was more like it. He still looked like a walking thrift shop.

I stopped by Cummings's office twice and left messages for him. The second time his secretary gave me a message back. She was about sixty and built like a Jeep Wagoneer. She reminded me of Dobie Gillis's mother.

She said, "Mr. Cummings said to tell you, and I quote, If he comes near me again, I will show him how to walk on his knees. End quote."

The sucker could draw a mental picture for you.

Had to give him that.

CHAPTER

18

THERE was Thomas Harrold's office on the 20th floor of GBC and there was his private suite next to it. We were in the suite. When we'd begun to set up, Marty surveyed the room and said, "They moved the Louvre."

The west wall wasn't a wall at all, but a window, ceiling to shag, facing the Hudson. The furniture was either early American or recent Arab, I couldn't decide. Chagalls, two of them, were fighting it out with the Monets; Jeannie was the art history major in the Finley household, but I knew the right French stuff when I saw it. And I knew they were not prints. The iced tea had been served up by Harrold's secretary in crystal. The late afternoon sun all but made Marty's lights unnecessary.

But the prettiest thing in the room was Thomas Harrold.

When it came time to mike him up, Natalie volunteered. Dreamily. Marty leaned over and said, "Lapel or zipper? I make it three to one on zipper."

Harrold had blond hair brushed straight back neat and gray eyes the color of stainless steel and the kind of perfect patrician nose you'd pick out of the cosmetic surgery catalogue. He either spent a hell of a lot of time in the sun, or had a full scholarship at one of Manhattan's ritzier tanning places. He even had an Anne Francis beauty mark near the right side of his top lip. Didn't mar the finished product, just made him look more like a matinee idol. The summer suit was three-piece, a shade darker than the eyes. Blue shirt, white collar, gold collar stay. The stay matched the cufflinks. Black wing-tips but not regulation wing-tips. I made them Italian. He was about five-nine or so and had to do a lot of gym and salads to look that lean. He could have been anywhere between thirty-five and fifty. The moment we walked in, Natalie looked like she wanted to be surgically attached to him. It was a side of her I'd never seen: Natalie goes Gidget.

I had to admit I thought he was kind of cute myself.

After Natalie stopped fumbling and got the mike attached and we all did sound checks to Marty's satisfaction, Harrold said, "May I say something before we actually begin?"

He was looking at me. Johnny Brant was right about the hardness and steadiness of the gaze. Tourists skated on worse at Rockefeller Center.

I said, "Sure."

Harrold took an unfiltered cigarette out of a gold case on the coffee table in front of him and lit it with a lighter the shape of a globe. It was like the GBC logo. Harrold did not drag on the cigarette so much as sip it. In the words of a magnificent old Boston columnist from my youth named George Frazier, this Harrold was a whole glass of style.

"I do not submit to many interviews, as you well know," he said. I nodded. "And we do have our special investigative news team from GBC working round the clock on Peggy Lynn's disappearance, in conjunction with the NYPD. But we do not want to leave any stone unturned in our desire to find out what has happened to a most valuable member of the GBC family, and a trusted friend. I am quite aware of your reputation, Mr. Finley. For me not to grant you this interview would have seemed contrary on my part. So here we are."

The voice was a baritone, but not too sweet. He reminded me of the sports announcer Bob Costas. I could tell it had been a long speech for him.

"Here we are," I said.

I looked back at Marty. He gave me thumbs-up. Natalie was just staring at Harrold. She looked like her headset was playing Nat King Cole.

I said to Harrold, "Is it true that you were considering making Peggy Lynn the executive producer of 'Midnite' before she disappeared?"

"Yes." Just like that.

"Why?"

"Because the show, despite the ratings, had grown stagnant, at least to my eyes. Despite what people thought about Peggy Lynn's technical weaknesses as a broadcaster, I had always found her instincts about the show to be dead-on and her creative input to be startling."

"Did you think she could handle both jobs, boss and star person?"

"Without any problem, since I have always been the real exec at 'Midnite.' As you know, there is currently no person holding that title on the show. I make the final decisions. No one else. I simply filter them through Sam Cummings. Nothing much would have changed by giving Peggy Lynn the title. But she wanted it as part of her contract negotiation, and I was ready to give it to her. Looking at the big picture, I considered it a small perk."

"Who would have made hiring and firing decisions?"

"She would have, with my approval."

I said, "Even though Cummings and Peggy Lynn were close, don't you think it would have caused some angst if she became his boss?"

"Sam Cummings's ego, his feelings, were hardly an issue." He sipped some iced tea out of a crystal goblet.

"What about Johnny Brant? The two of you have been together a long time."

"As I said, the show had grown stagnant. I saw it. Our board saw it."

"Was Brant going to be let go?"

Harrold raised an eyebrow and smiled a shark smile.

"It would have been up to the new executive producer."

"You said you'd have final approval."

Harrold raised the other eyebrow. Duet.

"Oh I did, didn't I?"

Again I said, "Was Brant getting the boot?"

Harrold said, "There had been some talk of that. Generic talk. Of course, everything has changed now."

"What about Kris Stanford?" I said. "What would her status have been in the reorganized hierarchy of 'Midnite'?"

"Kris Stanford was about to be fired from this network," Harrold said. "Peggy Lynn had outgrown her. She had become a tiresome bother."

I stopped and lit a Marlboro. I didn't like being surprised with the camera rolling, even though that's why the Lord invented the editing room. But no one had said anything about the late Kris Stanford getting fired. So far there hadn't been any other real surprises from Harrold. Brant was on the way out. Cummings was a nobody in Harrold's eyes. But I didn't know that baby Kris was about to hit the street.

So I smiled at Harrold and jumped ahead two spaces.

I said, "There are lots of people who work here who think Peggy Lynn handled you as easily as a princess phone. That true, Mr. Harrold?"

There was a little tightening around the edges of the mouth, but not much. Harrold wasn't the type to blink first.

"Preposterous," Harrold said blandly. He tried for bland, anyway. If I'd been closer I might have caught a little spittle. "There was a most unattractive tone to that question, Mr. Finley."

He was right. But the exchange was going to look prettier than the NBC peacock.

"I don't know what gets into me sometimes, Mr. Harrold."

"I am not here to trade flippancy with you."

"No, I wouldn't expect that to be your game."

Natalie was jerking her head back and forth like she was watching Evert Lloyd rally with Martina.

"So your relationship with Peggy Lynn Brady was strictly business?"

"Yes, it was."

"Always?"

"Yes."

From behind me, Marty said, "Real close." That meant we were getting near the end of the cassette. I didn't want to break up the heat that had blown into the room suddenly. If Harrold got time to compose himself, he was going to turn back into a mannequin in Macy's window.

I said, "You two did dine alone an awful lot, didn't you?"

"We were looking to make radical changes in a long-running hit show, Mr. Finley," Harrold said patiently. "That takes time. And I do have some other duties during the day." He sipped more iced tea. "I will not have you suggesting that innocent dinners were anything more than

that. I am a married man. I will not address myself to
malicious office gossip. As you know these are delicate
times around this network. It is hardly a secret that the
gentlemen who own the Global Broadcasting Company
are thinking of a sale to Reverend Endicott's Christian
network. The tragedy of Peggy Lynn's disappearance has
been enormously troublesome to both sides. I run an honest, aboveboard operation here, not Peyton Place. That is
why Reverend Endicott became interested in GBC in the
first place."

I said, "Exception noted. But I had to ask."

"Apology accepted," Harrold said.

"It wasn't an apology." I turned to Marty and gave him
a cutting motion underneath my chin. Natalie took off the
headset.

Harrold opened up his jacket and pulled a watch out of
his vest pocket. You don't see many pocket watches. He
flipped open the case. I thought, There haven't been moves
like this since Clifton Webb.

I said, "Can I ask you a couple of quick questions before
I leave, off the record?"

"Go ahead" is what he said. "Make it fast" was the
unspoken command. I figured that tone of voice usually
made GBC drones and underlings roll over and beg.

"Do you have any thoughts about who might have
wanted to bring harm to Peggy Lynn Brady, if it is someone who works here for you?"

He walked over and stood in front of the wall-window,
hands in the pockets of his slacks. He looked like a *New
York* magazine cover, headline "TV Biggies on the Go."

Natalie stopped packing up and was staring again.

"Johnny Brant wouldn't have the guts, even if it
meant his career," Harrold said. "Sam Cummings was,
or is, in love with her, even if he won't admit it to himself. I think Kris Stanford was in love with her too. I

frankly always wondered about that one. When I have
thought about all this, and I have thought about it a lot,
I thought it was Kris. She had been fiercely loyal to
Peggy for so long, almost to a degree of sickness, and
now she was about to be rejected." Harrold stopped and
offered something that was an exit short of being a smile.
"Television is turf, Mr. Finley. I have mine, Peggy had
hers and was obsessed with expanding it, no matter what
the cost. We all protect our turf in our own way. Kris
Stanford was about to lose hers, at a time when she had
every right to expect it to be growing. Peggy Lynn Brady
was about to take Stanford's loyalty and grind it into
dust. Yes, I think she could have brought harm to
Peggy, if Peggy had told her."

I said, "If you're right, then all the answers I'm looking
for could belong to a dead person?"

Harrold tried to look concerned. "Precisely," he said.

Natalie and Marty were waiting by the door. I did like
Columbo used to do.

"One last thing. Nothing to do with the story. Just
curious. Is it true that you were an actor once?"

For just a moment, he looked startled. Like a match
that didn't quite catch in the wind.

Harrold said, "What an odd question. I guess, yes, you
could call it acting. I was briefly the king of the walk-on
in some of the old black-and-white series filmed in New
York City. Unfortunately for me, they did not give out
Emmy awards for being the room-service waiter. Or siza-
ble paychecks. So I had to go out and find a real job." He
gestured around the suite. "I ended up with this one. I
suppose you could call it a real job."

I thanked him for his time. We left. As we headed
toward his private elevator, Marty Pearl said, "I don't
mean to be crass and vulgar in front of the womenfolk, but
I got a feeling that boy's dick is made of ice."

"Wonder what it would take to melt him down?" I said.

Marty poked Natalie.

"Got any thoughts about that, princess?"

Natalie blushed and said nothing.

Both were firsts.

"WE need a little bit more from this Sam Cummings, I'm thinking," Charley Davidson said.

We had dropped off the cassettes and gear at Channel A then decided to brave the Desperate Hours at O'Rourkes. Charley had decided to come with us. His wife was visiting her mother in Baltimore. Jeannie was in San Francisco giving a speech at the National Organization for Women and wouldn't be back for a few more days. It was boys' night out, plus Natalie. Everybody was on drink number one. In the front room, a lot of waspy-looking creatures were singing "Happy Birthday" for what looked to be the head wasp.

We sat in the back, underneath the television set. It was showing an Australian Rules football game. I didn't understand much of what was going on, except that about every thirty seconds an Aussie would kick a ball then get the shit kicked out of him.

"Charley," I said. "I would love to get more out of Sam Cummings. I'd like to run some of the stuff Harrold told us by him. But I make him cranky. Then he hits."

Charley sipped his martini and I sipped mine. When I didn't want to get drunk before it got dark out, I would have Seamus make me a Bombay martini in an America's Cup boat with six olives in it. I would nurse said martini.

"Boss is right," Marty said. He was slouched in the corner under one of my old newspaper columns. "We need to know if the slug really knew about all the shit—*all* the shit—that was about to go down on 'Midnite.' Peggy

Lynn's history. So is Kris Stanford. Brant's got all his theories, but he didn't know fuck-all about what was really going on. He's been so scared for so long his brain froze. We need to know if Harrold's telling the truth, or if he's got something to hide, like some people think. Cummings is the best shot."

He grabbed his bottle of Moosehead ale and pulled on some of it. I just looked at my friend. For Marty Pearl, that had been the equivalent of a filibuster.

"Natalie has to talk to him," Charley said. "Or at least make a run at him. No cameras. Just a chat."

Natalie had been filing her nails. She hadn't touched much of her drink, something called a sea breeze. It was a grapefruit juice and vodka, with a splash of cranberry juice. Natalie didn't drink anything that didn't have a nickname and come in watercolors.

She looked up when she heard her name.

"What is Natalie going to do?" she said.

Charley said, "Talk to Sam Cummings as soon as possible. Tomorrow if you can swing it."

"Uh uh," Natalie said. "No way. Noooo way. That guy gives me the creeps. I've seen him watching us the last couple of days. I'm not going anywhere near that lounge lizard. I haven't had my shots."

Charley smiled serenely at her. His fingers were clasped over his belly. He had his reading glasses on top of his head. He was wearing a red plaid bow tie.

"Natalie girl," he said. "This is not a debate. This is what you call an executive decision, middle-management level. I have a feeling that if Cummings will talk to anybody, it will be the charming Ms. Ferrare. He's in the business. He has to know that it's going to look bad if he's not in this piece. People are always wondering why folks go on '60 Minutes' and get their brains beat out. It's simple: It is better than having the audience wonder what you're trying to hide."

Charley got Little John's attention and made a circular motion with his hand, indicating another round. Natalie and I waved off Little John. Marty nodded from underneath the Brooklyn cap.

"What about the possibility of an affair between Harrold and Peggy Lynn?" Charley said.

I said, "I have no idea after talking to him. I know he's got a wifey up in Westchester and a whole country club *Town and Country* life, according to the clips. He seemed extremely uptight about the Endicott takeover, and that's been going on for some time. He doesn't strike me as the type who would take a chance on blowing his deal for a little kissy face, huggy body, even with the world-renowned Peggy Lynn Brady, star of mattresses everywhere."

"O'Rourke dig up any dirt yet?" Marty said.

"Not yet," I said, and plucked an olive out of the Bombay. "He's having drinks at Twenty-one with some lady lawyer from GBC. He'll be by sometime, unless he decides to trip the Lite beer fantastic."

Natalie wrinkled her nose. "That's it," she said wearily. "I'm out of here. I'll try with Sam Cummings in the morning. Thank you for the stimulating conversation. Thank you so much for the drink. Now you boys get good and drunk, say fuck an awful lot, and have an all-around grand evening. Maybe catch some pro wrestling on the tube." She checked her hair in the mirror. "It's always so difficult for a girl deciding between a night out with you swells and the ballet." And sashayed toward the front room. We all watched her.

I speared another olive with a toothpick.

"Somebody's lying here," I said. "Harrold says that Kris Stanford was out with Peggy Lynn, in all ways. Brant says the two of them were thick as ever. Harrold says Peggy Lynn was about to turn Cummings into a dishrag. Cummings told me they were full of plans about the new show. According to Brant, Harrold could have been messing around with Peggy Lynn on the side. Harrold says forget about it. Brant's a chickenshit, but if what Harrold says is true, Brant's ass got saved when Peggy Lynn went away or got whacked or whatever. So Brant's glad she's not around. Cummings seems to be the only one who misses her, but Harrold makes it sound like Cummings didn't have any right to feel that way."

Charley waved a hand at Little John and pointed to his empty glass with the other.

"How about we turn it around?" Charley said. "How about Harrold was going to get rid of Peggy Lynn, not Brant or anybody else? She's become more and more of a pain in the ass. Harrold's already worried about Reverend Endicott. So he's gonna go through the motions on her new contract, say they can't agree to terms, and let her go. But then she does have something on him, and squeezes him the way she squeezed Seth Parker, and she turns it all around on Mr. Thomas Harrold. Wouldn't that give him a motive?"

"Of course it would," I said. "But then I'm right back to wondering how you go about blackmailing a mogul."

Marty said, "Or Harrold is telling the truth, and it was Cummings who went nuts when he found out Peggy Lynn didn't need him anymore."

"Or Kris Stanford," Charley said. "Same deal. Like Harrold thinks."

"Or even Brant," said Marty. He was watching more Australian Rules.

I said "Fuck."

We had finished our burgers and were having coffee when O'Rourke came bursting into the back room. He looked like he had just come from a golf dinner. Kelly green jacket and red shirt and yellow slacks that looked to have bumblebees on them. He was a joke I'd heard once. Q: Why do Wasps play golf? A: So they can dress like pimps.

When he got near us I noted that he had overdone it with the Old Spice as usual.

"I have some interesting items for the Channel A newsletter," he said triumphantly. "I got a lady lawyer from GBC who is a dirty squealer."

O'ROURKE talked to me and watched the Yankees.

"The goddamn Christians have everybody scared shitless over there," O'Rourke said. "Anybody seen a score lately, by the way?"

Marty said, "Cleveland, one-nothing."

"Shit," O'Rourke said. "Anyway, the lady lawyer— Brynne Healey her name is, business affairs—tells me that GBC is quietly under siege. Harrold has become the Reverend Eugene Endicott's point man. If the Christians take over, they want the place clean as a whistle. They all just clutched their Bibles with the Peggy Lynn mess, then Kris Stanford getting killed. They weren't too thrilled about Finley and Brant and Billy Go to the Park, even if it wasn't Brant's fault." He sipped some of my coffee. "Endicott gooses, Harrold jumps. There's been a little drug testing here and there, for example. Harrold says it's voluntary, but the message is that if you don't pee in the bottle, you're guilty. Brynne says that some coke showed up for a kid in the mailroom. Sayonara. Harrold also bought out the contracts of a couple of homos, one a director, the other a makeup guy. Very quietly. Bottom line: Harrold is very uptight about the takeover, so he does what he's told."

"Why did Brynne choose to share all this with you?" I asked.

O'Rourke took his eyes off the set and trained them on me. Bassett eyes. Like I'd hit him with a rolled-up newspaper.

"Hey, she likes me," he said. "She's on the Jersey side of forty, which is a little old for me, but she could be an aerobics junkie. After she'd had her third Beefeater—straight, I might add—she took my hand and told me what a good listener I am. I think I might have to run her over to the River Café tomorrow night and show her the view."

I said, "She say anything about a back street program for Harrold and Peggy Lynn? Love nest maybe?"

"She says there was talk, but you've heard that too. If something had been going on, it was definitely over when Peggy Lynn went away. She says there was no way Harrold would've taken a chance, what with Endicott looking over his shoulder and Mrs. Harrold waiting for the train. Brynne Healey is of the opinion that Endicott has been watching Harrold and the other management guys as closely as Harrold has been watching everybody else."

I thought Charley was beginning to nod, but he looked up and said, "Sounds like a fun place to work."

"Yeah," Marty said drolly. "Like high school with money."

On the television screen a Yankee pitcher was striking out an Indian batter with the bases loaded. O'Rourke jumped out of his chair.

"Aw right, O'Rourke!" he yelled. O'Rourke had a way of personalizing all Yankee triumphs, great or small.

I asked for a check and paid when it came. Marty and I put Charley in a cab. He slurred something that sounded like "Good-night." Marty offered me a ride. I told him I was going to get the early papers and walk home.

"Where the hell are we?" I said.

"Sport," he said, "we're still in the middle of a fucking Japanese art film."

19

I WAS dreaming about the reservoir again. It was night in the dream. Raining. I was slogging through the mud again. There was someone ahead of me but I couldn't see who, and couldn't make any ground. There were bleachers all along the side of the path, filled with people cheering me on. Every few yards I would look up and see a face I recognized. Jeannie. Natalie. Charley. Marty. Seth Parker and David. Mick Dunphy. I ran harder and couldn't catch up. The mud kept getting deeper. I couldn't see through the rain. Then I was yelling "Stop!" and she turned around and it was Peggy Lynn Brady up ahead of me. She smiled and waved and jumped into the water. . . .

The phone rang.

"This is your seven A.M. wake-up call," the voice on the telephone said.

I mumbled, "Start talking. And this better be important." Standard material.

"Already did," the voice said. "Repeat: seven A.M. wake-up call, courtesy of New York's finest finest."

Dunphy.

I looked over at the clock radio. He wasn't lying about the hour. It was the first time I'd heard his voice since Billy Lynn. I sat up in bed, out of breath and sweating, and thought, You really are out of shape, Finley. Your ass gets worn out even when you dream about running.

"I repeat, this better be important," I said thickly. I took a slug out of the Coke can on the nightstand. It saved steps when I got thirsty in the middle of the night.

Dunphy said, "It is more intriguing than important, but it could turn out to be both."

"I'm listening."

"One," he said. "Somebody got into Peggy Lynn's townhouse last night and went on an Easter egg hunt."

"Is there a two?"

"Yup."

"Before we get to two, what did the intruder take?"

"Don't know. Maybe nothing. But there was enough of a mess for us to know that the somebody was looking for a something."

I said, "Okay. Two."

"Miss Peggy Lynn Brady had made a reservation on East Hampton Aire to fly from the Marine Air Terminal at LaGuardia to East Hampton Airport the night she disappeared," Dunphy said. "I gotta admit, we missed it first time around. It's like a Mom and Pop operation, the airline. Eight-seaters, fifteen-seaters, like that, and no computer. They'd lost the reservation. But then the other day, her last American Express bill came in and there it was, a sixty-buck charge to East Hampton Aire. See, when you make a reservation with them, they make you guarantee the seat with a credit card. You skip the flight and you pay anyway. There you go. She never got on the plane, but at some point she was planning to."

I cradled the receiver between ear and shoulder and walked over to the window unit and shut off the air conditioner. I had fallen asleep with it on, which was like an engraved invitation to bronchitis.

Mick said, "You there?"

"Why are you telling me this? You hate me."

"I ran into O'Rourke last night. He said you're back at work and actually making progress. I am also not overwhelmed with confidence for the colleagues of mine who are half-assing their way through the mystery concerning the aforementioned Miss Brady. I myself work in homicide. It is a full-time job. Right now I am dealing with the offing of an undercover cop in Brooklyn. So I decided to lay this on you and let you run with it."

I had read about the undercover cop. The execution-style—bullet to the back of the head, guy tied up—meant Colombians and drugs. Colombians and drug killings in New York took up more space in the tabloids than the ads.

"Does this mean I'm forgiven?" I said.

"Nah," said Dunphy. "But you might be coming to the end of your probation." Then he said, "I gotta go."

"Mick," I said. "How'd you find out about Peggy Lynn's house?"

"We had to take off surveillance finally. But I went over and had the locks changed, just for fun. I made the locks real easy. Then I had a couple of boys check out the house every morning. Somebody picked the front one. Which means that somebody must have been surveying my surveyors."

"Could be random."

"Maybe. And maybe not. I prefer to be sporting and think otherwise."

"You dust the place already?"

"Yeah. Nothing. Clean as a line single to left."

I said, "One other thing: Since you are in such a sporting mood, could you run credit card checks on some of the other GBCs for me? See if any of them had any interesting charges on or around Peggy Lynn night at the old ballpark?"

There was a pause.

"Who?" he said finally.

"Sam Cummings. Kris Stanford. Thomas Harrold. Johnny Brant."

Another pause.

"There is a lot of give and take in our relationship, Finley. Maybe you've noticed. I give. You take."

"C'mon, Mick."

"I'll get back to you."

"My hero," I said in falsetto, but the line had already gone dead.

It was probably for the best. I went into the shower and used the water massage gadget until I felt ready to face the day. Then I shaved in the stall, using my new steam-proof mirror. Then I tried out my new Mister Coffee.

It takes a big man to admit he's a slave to technology.

DELORES wasn't at her desk when I got to the office. I worked the phone some anyway. I wanted to know where Peggy Lynn planned to go in the Hamptons when she had made that reservation. Her getaway house was in Westport, as in Connecticut. The police had gone over it, and the grounds, and come up empty.

Brant's place was on the Jersey shore. I didn't know about Harrold. Or Cummings. Or Kris.

I called my friend Susan Wyner, real estate person, in Bridgehampton. She was a lifer out there, daughter of a

potato farmer, and sharp as a tack; a one-woman information bureau about the area.

"I need a favor," I said when she got on the line.

"Gee, Peter," she said. "I'm all out of tickets for the
Fire Department outing."

"My darling," I said, "you are much too quick for the
South Fork of eastern Long Island."

"I know, I know," she sighed. "But not when we're in
season and slickers like you are hanging over the bars."

I sketched out what I was working on, then asked her
to check out if Harrold or Cummings or Stanford either
owned or rented on the South Fork. It was a longshot, I
knew.

Susan said, "You just want to know about our sleepy
little village. I hope."

"I wish it were that easy, Suze. But methinks you gotta
check out the whole deal. Westhampton Beach to Montauk Point."

"When you ask for a favor, Peter, you ask for a favor.
If those people don't rent, you know I gotta go through
Deeds over in Southampton."

"I thought your first husband was big in deeds?"

"I think you misunderstood me one night at Van's," she
said. "I said he was big in greed."

I said, "Whatever. See what you can find out, okay?"

"If I turn up anything, can I get into your piece?"

"I can already see your name in headlines in the *Bridgehampton Sun,*" I said and hung up.

I spent the rest of the morning running into dead ends.
Neither SAG nor Actors Equity had any record of a
Thomas Harrold, or someone with a name anywhere
close, ever being a member. I stopped by Natalie's office
a couple of times but she wasn't there. I assumed she was
with Cummings. Or trying. I called Johnny Brant and
asked if he knew of any close friends Peggy Lynn might

have had in the Hamptons. Brant told me the two of them swapped weekend plans as often as they did pie recipes.

I called Mick Dunphy over at the precinct and asked him to run everybody's alibis for the night of the disappearance past me again. He grumped and did it.

"Harrold was at a United Jewish Appeal dinner at the Waldorf honoring Cosell," he said wearily. "Cummings and Kris Stanford were at Peggy Lynn's house working on the show. They ordered in Chinese. Spareribs and moo shu pork, as I recall. Delivery boy saw them both when he brought the junk. Brant was at Yankee Stadium in Steinbrenner's box; he's an Orioles fan."

"Could you run Peggy Lynn's credit card check by me again?" I asked as politely as possible.

"Affirmative," he said. He recited the list of charges. I wrote them all down. "If I get something else, I'll get back to you."

I tried Jeannie in San Francisco. She was staying at the Huntington. It was eight o'clock in the morning there. She was already out of the room.

Charley had called in sick. It happened to him a lot after O'Rourkes. Marty called it the Smirnoff flu.

I had verified one of life's truisms once again: Getting up early sucks.

So I went to the coffee machine one more time and came back to my office and did something I should have done earlier—read all the box scores in *USA Today*.

Box scores always have answers. Even if you don't know the questions.

NATALIE came back after lunch. I was on the phone with my father, who was back in Boston for the fortieth anniversary of his graduation from the police academy.

She came in, plopped into the chair across from my

desk, angrily lit a cigarette—Natalie Ferrare can make the most innocent of gestures into a hostile challenge—crossed her legs with a big show, and glared me into hanging up the telephone.

"Pap," I said. "Call me later. Miss Ferrare just came in and wants to discuss PMH."

Over the phone he said, "PMH, sonny?"

I said, "Pre-menstrual homicide," and gently replaced the receiver. Smiling at Natalie, I said, "You saw Cummings, I take it?"

Natalie nodded.

"It didn't go well?"

She slowly shook her head.

"You're upset with me."

She pursed her lips, nearly closed her eyes, and nodded again. Vigorously.

I slid an ashtray across the desk toward her.

I said, "We're not connecting here, are we, princess?"

She butted out the cigarette like she was squashing a persistent bug.

"Don't give me any menstrual humor, big boy," she said. "If I ever have to go near that man again, I quit."

I just let her go on.

"There is something seriously off with him, Finley," she said, absently recrossing the legs. "I mean, there might be a light on upstairs, but I've got doubts, *doubts,* that there's anybody home. When you're with him, you sit on the edge of the chair the whole time, wondering what harmless little thing you might say that might, you know, ignite him or something. He's like this crazy goddamn watch dog."

I touched the back of my head and remembered lunch at Summerhouse.

"I hear you," I told her.

She got up and went over and faced me from in front of the Ted Williams poster. "His basic position is that everybody is lying except him, if they're still around or alive," Natalie went on.

She smoked and paced, using the cigarette for emphasis. As usual, I was struck by how her nervous energy could be sexy in a confined space.

She said, "I tracked him down in the coffee shop at GBC. Trying to be sweet as could be. Like a buddy, you know? I came at him like a lot of his co-workers were talking a bunch of shit about Peggy Lynn and about him. For a while he just sat there slurping his coffee—God, he is a disgusting man—not saying anything. But then he got interested when I got to some of the tidbits Harrold offered when you interviewed him."

"Like him becoming a figurehead or something when Peggy Lynn took over the show?"

"Yeah. I thought he was going to slap me. His face turned white. At least I thought it did, underneath all that awful hair. Said Harrold was a fucking liar. Said that no way in this world would Peggy Lynn ever do that to him. Said she was just playing along with Harrold, getting the title, because Harrold was going to be on the street when Endicott took over. He said, 'It was our show and it was going to stay our show.' "

I leaned back in my chair and crossed my legs.

I said, "He say how he knew such things? I sort of find it hard to believe that Cummings and the Rev are partners at prayer meetings."

"I asked him that," Natalie said. "He just told me that Harrold was gonna be out, that it was gonna come down to a choice between Peggy Lynn and Harrold, and Peggy Lynn was definitely going to win that one."

"You ask him about his pal Kris getting the ax?"

She dive-bombed back into the chair. Slid so far down I thought she was going to end up on the floor. Mussed her hair so that it covered her eyes. Put her cigarette into her mouth and let it dangle. I knew she was doing a Cummings impression. She made her voice gruff and low-down. I grinned.

"Another fuckin' lie," she said, as Cummings. Then she sat up and became Natalie again. "Fuckin' lie, as you can see, was sort of a recurring theme in our chat."

"You believe him?"

"Who the hell knows? You've been there. It's like talking to one of the animals at the zoo."

The phone buzzed. I ignored it.

"Why do you suppose he opened up to you at all?"

"Other than my wiles?"

"Yeah. Other than them."

"I think he was just covering himself. That's the way I read it. I don't know who did what to whom over there —that's your department—but Cummings must figure that it's his word against Harrold's. His and Peggy Lynn's and Kris's, and the other two aren't around to contradict him, even if he is fibbing." She stopped for a breath. "Plus, he says he's quitting."

I uncrossed my own legs.

"Really," I mused.

"He said he's fed up with Harrold. Said the thought of working with Brant anymore makes him want to puke. That's a quote, incidentally. I'm sure you'll want to use it. He's got another year on his contract, but he's going to go in and offer Harrold a chance to buy him out. Then he says he's gonna find a quiet beach somewhere. I just hope it's not mine. The thought of him even semi-undressed makes *me* want to puke."

"Anything else of note?"

"Not really. After he told me he was quitting, he asked what else Harrold said. Wanted to know everything. I gave it to him best I could. Then he just got up and left me sitting there with my tea. I thought about getting fumigated, decided against it, then came back here to rejoin the human race."

I went across the desk and kissed her on the cheek. Not smart-ass or patronizing. Just nice.

"You done good," I said softly. "Look at it this way, I ended up in the emergency room, you ended up with stuff. Done good."

Natalie said, "Thank you."

"Now go back to your office," I said. "Deep breathe for a bit. Then try to set up an interview with the Reverend Eugene Endicott as soon as possible. If you do that, you can take the rest of the week off."

"Do they give out awards for working princesses?" she said as she got up.

"Not that I know of. It's not a fair world, Nat."

"You're telling me," she said and left.

I sat back down and stared at Ted Williams.

"Kid," I said out loud to the Splendid Splinter, "curiouser and curiouser."

Williams just stared back at me, mean-like. He really hadn't done a thing for me since 1960.

I WALKED home about five o'clock. No one I wanted to call me had called me back, so I went home. Home is where you can lock the door and close the shades and think. Home is where you can fix yourself a weak Jack Daniel's and water and put Sinatra on the stereo, my favorite album in the world—"After All These Years, Francis Albert Sinatra Finally Conjoins with Edward Kennedy Ellington." Frank and the Duke. Conjoining. Four songs to a side. Billy May arrangements. Every song at least four minutes long. I shut off the phone and stretched out on the couch in the living room.

Somebody at GBC was lying. I had stayed at GBC

because I had to. There was no edge for Brant to say Peggy Lynn had no life outside the station. The letters had talked about a secret lover and so had Cummings. But the lover was making her happy. She'd written that, two weeks before she went away. He was a phantom, but he sure as hell wasn't a jilted phantom.

Repeat: somebody was lying to me.

And somebody was hiding something.

Brilliant, Finley.

Harrold was lying. Or Cummings was lying. I had narrowed it down to the two of them, mostly because I had no other way to go. Kris Stanford? Unavailable for comment. Was she in, or out? Could she have done it somehow? Maybe. If she had, I might never know what happened.

No. Correction. I *would* never know what happened. Kris wasn't going to give me the lover's name either.

I sipped some Jack. Sinatra was having light fun with "All I Need Is the Girl" from *Gypsy*. Had I turned off the phone? Yeah. Master of detail.

I had no evidence on anybody. Who had more to lose? Answer, Harrold. But if Cummings thought he was about to lose his whole stash, position and power and the clout that came with being Peggy Lynn's sergeant-at-arms, then he had more to lose. Same with Kris Stanford. It was simple perspective. The one with the most to lose was the one who was going to lose it, dummy. It was like the time when I was in high school and found out that my grandfather only had a few months to live. My grandfather was eighty. Using all the wisdom of my years, all sixteen of them, I said to my father, "Well, Pap, eighty is a good long life."

Jack Finley said, "Not if you're eighty, it isn't."

I finished my drink and decided against another. I went to the refrigerator and got a bottle of Kaliber. It is a nonalcoholic beer made by the Guinness people. I don't know how they do it, but it tastes like beer. Sinatra and Ellington were on "Indian Summer." Frank was just stroking it. It was getting dark outside. I didn't put the lights on.

Sam Cummings was quitting. Peggy Lynn was going somewhere in the Hamptons, then canceled. Brant got a reprieve when Peggy Lynn got deleted. Somebody broke into Peggy Lynn's home, which she shared with Kris Stanford. Pattern? Connection?

Where?

One of the lights on the phone blinked noiselessly. I let it blink.

I must have drowsed away. The ringing of a phone startled me. It was like an alarm buzzer going off. Someday, they were going to discover that waking up did more damage to the heart than smoking, jogging, stress, obesity, dieting, cholesterol, crosstown traffic. Or worrying about which one of those things was going to do the most damage to your goddamn heart.

It was the house phone. Couldn't shut that one off.

I found the switch on the lamp at the end of the couch and stumbled across the room. I checked my watch. It was near ten. I had been asleep for a while.

I picked up the phone and mumbled, "What is it?"

It was Lenny Morrissey.

"Package for you, Mr. F."

"You're shitting, Lenny," I said. "At this time of the fucking night? Who brought it?"

Lenny said, "Damned if I know. I was helping the Drums—they're ten-F, you know—unload their car out front. They been away. I put their stuff on one of them dollies, I wheel it over to the elevator, I come back, the thing is sitting on my stand. Your name typed on the front, that's all."

"What's it look like?"

"Brown wrapping paper. About the size of a book, like that. You want I should bring it up?"

I told him to do that. When he did, I unwrapped the package. It was a cassette. VHS size. No identification of any kind on it, except for the brand name, Fuji. I was a two-VCR man. VHS in the living room, Beta in the bedroom. I turned on the big Sony in the living room and put the cassette in the machine and hit "Play."

It was an old black-and-white porno film, the kind you used to get in the mail for bachelor parties before smut became mainstream and came in color.

The title was *Lady of the House.*

I sat on the floor in front of the set and watched. It was all fairly standard stuff, until about fifteen minutes in. A bored housewife in expensive home. A delivery boy. They do it on the kitchen counter. Then the kitchen table. Then the kitchen floor.

Enter the handy man.

They do it in the yard.

Then came the electrician. I assumed they were perhaps going to try it while hanging from the light fixtures in the dining room.

And then I looked hard at the set and nearly put my nose against the screen and said very quietly, "Holy shit." I stopped it and rewound and hit the pause button and froze *Lady of the House.*

I said, "Holy shit" again.

The electrician had very impressive equipment once he shucked his jeans. Breeding farm equipment.

The electrician, getting ready to pump away, was also a much younger Thomas Harrold.

Right up to his Anne Francis beauty mark.

CHAPTER
20

I MADE myself watch it all the way through. It was Harrold, no doubt about it. Then I rewound *Lady of the House* to the opening credits. The name he used then was Tommy Long. Cute.

But appropriate. No getting around that.

It was eleven-thirty. I fixed myself another drink. Now I knew what leverage Peggy Lynn had on Harrold.

Was it big enough to kill for?

Damn right it was. *Lady of the House* wouldn't just ruin a career. It could ruin a whole life. I didn't think the Reverend Eugene Endicott would like the movie as much as *Bambi*.

So Harrold had a motive. He'd said he planned to give Peggy Lynn everything she wanted, but maybe he really planned to get rid of her and had lied to me. He tells her he's dumping her. She says, "Forget it," and produces the movie. He gives her the new contract, makes her executive producer, et cetera, et cetera.

I asked another question, aloud.

"So why kill her?"

Maybe he was afraid she'd use the movie again somewhere down the line. Okay, so he had motive. But where was the opportunity?

Interviewing myself was making me tired, as usual. But I kept on. Who sent the movie? Not Peggy Lynn. And certainly not Kris.

It had to be Cummings. He was a team player. He said the only secret Peggy Lynn kept from him was the new boyfriend. If she had the movie, he knew. Mick Dunphy said her apartment had been boosted. Cummings would have known where to look for the cassette if she had it there. He was about to leave the Global Broadcasting Company. He had no use for Thomas Harrold. Maybe he wanted to take a souvenir with him. Maybe he wanted Harrold's scalp instead of a gold watch.

I had frozen the movie on the VCR. I walked over and hit the stop button. I must have left the set on Channel G, because the first thing I saw was the opening of "The Living God Live!" From one kind of porno to another. I sat back down and watched. Maybe if I opened my spirit, the Lord would give me answers.

On the screen, Endicott, in bright green robe, was spreading his arms, as usual, wide to his flock.

"Is your house *cleeeeeean* today?" he boomed.

I stared at the television. It was a night for doing that.

"I repeat, brothers and sisters," Endicott screamed, "Is your spiritual house *clean*?"

"Jesus H. Christ," I said.

I went into the bedroom, reached into the top drawer of my bureau.

The search didn't take long.

There it was.

"Jesus H. Christ," I said softly.

I had been wasting my time with the first half of the double feature. I had one more drink and set the alarm for seven-thirty. And dreamed about an old saxophone man, sitting on a beach, playing for the ocean.

NATALIE called me at eight-thirty as I was walking out the door.

"The Reverend Eugene Endicott will grant you an audience at noon," she said. "Dorset Hotel. He's giving a breakfast speech there. One of his aides says it's gonna be just the two of you. Says Endicott would like to go one-on-one with you before he consents to an actual interview. Apparently he is well versed in your recent comings and goings."

"Perfect," I said into the phone. "Pluperfect, in fact. When the dice get hot, a boy can make pass after pass."

Natalie said, "What are you talking about, Peter? You been up all night?"

"Darling girl," I said, "I slept like a baby."

"You're crazy, you know that?"

I said, "Not anymore."

"You coming into the office?"

"Nope. Got some errands to run."

"Where are you going to be?" she asked. Accusingly.

"Tell you later."

"You're up to something, Peter."

"Up to my fugging eyeballs."

I was at Harrold's office by nine o'clock. His secretary, a red-haired bug of a thing named Megan, told me he was in conference. I told her I would wait. She told me she didn't know how long Harrold would be. That he had a busy morning.

"I think he'll see me," I said. And sat down on the

couch across from her, picked up a copy of *Variety*, and read it.

I was humming now, but there was no need to rush anything.

I was still reading when the door to Harrold's office opened. A bald man who was too fat for his double-breasted suit came out first. Then Harrold. They shook hands. The bald man said, "I'll look over the trend in the overnights the last couple of months and get back to you by late this afternoon."

"*Early* this afternoon," Harrold said casually. The bald man took it like a shove in the small of his back. He scurried past me. I couldn't decide whether he reminded me more of Tom or Jerry in the cartoons; I never could remember which one was the mouse.

Harrold started to go back into his office, then noticed me as I stood up.

"Do we have an appointment?" he said. He looked as pretty as before. The darker suit set his hair off better.

"We don't," I told him.

"I really don't have any time for sparring this morning," he said. "Reverend Endicott has scheduled a press conference for next Monday. You can guess what it's about."

Behind her desk, I thought Megan might cry.

"I tried to tell him, sir. . . ."

"I don't have a lot of time either," I said brusquely, heading straight for the door. "But we're gonna talk. I brought you a present from Tommy Long."

I watched his face. I had seen a look like it before, the first time Natalie saw a dead body, after a shooting in Brooklyn. It was like a quick scuffle between nausea and control. Natalie didn't throw up. Neither did Harrold. But he looked as if someone was pulling all of his face from behind.

"Come in," Thomas Harrold said in a dead voice. "Hold my calls, Megan."

The man could take a punch.

The office was as opulent as the suite, only with more televisions. It was about half the size, like Harrold had become in front of my eyes. The office and all its mogul trimmings just seemed to swallow him up. The last ounce of polish he had had been used in the outer office for the benefit of little Megan.

I didn't much relish cutting off his epaulets in front of the troops, but I had to be sure about him, once and for all. It was time to dot the *i*s and cross the *t*s.

Harrold said, "How did you get it?"

"Someone dropped it by my apartment late last night. I watched it and came by here. I want you to tell me why I shouldn't think you killed her because of it."

Harrold was absently flipping a pen over in his right hand. I couldn't tell whether he'd heard what I said.

"Have you told anybody about it?"

"No."

"Why would someone do something like that, do you suppose." He was musing out loud, to himself.

I laid out a scenario for Harrold: Peggy Lynn had tried to use the tape on him. Harrold, or somebody working for Harrold, had killed her. Peggy Lynn was gone, but Cummings, who maybe had been in on it with her, went and got the tape, and was going to take Harrold down anyway.

"I have no idea what you're talking about," Thomas Harrold said when I finished.

I lit a cigarette.

"Why not?"

He said, "Because I have not set eyes on that piece of garbage in twenty-five years."

"Peggy Lynn wasn't using this tape as leverage against you?"

Harrold straightened some in his chair. It was as if he were coming out of a hypnotic trance. You're a real boy again, Pinocchio.

"No," he said. "You've got to believe me, Finley. I'm not discounting that she may have had it in her possession. You may be right about that part and Cummings knowing about it and handing the tape over to you because of some twisted, lingering loyalty. Peggy Lynn had even bragged to me once, a long time ago, about how she used some kind of tape against Seth Parker. Maybe she did consider using it against me if it ever came to that. But I am telling you the truth. I was going to give her what she wanted. Even if I had wanted to do otherwise, Reverend Endicott had made it abundantly clear to me that she was the cornerstone of the network in its present state. He wanted a housecleaning at 'Midnite,' but he wanted Peggy Lynn. He's a man of God, but a bottom-line accountant too. He met with Peggy Lynn to lay out his program for her. She could have the show, but he wanted her little army disbanded. He was going to eliminate the problem with Brant by simply eliminating Brant."

"Why should I believe you? Because you say I should believe you?"

"You're not listening to me, *dammit!*" He slapped a hand on the desk. "Endicott has been calling the shots around here. He wanted Peggy Lynn. So I wanted Peggy Lynn. I was stuck with her, Finley, if I wanted to keep *my* job. I wasn't going to strengthen my position by eliminating her. There was no percentage. She didn't need me, because she had Endicott on her side. Go ahead. Ask him. I know you're meeting with him today. He told me. There was no reason for her to blackmail me."

Off to my right, the five television sets built into the wall showed morning things noiselessly. GBC had a black-and-white western. Phil Donahue pranced about on NBC.

CNN had news, of course. CBS and ABC had people jumping up and down on game shows. PBS had a close-up of a fern.

Harrold said, "Sam Cummings could have given you *Lady of the House* for any number of reasons. He could just be acting like the vindictive son of a bitch that he is. He tells people he's quitting the network. Well, friend, he's quitting because he is about to be fired, and he knows it. And he hates me for it."

"Why wouldn't he hate Peggy Lynn?" I said. "She was the one, ultimately."

"I told you before. He loved her. I think he always did, from the time the two of them were together at Channel Two. Oddly, I think it's the same sort of mindless obsession that Billy Lynn had for her."

Harrold placed his palms on the desk in front of him and stared hard at me. His executive face was working again.

"Let me lay out a scenario for you," he said. "Let me be the prosecutor for a moment. Say Cummings hadn't been told by Peggy Lynn that she didn't need him anymore. Say in his mind they were a team, as always. If she had the movie, he had to assume that she had used it with me, or at least let me know she had it. In his mind, I would have motive. In his mind, maybe I did do it. He begins to think I'm going to get away with it. There's not even a body. What's the best means for him to put suspicion squarely on me?"

I said, "Hand *Lady of the House* over to me. Then wait for me to hand it over to the cops."

Dotting *i*s. Crossing *t*s.

"You still think Kris Stanford did it, don't you?" I said.

"Yes. I think there is an excellent chance that Peggy Lynn told her she was being fired, and she could not deal with it. If Cummings sent you this movie, he couldn't have known."

Neither one of us spoke.

Harrold finally said, "What are you going to do with that film?"

I got up and tossed *Lady of the House* into my satchel.

"I'm not going to tell Endicott about it, if that's what you're worried about. I think you are wrong about Kris Stanford. I think I have it all figured out. If I have, I'll drop this piece of shit by tomorrow, and you can burn it for all I care. 'Cause by tomorrow, porno is probably going to be the least of everybody's problems."

Harrold stood up.

"I take it you're not interested in the circumstances of me . . . having to be a part of something like that?" He pointed at my satchel.

I said, "Not in the least. I'm just like you, Thomas. It doesn't do no good at all to know the rules of life, 'cause somebody is always rewriting the damn rule book."

I left him standing there behind his desk, another one like the rest, scared as hell. Harrold just had a better office, better expense account, more to lose.

I STOPPED by Cummings's office. Dobie Gillis's mom told me he wouldn't be in today. I didn't expect that he would be.

I said, "Get him on the phone for me."

She raised a quizzical eyebrow at me. She was very good at it. I try it and I look like I have palsy.

"For you?" she said. "Are you making some kind of joke?"

"Yeah, I guess I am," I said. "Listen, if he calls in, tell him thanks for the movie, but I'm just going to go ahead and wait for the book to come out."

I left the office, took the elevator down to the street and thought about Billy and Seth and David, Cummings and Harrold and Kris Stanford. Johnny Brant. Peggy Lynn. Some of them gone. Some of them still around. All of them had tried to protect their asses in their own ways. Cross and double-cross. Triple-cross. Fingers being pointed in all directions. Me? Rat caught in a fucking maze.

Not anymore, I thought. Now I knew.

I stopped at a pay phone on the corner of Forty-second and Seventh and called Susan Wyner in Bridgehampton and asked her what I wanted to know.

It was an easy answer. I jotted down the address and the directions. I remembered a line from *Butch Cassidy and the Sundance Kid* as I walked uptown toward the Dorset to finally meet the Rev.

"I got vision," Butch said. "And the rest of the world wears bifocals."

On the way, I stopped at one more pay phone and called Natalie at the office and told her to give the World Christian Network a call in Dover.

"What do you want to know?" Natalie asked. "You planning to join up?"

"Not exactly."

Then I told her.

CHAPTER
21

I EXPECTED to find Endicott in the dining room of the Dorset, which is on Fifty-fourth between Fifth and Sixth, just around the corner from CBS and ABC, six blocks from NBC. The dining room is the home office in Manhattan for power network breakfasts and power network lunches. It is a big, ornate room with good food, prompt service, no tourists.

But Frank, the maitre d', told me Reverend Endicott was waiting for me in a private room upstairs.

"Frank," I said, "he try to do anything tricky with the water, or just ask for a wine steward?"

Frank said something that sounded like "Commie blasphemer" and showed me upstairs.

It was a banquet room, with just one table set in the corner. Endicott, a vision in a white suit, was sitting at it. I had expected an entourage, or perhaps the World Christian Network chorus. But he was alone. The shirt was also white. And the tie. If I peeked under the table

I was fairly certain I'd find Pat Boone's white bucks. If they had tailored suits in heaven, St. Pete was going to look like this.

"Reverend Endicott, sir," I said, putting out my hand.

He rose imperiously, like on "The Living God Live!," and took my hand with both of his. There was nothing wrong with my hand, but it felt healed anyway.

"Mr. Finley," he said.

The Voice.

"I'm a great admirer of your work," he said.

The simplest sentence was all rolling thunder and the acoustics in the banquet room magnified it.

"And I yours," I said.

A waiter appeared from a side door. I ordered a tomato juice. Endicott said that water would be fine.

"I've been reading the papers," I said. "Your European tour was a great success."

Endicott smiled benevolently. His big hands were folded on the table in front of him. "It was my first trip away from this country," he said. "It was gratifying to learn that the word of God indeed has no geographic boundaries, no language barriers, nor is it restricted by denominations or politics or life-styles, no matter how divergent from our own. I simply spoke to them in the language of the soul."

I really had followed the tour. He had packed stadiums in London and Paris and Frankfurt, in West Berlin and Bucharest, Dublin and Edinburgh, and Barcelona and Madrid. The only minor controversy was when he couldn't get an audience with the Pope. I liked the Pope's style, as always.

"You must be very tired," I said. "When did you get back, about a week ago?"

"Yes," he said. "And I am a little tired. Even the messengers of the Lord are subject to jet lag."

"You been resting up?" I said. " 'Cause I'm hearing that you called a big press conference for next week."

He smiled at me, a one-of-the-flock smile. In person he was better than the show.

"I guess the press conference is no big secret to one such as yourself," he said. "I understand you have been putting together some kind of documentary on the Global Broadcasting Company, built around the tragic disappearance of Peggy Lynn Brady. Well, we have not set an official date, but there will be a major announcement, yes. I think you will want to be there."

I said, "You got that right, Rev." I sipped some of my tomato juice and lit a Marlboro.

Endicott's eyes opened up a little when I called him Rev. They were cornflower blue. The Lord might have given them to him, but I thought Bausch and Lomb, the contact lens company, was a better bet.

"I beg your pardon," he said.

I said, "Just trying to lighten things up. Where'd you rest up after you got back from the Continent?"

"The church has a retreat on Hilton Head Island, in South Carolina," he said. "Very private, very secluded. It is a place where I can recharge my spiritual batteries, I suppose you could say."

Hilton Head. I tried not to look interested.

"Reverend Endicott, if we could get down to cases, isn't taking over GBC a gamble for you? Even with all the money they've got behind them over there, they can't get out of the red. You've got your own empire at World Christian. Why take the risk?"

"It is all a risk, isn't it, Mr. Finley?" he said forcefully. "The calling that was chosen for me by God makes me welcome risks. It was a risk to set out from a small church in Morgantown, and a tiny Sunday morning radio show. It was a risk to test the waters of television."

The Voice picked up a head of steam.

"It is a risk to heal, a risk to save. A risk to court ridicule by making Jesus an attractive product to souls found and not yet found. I did not choose show business as a means of spreading the gospel, Mr. Finley. *But the times demanded it!* I offer entertainment as a means of offering salvation. The music, the glitter—it is only an inducement to walk into my church. Once inside, they see that I am still a minister of God. Yes, it is a risk." He sighed. "But our message can be even broader, given the power of Global Broadcasting. Five years ago, the times demanded a beginning on cable for the World Christian Network. Now the journey must continue, cannot stop. We have outgrown cable, quite frankly. The situation at Global presented itself. I availed myself of it."

He was out of breath. A fine line of sweat showed at his hairline. I looked at his shock of white hair more closely.

It was a wig. I was surprised, I must admit, even a little disappointed.

I said, "My understanding is that you have had GBC under quite close scrutiny for some time."

The smile was almost beatific.

"They are right about you," he said. "You *do* do your homework. Yes, I had heard that about Peter Finley." He had been using his hands a lot in the sermon about risk; he relaxed them back into a clasp. "Yes, we have done some research. Important research. You see, Mr. Finley, the people who work at the World Christian Network *want* to work at the World Christian Network. They have given themselves over to the work of Jesus. Now, at the beginning, we could not reasonably expect to have that sort of, well, Christian unanimity at Global. But before we went forward, we did want to do some preliminary weeding out."

"Get rid of some of the bad seeds, so to speak," I said.

"So to speak."

"How come you weren't going to weed out Peggy Lynn Brady?" I asked. "If you did the important research you said you did, you know she had been a very bad girl. A slut, in fact."

He sighed again. It was a big show, like everything else about him. I thought he might be buying time. I didn't think he liked "slut" one bit.

"Of course it was no secret that her life, especially her life in television, had been poisoned by her own success," he said. "But I had spent some time with her before her disappearance, and I believe firmly that she was honestly trying to change. In my heart, I was certain that she was on the verge of a conversion, a spiritual upheaval. A new life. It was why I was so sick when she left us."

"Bad timing for you, huh?"

"It is heartless and cruel to speak that way about the dead, Mr. Finley," he said.

"You think she's dead too, huh?"

"Sadly, there is no earthly evidence to the contrary. She could have been a force for such immense good, if my reading of her was correct, and I think it was."

I said, "Transform her, transform one hell of an interested viewing audience, something like that?" I lit another cigarette. The waiter appeared again. Endicott sent him back into the anteroom with a look.

"She was a lost soul, but a famous one," Endicott said. "People idolized her. It would have been a marvelous thing for her to join our spiritual army."

I smiled.

"A pin-up girl. Betty Grable for Jesus."

Eugene Endicott looked at me like I'd hit him in the teeth. I remembered the look Billy Lynn gave me in my office when I was irreverent about the Lord. But Billy had only been a foot soldier in the spiritual army. I was in with the top cat.

"I did not come here for you to insult my beliefs," he said tersely. "I am a busy man. I have attempted to be helpful with you. Mr. Harrold was concerned that the piece you are doing might require a certain balance, in light of what is going to happen next week. But another remark like that and I shall leave."

"I'm sorry," I said. I wasn't, but I needed more answers from him. "I'm too much of a cynic sometimes."

"It can be a terrible, crippling disease."

"I'm working on it."

We sat there. He drank some water.

"Reverend," I began again, "you say you had gotten to know Peggy Lynn. You must be aware that people quite close to her were about to be let go from 'Midnite.'"

"That is the case," he said. "In fact, I had even discussed this matter with Peggy Lynn myself. If she really had the courage to change, she had to let go of the trappings of a sinful past. I assume you are referring to Mr. Cummings and the late Miss Stanford. So am I. I had found out things about them, from Mr. Harrold and my research. They are not, were not, our kind of people. And, frankly, Peggy had outgrown them."

"Had she told them?"

"Kris Stanford, yes," he said. "Peggy told me the day before she . . . left. I am not so sure about Mr. Cummings. But I think he knew too."

"It must have been very hard for her," I said.

"But practical. In the long run."

"You're a most practical man, aren't you, Reverend Endicott, sir?"

A nice bronze glow came over his face, like two mornings after sunburn. I wondered if he could do it on cue.

"I am hearing the word 'practical' from your voice," he said. "But your attitude is saying 'calculating' to me."

"I'm just looking for the truth," I said blandly. "Just like you. Whatever works."

"It is not the same truth, I gather."

Again I said, "You got that right."

"You have seen 'The Living God Live!' I take it?"

"It's replaced the network news and 'M*A*S*H' reruns for me at seven o'clock."

He frowned, almost audibly. It wasn't going the way he'd planned.

"What do you think of it?"

"I think you are the best public speaker I have ever seen. I think you are aware that television, televised religion in particular, is all about storefronts. Most everybody is selling the same products, whether they're new sitcoms, made-for-TV movies or sweet Jesus Himself. You know what the most popular show on all of television is, Reverend Endicott? Yeah, you probably do. It's 'Wheel of Fortune.' A game show. It's got a syndication you can't believe, and it's watched by more people every week than anything else. Every time I watch you preach or rake in the pledges or heal or whatever, I can't get 'Wheel of Fortune' out of my mind."

He didn't get up, I had to give him that. The man had supreme confidence in his powers of persuasion, even with an infidel.

"I save *souls,*" he said. "I make religion *attractive.* I make it *enjoyable,* because I offer people who tune into our show the big moment, the grand moment. People have become convinced that the religious among us are odd, lifeless. Boring. I have shown a new way. I have used entertainment. Is that so wrong, Mr. Finley? Are the means so horrible for such a worthy end? Talk to those who have seen our light, embraced it. Watch the faces in our studio audience. I have united our followers into a spiritual culture. I have coordinated religion with the electronic times."

"Salvation as jackpot prizes," I said.

"But salvation," he said.

"So you say."

There was an awkward pause. It was clear we weren't meant for the buddy system. "The announcement next week will be your grandest moment, won't it?" I said. "It will be like the beginning of your greatest healing. You're going to save a whole goddamned network, aren't you Reverend? And all the ones who watch it?"

"The Lord does not allow us to plan results, Mr. Finley," he said. "We can only plan plans."

He pulled up the sleeve of his white coat and checked the time.

"I must go now," he told me. "I am truly sorry this did not go better. But you came here with a closed mind. I see no purpose in us talking again. A version of this with cameras rolling would be fruitless, don't you think?"

"Like scattering seeds over rock."

"You should come to our press conference."

"Rev," I said, "I wouldn't miss it for the world."

I walked out before he did, left him there, waiting for the stage manager to hit the lights. Waiting to disappear, like on television.

He had been just what I expected.

All God's children is perfect, I thought. Some is just more perfect than others.

I WENT to the bank of phones off the lobby, around from the front desk. I used the number Natalie had given me and called him at home. He picked up after the fourth ring.

"Don't hang up," I said.

There was silence. But he didn't hang up.

"You sent me the tape, didn't you?"

After another pause, he said, "Maybe I did."

"You ever ask Peggy Lynn whether or not she used it with Harrold?"

"She must have."

"You think Harrold did it, don't you?"

"Fucking right."

"He didn't, Sam."

I hung up on him. I called Natalie at the office. She had done everything I asked.

"You were right about the car," she said. "And the rest of it. I called the airport."

"Is Marty there?"

"Uh huh."

I had sent him over to the 17th Precinct earlier, just in case.

"Tell him to make sure the stuff works, then the two of you come by the Dorset and pick me up. Now switch me to Charley."

She switched me to Charley. I told him the last thing I was going to need.

CHAPTER
22

THERE wasn't much traffic going out. We took the Long Island Expressway to Exit 70, then the connector called Manorville Road, then Route 27 the rest of the way. Marty drove. Natalie asked a lot of questions. I gave her the answers. We went through the little village, past the high school, took a right at Sag Main's blinking yellow light, went past the Loaves and Fishes store, up past the Sag General Store. I saw the cemetery up on the left. When we saw the horse farm, we took a right on Bridge Lane. Before we got to the bridge, we saw Seascape Lane on the left.

"Here," I said to Marty Pearl.

On the right, a sign said "Dead End." I thought, Hope not. It looked like a neighborhood at first, a new development, houses on both sides of the street, set close to road, featuring a sort of ocean community architecture of split level monstrosities that was making the whole area resemble Scarsdale. One of the front lawns on our left was

247

dominated by a huge sculpture that looked like a ball and chain.

After about a mile, Seascape ended in a shrubbed rotary.

The gravel driveway was right where Susan said it would be. A tiny sign attached to a tree said PRIVATE.

The drive was just big enough for the van and went for another mile at least. Nothing on either side except for a lot of green, lush foliage, marsh weeds over six feet tall. It all stretched back from Sag Pond. Private indeed. Finally we came to the gate. It opened easily after Marty jimmied it a little.

"You want us to wait here awhile?" Marty said.

"Natalie knows how to work it. You handle the rest like I said."

He nodded.

I walked up the path as softly as I could on the gravel and saw the house. It was a grand version of a saltbox, two stories high, with a circular drive in front. The lawn hadn't been cut in some time and needed work. Figured. There was a wooden gate leading around to the back that had become overgrown with rose bushes and lilacs. No sign of anyone. I decided against knocking on the front door and carefully made my way instead through the roses and lilacs. The backyard was a magnificent expanse, with tennis court and pool, stretching the length of a football field down to a beach that was the open end of the horseshoe-shaped property. I could see the water. I played a last hunch—why not?—and walked toward the beach, which was completely secluded by more foliage and weeds. Out at the end of the pond I saw a sand bar. Beyond the sand bar, in brilliant late afternoon majesty, was the Atlantic.

The Rev lived well. But I had expected that he would. The person I was looking for was on a beach towel, taking the last of the sun. My sneakers were a whisper in the sand. There was just the muted crash of the ocean.

I stopped six feet away and took a deep breath.

Bingo.

So to speak.

"Long time no see, Peggy Lynn," I said.

CHAPTER

23

SHE wheeled around on the towel in terror, and then scrambled to her feet. But there was no place to run, unless the Rev had fixed it up so she could walk on water too, and she figured she could make a break across the ocean toward Spain or Portugal. I could never remember which came first, if you headed east.

"My God!" she said finally, when her lungs worked again.

"Aw shucks, baby," I said. "We're alone here. You can just call me Peter. And please don't think about going anywhere in a hurry. I'm a little tired, I'll admit, from running after you in circles, but I would catch you and hold you down. Maybe I'd even lose my temper and blacken one of your eyes, just to add a little life to the press conference."

Her hair was shorter than I remembered, in a style that used to be called pageboy. She had a terrific tan around a simple one-piece red bathing suit. There were more freckles than I remembered: still a touch of Doris Day. On the towel was a Bible, opened, back and front leather covers facing up. Next to the Bible was a simple gray sweatshirt.

"The Lord," I said, "He moves in mysterious ways."

"Peter," she said, "you don't understand. You couldn't possibly . . ."

"Yeah, I do. Maybe not all of it. But enough of it to get my ass out here and find you. Enough so's I'm going to blow yours and the Rev's shitty scheme sky high. To the heavens, you could say." I picked up the sweatshirt and flipped it at her face. "Put this on. Don't want you to get a chill."

She put it on.

"Sit down," I said.

She did. I sat in the sand across from her, close, like we were in a two-shot. It should be close enough.

"Peter," she whimpered, "you've got to listen to me." I ignored her.

"See," I said, "I was like everybody else. I thought you were dead. I went from there. And started to line up all my little suspects, like ducks in a row. Billy first. But crackers as he was, he really thought you were dead. It's why he came. He was going to *avenge,* say amen. Then he got whacked trying to kill Brant, but he'd taken care of Seth and Kris first. It was easy for him. I made it easy by not telling the cops about him. Thanks to me, nobody knew he existed, 'cept our family at Channel A, and they were following my lead."

She tried again to interrupt. "Peter . . ."

"Shut up!" I snapped. "Slowly, very slowly, I came to some significant conclusions. One, none of the people I wanted to have done it had the balls to do it, no matter what was going down at GBC. They're all insecure little show weasels, just like you. And two—big two, baby—

they all thought someone else did it. Cummings thought
Harrold did it. He even sent *Lady of the House* to help me
out. You remember the flick, don't you? Sure you do. You
and Sammy and Kris were the ones who found it, right?"

"Yes." In a whisper.

"Harrold, he thought Kris Stanford did it. Or maybe
Cummings, until *Lady of the House* turned up. Me too. I
kept remembering one of the last things Billy said before
he got shot. 'She had figured it out,' he said. He had to
mean Kris Stanford. 'She was afraid he was going to get
her too,' he said. Kris must have thought it was Cummings. You told her that she was getting dumped, didn't
you?"

"The night I left."

"But you hadn't told Cummings."

"I didn't get the chance."

"But she must have thought you did. And afterward, it
probably made sense to her that Cummings maybe freaked
and killed you. The boy's got some temper. She knew. She
probably was afraid if she asked Cummings anything
about it, or getting let go, he might tap her too."

"I don't know. Perhaps. I guess it makes sense."

I said, "Shazam, shazam."

Peggy Lynn looked around, maybe to see if I'd come
alone.

I said, "But Cummings couldn't have done it. If it was
him, he wouldn't have taken the chance of going to your
apartment to lift the cassette of *Lady of the House*. No
reason to. Because nobody suspected him. He just would
have left well enough alone."

Off in the distance I saw a sailboat. The wind had come
up. The sun had gone behind the clouds. There was a
single swan in Sag Pond.

"Should I go on?" I said.

"You're doing so well," Peggy Lynn Brady said. "It's your story."

"But you started it, baby. You started it by taking your summer vacation in the Hamptons. Little by little, there were pieces that didn't fit. The change that people said had come over you at the end. The certain someone that you were supposed to be seeing on the sly. A weekend trip to Hilton Head a month ago, where the World Christian Network has a retreat. Mick Dunphy—remember him?—turned that one up in your credit card receipts. All of a sudden I said to myself—I've been talking to myself a lot lately, worrisome habit, don't you think?—what if it's the Rev himself? He left for Europe when you disappeared. They said he'd been spending time with you. I said to myself, 'Hey, Finley, what if the Rev planned the whole fucking thing?' He could kick off his brand-new network by bringing back Peggy Lynn Brady from the dead!"

I stopped and lit a cigarette.

"Hey, Peg," I said. "He convert you one night while he was fucking you?"

She was close enough. She tried to throw a big round-house slap with her right hand. I grabbed it easily with my left. Got her by the wrist and squeezed.

"You're hurting me," she hissed.

"Don't tempt me, Peg," I said, still holding her wrist. If I let go, I was going to hit her.

It was a variation on turning the other cheek.

"Eugene saved me," she said. I thought I saw tears forming. "He could not have known, *I* could not have known, that people would die because of our plan." I let go of her wrist. "It was just that I had to die, symbolically, to begin my new life."

Aimee Semple Lynn McBrady.

"You and God and the Rev are a threesome," I said acidly. "Is that the deal?"

She sighed and shook her head at poor, lost soul Finley.

"You can make all the jokes you want," she said. "I'm a different person now, Peter. The Peggy Lynn that you once knew, that everyone knew, is gone for good."

For good. Illusion upon illusion upon illusion. I stared out at the ocean. There were still bright swashes of sun streaking it here and there.

There was still a lot I wanted to know.

I said, "You kept in touch with Billy all those years, and you didn't know he had a screw loose for you? He told me he was your husband, you know?"

"Eugene told me after . . . Billy died," she said. "I had no idea."

"You two slept together when you were teenagers, didn't you?"

She put her head down. I barely heard her say, "Yes." She looked up at me with the glistening eyes. "It was the first time for both of us. We had to stop finally because we knew it wasn't right, and that it would kill his father if we ever got caught."

"Why the hell did you stay in touch with him, tell him what you did in those letters?"

Peggy Lynn started to reach out for my hands, thought better of it, put her arms around her knees instead.

"Don't you see, Peter? I must have been reaching out even then, without knowing it. Despite Billy's and my . . . sin of the flesh, we had God with us in that house in Guertin. But then I left it all, searching for false values, finding them, and sin. By corresponding with Billy, I was reaching out to the last time I was the person I was meant to be, could be again. Eugene made me see that. He has made me see so many things."

"The Rev," I said. "All seeing. All knowing. All seductive."

She glowered at me.

"Go ahead," she said. "Scoff."

"You feel bad when Billy ice-picked your friend Kris, Peg? You feel a little pang when Mick Dunphy shot Billy through the heart? How about Seth? You think even he deserved to get it that way, in the back of the fucking neck? Did Eugene find a passage in the Good Book about ice picks?"

"I know how it looks to you now, Peter," she said. "But who could have known how truly disturbed Billy was, that his idea about my death would, I don't know, disconnect him so? You cannot blame me for that. You cannot blame Eugene. It was going to happen with Billy sooner or later. Maybe it was going to happen to me."

I said, "No such luck."

She looked at me, confused. The Rev wasn't here to give her all the right words, all the healing platitudes.

"You don't mean that," she said.

"Oh yeah, I do, baby," I said, burying my cigarette in the sand. Then I said, "What about your little secret police, Peggy? You were a big star. Why did you think you had to keep fucking with people? Why did you think you had to go find that porno flick on Harrold? What did he ever do to you except give you a show?"

"I told you," she said. "That Peggy Lynn is gone. I don't want to talk about her."

"Humor me. Resurrect her for a coupla minutes."

She stood up. The legs were still something to behold. She walked down to the water, hugged herself against the ocean breeze, slowly walked back to me. It was all real, or it was posturing. I didn't much care anymore.

"It was six months ago, around there," she said. "Thomas was going through a bad time with his marriage. Our contract negotiation was going badly. And then he hinted one night that everything could be worked out all the way around if I had an affair with him. And it was like an old nightmare, Peter. I had done it before. I had done it with Seth because he had filled my head with ideas about Broadway and I had let him. I admit that, Peter. I allowed myself to be used by him, even though it was obvious to me what his preferences were. When I saw it happening again with Thomas, I looked for ways to protect myself, the way I had with Seth to get out of that marriage."

"So you told Cummings and Stanford to get something on Harrold, just in case?"

She looked off toward the water.

"Yes. I remembered that a long time ago, one of Seth's friends had hinted that there might be such a movie. Sam worked on it for a couple of months. Found the movie. But I never had to use it. I met Eugene, and things began to change for me."

"Sam thought you used it. Had to. It's the only reason he'd break into your house looking for it. It's why he thought Harrold killed you."

"I guess."

"He was still being loyal to you. You were going to give him the bounce, but he thought you were dead, and he was still covering your sorry ass."

"He was part of another life," she said patiently, reciting. "I did feel badly about it. But I *had* to sever ties with the weak, scheming person I had been. Only then could the spirit of God guide me. Eugene knew so much about me, understood me, understood so much of what had gone on at Global. He opened my eyes."

"The prince of fucking light," I said.

"Don't talk about him that way."

"Or what, baby? He's going to yank out my eyes? Turn me to stone? Jesus, you should pardon the expression. You bought the whole package, didn't you? You bought the package from Parker about Broadway. You bought all the phony television dreams. Now you're getting salvation.

Wholesale." I picked up a flat stone and scaled it toward the pond from a sitting position.

"Tell me about Endicott," I said.

"It's none of your business. You only want to know so you can hurt us both. You're jealous of what we have."

I leaned close to her. I put my hands on her shoulders. And very slowly I said, "Tell me."

They had met a few months before, when Endicott got serious about GBC. She had just broken off an affair with an investment banker. Said she was drifting. It didn't take long for Endicott to cast his spell and them to become lovers. He got the body first apparently, then set his sights on her immortal soul. He thrilled her with ideas about the future, about his grand design for "one true network of good." She went for it.

Then one night he tried out his plan for her to go away for a while.

"I resisted at first," she said. "My mind was still closed. I couldn't see how misleading people could be turned into a positive force. But again Eugene made me see. The network was failing. He needed something dramatic, a modern-day miracle, to begin his crusade. He needed a symbol to grab the world's attention. People loved me on television. If I could stand up to the world after a time away, and tell how I had found the true way, which I had, there was no telling how many souls we could save."

I said, "A veritable bonanza. And how were you two crazy kids going to account for your absence?"

"I can't tell you."

"Sure you can."

She shook her head. I let it go.

"How long had you planned to stay away, at the start?"

"Not that long. Just until Eugene had finalized the sale." She shrugged. "Then things started to happen. Kris. Seth. Billy. So I stayed here and waited."

"Why the hell did you make a plane reservation on East Hampton Aire? Endicott had to know people would see you."

"It wasn't supposed to be that weekend. We were just going to be together out here, the way we were at Hilton Head. Eugene thought he was going to have to be away that weekend on business. But he came up to New York on Friday. And we just decided to go ahead and do it. He didn't want to use a private plane, because then another person, the pilot, would know. So Eugene drove his own car, picked me up after the show, and we drove out. I've been here ever since."

Natalie had called around, finally verified that Endicott had given his New York driver that weekend off.

"Waiting to rise from the dead," I said, spitting out the words. "Shit, I can't believe it took me so long. There were just too many times when the Hamptons kept making cameos in everybody's stories. And then Hilton Head." This was for me, not her. "And the strong and good man in your life. It was right there for me, in the letters. He flew up here in his private plane when he got back from Europe, didn't he?"

"Yes. There would be no reason for the pilot to be suspicious about that. He comes here often."

Natalie verified that too, but Endicott told me he'd gone to Hilton Head after Europe. The Rev had no reason to think I'd already checked that part of his story before our lunch.

"And now the big press conference next week?"

A pause.

"Yes."

I stood up and brushed sand off my blue jeans. "I'm going to blow you both out of the water."

"You can't," she said. "You can't keep me here. I am going to leave here now. Eugene told me what to do if I was ever spotted. It will be your word against ours. I know you. You wouldn't have brought the police with you. You go alone. You just came out here today to see if you were as brilliant as you thought you were."

I patted her pretty blonde head. "Not always, baby. Not always. Those people over at GBC are right about you. You still don't understand a thing about television."

"Marty!" I yelled.

He was about thirty yards to our right, in the woods. He came out from behind a big tree. For once, the fatigues and khaki painter's pants were required dress. The gray Sony Betacam was on his shoulder.

Big chunk of the forest, stepping out of the receiving line.

"Say hello to Marty," I said.

"My God!" she shrieked again.

"You're repeating yourself," I said mildly.

She ran toward the house. I let her go. There wasn't any place for her to hide anymore.

I called after her, "I hope you get cable out here."

She kept running.

Marty and I walked back to Natalie in the van and then we all drove the five miles to East Hampton Airport after I did a standup in front of the house and Marty made enough establishing shots of the area. The plane that Charley had ordered, a cute little single-engine Bonanza, was waiting.

In the plane, Natalie said, "You gonna use all of it tonight?"

"Some," I said. "But not all. I'm gonna let the Rev play his hand. Then I'm going to flip over the king in my very own full house."

We flew back to the six-thirty news at Channel A with all the goodies.

CHAPTER

24

THE last shot was Peggy Lynn running from the beach toward Endicott's backyard. On the voice-over I was saying, "Once more Peggy Lynn Brady was running away to hide, perhaps to ponder her next publicity stunt. But when she reappears, what can she possibly say that will make us believe her ever again? When she reappears, she will be at the side of the Right Reverend Eugene Endicott. They will try to cloak themselves in old-time religion, but won't it just be another con? It will be as if the new emperor and empress of the Global Broadcasting Company have no clothes. This is Peter Finley for Channel A . . ."

We were in Charley's office, watching a replay of the six-thirty. Me and Marty and Natalie. Dwan and Charley and Jack Finley. Charley walked over to the cassette machine in his office and stopped the tape.

The little man was glowing as if the second mortgage were paid off. He said the same thing he'd said when he saw the piece the first time, fifteen minutes before air.

"Kicking ass and taking names," Charley Davidson said.

I sat on the edge of his desk, legs dangling over the side, sipping some of the champagne Charley had broken out when the six-thirty ended. I looked down at the buttons on Charley's phone. They were all blinking, one after another, like I'd said "cocksucker" on the air. Beyond the newsroom, in the outer lobby, were reporters and camera crews from everywhere, papers and wire services and radio stations and television stations. We had national waiting and we had local waiting. Waiting to interview me. I let them wait.

"Kicking ass," I said softly. "Taking names."

"Sonny," my father said. "I call it the best deal since Lepke turned himself in to Winchell."

I said, "Thank you, thank you."

"White boy forty-nine, God Squad nuthin'," crowed Dwan.

Natalie raised a glass and said, "Show business is my freaking life."

We all drank more champagne. Marty Pearl walked over to me and shook my hand.

"Friend," he said quietly. "You the best they is."

We had gotten back to the office a little after five, and mobilized from there. Dwan had already put together the body of the piece. Scene on Seventy-fourth after Kris Stanford's murder. Scene at 1515 Broadway. Shot of me at the reservoir after Billy had been killed. The opening was me doing the standup in front of Endicott's Sagaponack home, then came a lot of Marty's shots of me chatting with Peggy Lynn Brady on the beach. No voices. We went to Dwan's background stuff after that. Then closed with the chase, just like in the movies.

Kicking ass, taking names.

Endicott's lawyer called at six-forty, threatening a lawsuit. "Nightline" called; I'd be going on with Ted Koppel later. Jeannie called from San Francisco. She hadn't seen the show, of course, but the Peggy Lynn story was already all over the network news. Brokaw and Rather used it at the top of their shows. Peter Jennings let it bat second.

"I think I'm going to be a pushover for you when I get back, big boy," Jeannie said on the phone. "For a lengthy temporarily."

"And when might you be coming back?"

"Tomorrow," she said. "The American that gets in about five-thirty at Kennedy."

"I'll bring the limo, Mrs. Finley," I said.

For a moment there wasn't any sound at the other end of the line.

"I'm proud of you," she said.

I said, "See you tomorrow. If I'm not there, the car will be. I've got one more piece of business with the Rev."

Endicott's lawyer had told us that the press conference had been moved up to Saturday noon, in the big ballroom at the Waldorf. Nobody could prove it, I figured, but the Waldorf was probably where he was holed up with Peggy Lynn.

"How do you think he'll play it tomorrow?" Charley asked after I hung up from Jeannie. He meant Endicott.

"The only way he can," I said. "He's going to deny everything except that she's back. Shout that she's been saved, brothers and sisters. He's gonna say that she was wandering in the wilderness like whoever it was that wandered in the wilderness in the Bible, and that she called him finally, and he took her into the Bridgehampton-Sagaponack chapter of the Lord's house."

"Like she said," Charley said. "Your word against theirs."

"So they think." I smiled.

"Yeah," Charley said. "So they think."

"You can say anything you want to on cable, can't you, Charley?" I said.

"Even the f-word, if used tastefully."

"Always," I said and hopped off the desk and headed for the door, straightening my tie as I went.

"Hold all my calls," I said.

I went out to play Meet the Press with my colleagues.

KOPPEL made me work on "Nightline." He is the best television newsman since Murrow. He'd tried to get Endicott and Peggy Lynn, failed with both of them, went instead with the history of the disappearance and me for the entire half hour. He kept pressing me about how I was going to prove my allegations, pounding away at what he said was a lot of circumstantial evidence and suppositions on my part.

"Because I can," I said.

"But how exactly?"

"Ted," I said. "Are you a baseball fan?"

He said yes.

I said, "Tomorrow, when Eugene Endicott and Peggy Lynn Brady hold their press conference at the Waldorf, I'm going to my bullpen. And you'll just have to wait and see exactly what I got out there."

Koppel did a closing commentary about all the questions still surrounding the case. I got into the ABC limousine and went home. The rest of Channel A was at O'Rourkes. But I'd had a big day.

Lenny Morrissey was in the lobby of my building when I got there.

"Congratulations, Mr. F," he said. "I call it a second-round knockout is what I call it."

I rapped two knuckles on his concierge pulpit and said, "Knock wood, Lenny. I'm still only way ahead on points. But I think I knock his ass out tomorrow."

I went up to the apartment. The door was unlocked. Jack Finley was waiting for me, in blue robe and slippers, looking like a sandman with a case of the cutes. Holding a drink.

"I thought it went well with the Koppel fellow," he said. He went and got me a cold beer from the refrigerator.

We went into the living room and got comfortable, me in the big armchair, my father stretched out on the couch. Johnny Mercer was on the stereo. It is mostly always Johnny Mercer for Jack Finley.

"So how *did* you know, sonny?" my father asked.

"It was just a whole bunch of little things that organized themselves at the end," I said. "Like leftovers becoming a real dinner. The Hamptons kept popping up here and there, but I didn't realize how much until Mick called with the stuff about the reservation on East Hampton Aire. When I asked Susan Wyner—she's a real-estate pal out there, Pap—to check on houses the first time, I really thought she'd find out that Cummings or Kris Stanford had a joint out there. Probably Cummings. I'd gotten it into my head that he was the one. I'd seen him blow up at me. I figured he could have snapped if Peggy Lynn told him to go find another job. I thought he might have worked out a scam to get her out there and talk about it with him, maybe try to change her mind. Then he'd gone nuts, like a variation of Billy, and killed her. Something like that."

I dragged on the beer.

"I had just skipped Endicott. But then it all finally clicked when I was watching the Rev's stupid show the other night, after I'd gotten the porno movie. His big catchphrase is 'Is your house clean?' Hell, it's like when Gleason used to shout 'And awaaaaay we go!' It was in the letters all along. The new man in her life was there, in a real letter. And she had written Billy that her house was clean. By then it was coming back to Endicott. I even remembered something the old sax player had told me, something I hadn't paid any attention to at the time, 'cause I thought he was rambling. He'd talked about cars, big cars, pulling up to Peggy Lynn's house, and how sometimes the Lord himself would get out. It was easy enough to check out a house for Endicott through Susan. And then it was all official. I was the one yelling 'away we go.' "

My father grinned. "Your memory got you through college, sonny. I never thought for a minute it was your study habits."

"Yeah, it turns over real nice if I keep pumping it. Cummings took himself out of the running by sending the movie. He really had to think Harrold did it to pull a stunt like that, because otherwise he would have been drawing needless attention to himself. He had to think Harrold was going to get away with murder, or else he wouldn't have broken into the house to get the damn movie."

"Makes sense," my father said. He leaned forward and sipped some of his drink from the glass on his chest. There was no spillage. Jack Finley refers to it as "grandfathering your cocktail" if you spill.

"Why not Harrold?" he said.

"Because there was no point. He'd become an errand boy for Endicott. Do what he was told, keep his job. If the Rev wanted Peggy Lynn to stay, so did he. He was right when he told me there was no percentage in him wanting to get rid of Peggy Lynn. And Harrold was genuinely shocked to have *Lady of the House* come back into his life when I stopped by his office with it."

I kicked off my sneakers, and draped a leg over the arm of the chair.

I said, "By the time I sat down with Endicott, I didn't need a hell of a lot. And when he lied to me about going to Hilton Head after he came back from Europe, I knew I had him. There was no reason for him to hide going to Bridgehampton if Peggy Lynn wasn't out there."

My father said, "Ah-hah."

"See, Pap, there were just too many inconsistencies with the crap I'd found out at GBC. This one arguing with that one. Peggy Lynn threatening this one, then that one. Finally I just reminded myself that they're all television people. They're all full of shit, and they're all scared. Illusion, that's what I decided on at the end. All illusion. And Endicott is the living king of that. It had to be him. And she had to be alive. When Natalie ran down the stuff about the plane and him driving his own car the weekend she disappeared, I knew I was holding him by his holy balls."

My father sat up, beaming.

"Peter," he said, "I couldn't have done it better myself."

"Yeah, Pap. Yeah, you could have. You could have done it somehow so nobody ended up in the morgue."

I walked over to the television set.

"You tape it like I asked?"

"Of course. Right after 'Nightline.' "

I hit the play button. It was that evening's installment of 'The Living God Live!' It was a rerun. Endicott obviously hadn't done any new shows since he got back from Europe. I wanted to watch it anyway. Get angry enough for tomorrow, and the showdown at the Waldorf.

On the screen, Endicott was standing in front of his throne in all his glory, arms stretched out to all of us. He was in perfect voice. His robe was scarlet.

"There is but one *truth*!" he was shouting. "There are misleaders all around us, falsehoods and sinners all around us, but *we* are the blessed! *We* are the fortunates! *We* are the *chosen*! We have embraced the truth of *Jeeeeeeeeeesus*. . . ."

CHAPTER
25

BEFORE he went back inside the van to baby-sit the equipment with Natalie, Marty walked me into the grand ballroom of the Waldorf. Jake Connolly, a Channel A cameraman almost as slick as Marty and almost as big, was with us. Marty came because he thought Endicott's people might try to roust me at the door. He was right.

There were a couple of bouncers for Jesus standing on each side of the entrance being used for the press. They were wearing WCN blazers and trying to look menacing.

I showed my press pass to the woman, also in WCN blazer, checking names against her list. She saw "Finley" and nodded toward the Jesus bouncers.

They started to move toward us, like tag team muscle. Marty casually stepped in front of me. Standing off to the side was Mick Dunphy, grinning the wise-guy grin as he watched the show unfold.

Marty said to the bouncers, "Which one wants to go first?"

They each looked Marty up and down and let us pass. The way and the truth and the light occasionally run into roadblocks. Marty Pearl was one. We went inside.

Marty said, "Good luck at commencement. Your mother and I are so proud of you, son."

The World Christian Network Chorus had situated themselves on two rows of chairs set up on the stage. The singers wore white robes. The curtains on the stage were a combination of white and gold. A pulpit was set up in the front, one chair to each side of it. There was a thicket of microphones attached to the microphone on the pulpit. There were two stationary cameras on the stage, left edge and right. And the ballroom was already packed. Yeah, Graduation Day.

Endicott was going to try to brazen his way through. I was more sure than ever. But he wasn't going to announce any purchase of the Global Broadcasting Company. I had talked to Thomas Harrold in the early morning. The Global board had put a hold on everything.

"You still think he'll go through with his version of the resurrection?" Harrold had said.

I told him, "He's got no other way to go."

Now in the auditorium, Marty said, "You gonna be all right?"

"I have such a small part," I said. "I should be able to remember my lines." Marty went back to the van.

Jake Connolly and I walked up the side of the ballroom. When we got near the front, Mick Dunphy joined us.

"The thing work?" he said.

"Like a charm."

"Anybody know about it except you and the big guy and Natalie?"

"I told Charley and Dwan. And my dad."

"So you got them by the balls?"

"Him anyway. She's pathetic is all. She won't even get

it. She thinks she's had her passport stamped for heaven. It's just one more version of Peggy Lynn Brady she made up. It's him I want. The Rev is gonna fall from the state of grace today. Live, via satellite." I turned to face Dunphy.

"Hey, Mick," I said. "Thanks for letting us use that stuff. I'm sure there's not anything in the manual about loaners like that, especially the way I kept screwing up on you before."

He waved it off. "Sometimes, pal," he said, "the pull of heredity is strong with you. Sometimes I even think you might have made one hell of a cop. And if anybody tries anything when you make your move, I will cause an official commotion."

We waited for the show.

And at a couple of minutes after noon, there was a gasp from the audience, then a thunderclap of applause. Endicott had clearly filled the audience with his own people. He came out first, dressed in the same white suit he'd worn at the Dorset. A couple of steps behind was Peggy Lynn Brady, wearing a simple white dress, hair pulled back, no jewelry. Humble she was, but radiant. The WCN chorus rose and softly began to sing "The Lord's Prayer." It sounded radiant too. When they finished, Peggy Lynn took a seat.

Endicott stepped to the pulpit.

He threw open his arms and shouted, "I will tell today of *salvation*!"

Another burst of applause.

"I will tell of how the word of the *living* God can reach anyone, if they are *willing*!"

He stretched out "willing" pretty good, Jesused it.

"I will set the world straight on the saving of a single *soul*!"

He turned and smiled at Peggy Lynn Brady.

She smiled back at him.

Then he went fully into it, the fable he'd concocted. The theme was as I expected. Peggy Lynn had been alone on her own secret island—he didn't say which one—away from newspapers, away from television or radio, away from all the media trappings that had made her a sinner. She kept busy trying to find the path to goodness and salvation.

Finally, just a few days before, she had decided to come back to civilization, had called him, a recent friend in God, and asked to be taken into his church.

"There is always room at our *inn*!" he boomed.

Now the applause was deafening.

"Is he kidding with this shit?" Mick Dunphy shouted into my ear.

"I'm afraid not, Lieutenant," I shouted back.

On and on Endicott went.

Finally he got to me.

"There is an enemy among us," he said, taking the Voice down, sadly shaking the white-haired head. "I see him in this auditorium today. He is the sort of devil who embodies most of mass communication as we know it, who uses the power of television as an instrument of evil, just as we are on the threshold of making it over into an instrument of God. I will not even soil this memorable day with mention of his name. You who live in this city already know that name. The name has become a curse. He is the great blasphemer."

Blasphemer was as good a cue as any.

My heart was beating to some nifty calypso rhythm. Jake and I walked forward and up the side steps of the stage. Natalie had come early and put a Channel A mike in the thicket on the pulpit, though it was just backup. Jake stopped at the right side of the stage.

I walked toward the pulpit.

Endicott turned when he heard the gasp from the audience. Peggy Lynn looked like she was trying to swallow the Red Sea, or some suitable Biblical body of water, through a straw.

Endicott pointed a finger at me and screamed, "The blasphemer takes the stage!"

I gave him an A-OK sign with my fingers and winked as I got to the pulpit.

Endicott, chest heaving, face red, took a step toward me.

I said, "Don't even think about it, you son of a bitch." Past him, across the stage, I saw another Jesus bouncer start to move out. Dunphy, who had circled back around through the wings, put a hammerlock on his arm, showed him a badge, and shook his head no in a nice, relaxed way.

"Leave this stage!" Endicott screamed. He wasn't the Rev anymore. He was beginning to sound like a fishwife.

I pushed him aside and stepped to the pulpit.

"My name is Peter Finley," I said. "I work for Channel A in New York City. I'm the one who found Peggy Lynn Brady at the Reverend Endicott's home on Long Island."

There wasn't a sound in the Grand Ballroom. Endicott seemed paralyzed.

Biggest room I've ever worked, I thought.

"And now I would like to ask Peggy Lynn Brady a couple of quick questions."

She was jerking her head back and forth between Endicott and me, in panic.

I roughly pulled her up by the arm.

"Is your name Peggy Lynn Brady?" I kept her at arm's length. I wanted to have the distance be right.

She looked at Endicott, then said, "Yes, it is." She started to move away. I gave her arm another jerk.

"Not so fast, please. Where did you work before your disappearance?"

Endicott yelled, "This is an outrage!"

I turned to him and said, "Please be quiet, Reverend. I'll be off your stage soon enough." I looked back at Peggy Lynn and repeated the question.

She said, "The Global Broadcasting Company." She said it quietly, almost like a question.

I didn't need much more than that.

"Do you like ice cream?"

She cocked her head to the side.

"What? I don't understand what you're talking about."

I let go of her arm and shoved her back toward her chair.

I turned back to the Grand Ballroom and pulled back my jacket to show everyone the police wire I was wearing, the same one I'd worn at Endicott's beach house. The one Mick Dunphy had been nice enough to loan me, along with the receiver Marty and Natalie were manning in the van.

I had known she wouldn't let me interview her when I found her at the beach. And I knew that without her own voice I didn't have a thing. Marty would never have been able to get close enough with the gun mike from where he was hiding in the woods that day.

So I had gone state of the art.

I explained all this to the audience.

"The voice I have on this tape," I said, "will be the same voice I have on the recording I made when I found Peggy Lynn Brady yesterday. And when she tells quite a different story than you have heard here today, when she tells it on Channel A tonight, then the world will know that the blasphemer isn't me, but the big fella here."

I stepped away from the podium. Endicott looked like

he had a bad case of the dry heaves. He grunted at Peggy Lynn, "You stupid bitch."

I thought I might have heard "bitch" come back from the Waldorf PA system.

I pushed past Endicott.

"Thanks for the use of the room," I said.

His press conference went all to hell after that.

CHAPTER
26

"**W**HAT if the ball comes over here?" Jeannie asked.

"I'll put down my beer, hand you my scorecard, and catch it."

She broke apart another salted peanut and ate it, then washed it down with some of my beer.

"It still seems like it would be more sensible to bring gloves," she said. We were sitting behind the third base dugout at Yankee Stadium, in the Channel A seats. "We're closer to the hitter's box than the three men in the outfield, and *they* have gloves."

"Batter's box," I said.

"What?"

"It is known as the batter's box."

"Fine. But you're dodging the glove issue."

"Gloves are for wussies," I said. It is my own word, a combination of wimp and pussy. "Besides, it would be like wearing a helmet and shoulder pads to a football game. Or carrying a tennis racket out to watch the Open in Flushing. Wussie stuff."

"Let me ask you a question, since you're such an arbiter of taste in these matters," she said, adjusting the world-class legs on the empty seat in front of her. "If we're *not* wussies—it's a silly word, Peter, and I won't be using it again ever—how come we didn't wear our Red Sox caps today?"

I squinted at her over the tops of my sunglasses, and took the beer cup back.

"Screw up our tans, for one thing," I said. "Then there's the other thing. Rooting for your team is fine. Suicide is another. You wear a Red Sox cap to Yankee Stadium, they take you out of here on a stretcher. I've been racked up enough lately."

It was top of the fourth. Sox against the Yankees. Still 0–0, second of a three-game series. The Sox had won 8–7 the night before, though the Yankees were still two games in front of them. The Tigers and Orioles were still tied for second, just a game behind the Yankees. They were playing each other later on, in Baltimore. When the game was over, Jeannie and I would get into the rented Thunderbird and drive to Bridgehampton.

We were exactly a week removed from Endicott's press conference. Saturday to Saturday. My three-part series on Endicott and Peggy Lynn and the rest of the shooting match had ended on Wednesday. Endicott had gone into seclusion. So had Peggy Lynn, right after Thomas Harrold fired her. The Global offer to Endicott had been officially withdrawn by the Arabs. Now Ted Turner said he might buy GBC. The Federal Communications Commission had descended on the World Christian Network's headquarters in Dover as if it were the beach at Normandy, and the FCC was the Allied invasion force. Already three people that Endicott had allegedly cured had stepped forward to say they had been paid by Endicott.

Jeannie and I had been talking about that before she brought up baseball gloves.

"It looks to me like Endicott's next job might be selling Hoovers door to door," Jeannie said. "If he catches some breaks."

"My sentiments exactly," I said.

She said, "What's going to happen to everybody's favorite family show, 'The Living God Live!'?" She was staring curiously at my scorecard. "Why does the K look so funny there?"

I sighed. I was happy enough that she'd agreed to come to the game. I couldn't have everything.

"When the batter swings at strike three, you make a regular K. When it's a called third strike, you turn it around."

"That's silly."

"You didn't hear about the show?" I said. "I thought I told you. They made the young minister who was working as emcee the host. He's taken a lot of the glitz out, but the show must go on, and all that. His name is O'Malley. Like Bing Crosby in *Going My Way*. This O'Malley looks like a real comer."

Jeannie said, "So it goes on and on."

"It's television, honey. One car chase show goes off, another takes its place. One private eye show gets canceled, they come along with a new private eye, who's like all the other private eyes, except this one can't hear out of one ear or something. I take out a phony preacher, they bring another one up from the minors."

"What's going to happen to Peggy Lynn?"

"There was a blind item in the trades yesterday. Or maybe it was Liz Smith's column. The USA network is talking about giving her a morning talk show. Woman oriented. A little religion, some recipes, interviews. It's a beautiful business, I tell you."

Jeannie turned to me. Her nose was getting pink. It was the color of her "Miami Vice" T-shirt. "Do you feel badly about what you had to do to her?"

I had not only used the beach tape, which Dwan matched up nicely with Marty's pictures. I had used the sound from the Seth Parker tape. I had used some of Billy's letters, the real ones.

"She had it coming," I said flatly. "I looked for some remorse out there when I found her but I couldn't find any. I thought of her sending Cummings and Stanford out to get that porno film. She started using with Billy and never really stopped. She had it coming. So did Endicott."

I waved to a vendor and got another beer for the two of us and another bag of peanuts. Hoffman, the shortstop, was on first with two out.

I said to Jeannie, "Are you going to move back in full time or not?"

She flipped down her own sunglasses and her squint might have been a smile.

"Just because you solved a whopper doesn't mean you've changed," she said.

I looked back at the field. Wade Boggs had taken ball one.

"Anyway," she said, "can this be the real Peter Finley talking? You say *I'm* the one who wants happy endings all the time. You say *you're* the one who just wants endings."

"That's not an answer, J.B."

"You're right. We'll see, okay? But let's just say you've got a hell of a shot, ace."

The noise in the Stadium built suddenly. Had to be a strong, brave core of Red Sox fans. Boggs had laced one up the alley in right-center. Hoffman had been running on the pitch.

Maybe everybody's got a hell of a shot, I thought.

I smiled as Hoffman rounded third and headed for home.